The Well at the Bottom of Everything

Michael James

ALSO BY MICHAEL JAMES

Trapped

Books in the Hotel series

The Hotel at the End of Time
The Well at the Bottom of Everything

The Well at the Bottom of Everything
Copyright © 2021 by Michael James

Cover Design by https://damonza.com/

ISBN: 978-1-9990544-6-5 (eBook)

https://www.michaeljamesauthor.com/
Twitter: @MikeJamesAuthor

For everyone who persevered through Covid.

We got this.

Contents

Chapter 1: Vain orders coffee.

Vain had survived things that would have killed other people.

She'd been taken to the Hotel at the End of Time and used as a human battery before escaping. She'd jumped off a roof. Blowing up the Portal should have killed her, for sure. Once, she'd even destroyed a gas station, although that was more awesome than crazy. Clearly, she was a no-nonsense badass who could do anything. So, she could do this. Nothing to be afraid of.

She could order coffee.

Even at eight in the morning, the coffee shop was packed with trendy idiots, and everything about the experience pushed her close to panic. The name, for example. The Wrecking Brew. Did that imply their coffee wrecked people? Or that the people making the coffee did the wrecking? Mark said it was only a stupid pun, but that was like saying it was only a wet pool when she'd asked about the crocodiles swimming in it.

He waited for her on the couch because instead of normal things like chairs and tables, this horrible place had couches and recliners and weird boxes. Everyone had a beard, and the walls were covered in things that didn't belong on walls like bike tires and spatulas.

She hated it there, but Mark wanted to play at dating. He wanted to play that game more and more often, whereas she preferred when he taught her to fight, or when they worked out together. But he'd insisted on grabbing a coffee before meeting their friends for brunch. She swallowed her annoyance and stepped to the counter.

"Can I help you?" The perky girl behind the counter smiled like she enjoyed her job. Vain was immediately suspicious.

"Two coffees, please."

"Sure, what size? We have mediu, moyen and mittel."

"Are those real words?"

"Yes."

Vain waited for a more detailed explanation. Sweat pooled in her lower back. A man behind her in line coughed, and she flinched. The perky girl offered no further details, but smiled more aggressively. Vain examined the menu for clues with growing distress.

"I don't know. The third one. Mitten. Two mitten coffees, I guess. Oh and Mark said he wants an everything bagel, but I'm not sure if he meant he wants all the bagels or if he wants everything on the bagel."

"One everything bagel and two mittel coffees. No problem. How do you take them?"

Vain wiped her forehead. A car started outside the shop and she bit her cheek. "In my hands, please. That's fine. Hurry."

"Cream or sugar?"

"Why are you saying those like they're opposites? Give me two mitten coffees with cream and sugar and all the bagels in my hands. Here is some money. I'll be on the weird couch."

Vain thrust a handful of cash at the perky woman, not caring how much she handed over. Breathing hard, she scurried back to the couch and Mark, and tried not to die of shame. Roman always ordered when they went out in public, but Mark was trying to 'push her out of her comfort zone' as if that was somehow a good thing. But she loved training with him, so she'd need to find a way to make this work. Anyway, Roman barely talked to her anymore. Sometimes, if she were lucky, he'd come down from his high and mighty perch with Queen Emma and gift her with his presence. She had no problem with that because didn't bother her in the slightest.

"All done." She plopped down and wiped sweat off her forehead. No one had tried to sit in her spot because Mark was enormous and sort of scary looking.

"I'm proud of you, Vain." He smiled at her, and she attempted to do the same. People smiled on dates. She'd also dressed up, if only to demonstrate how seriously she was taking this. She wore her standard comfortable outfit; jeans and a black tank top. Instead of her usual gray hoodie, she wore a smoking hot black leather jacket Charm convinced her to buy. If the queen herself walked in, she'd mistake Vain for royalty, she was so formally dressed.

"I threw money at her and got you a weird bagel. I think they're bringing the coffee over."

"Good girl. Are you okay?"

"Totally. I'm not at all nervous and I love being in a store with a dumb name that only sells one drink and is filled with hundreds of people sitting on milk crates.

"You're sweating and your face is bright red."

"They've got the heat turned all the way up."

A server approached and set two cups down on the table in front of them that wasn't actually a table, it was a door stacked on top of hobby horses. Vain hated this place more than the Hotel.

"I'm proud of you, babe. A few more of these and maybe you can get your own place."

Mark had been pushing her to get her own place for months now, as she lived with the twins and Charm above the restaurant. Roman moved out a few weeks earlier because they were practicing being apart. Both of them hated it, but they also both agreed it was probably necessary. Vain didn't mention it to Mark, but she wanted to stay in the restaurant forever. The thought of being alone in a strange apartment terrified her. That said, Charm did seem to be losing patience with Vain crawling in to bed with her at night.

"Can we train again after lunch?"

Mark checked a sigh and blew on his coffee. "Do you want to do anything else? It's all we've been doing lately. Maybe we could see a movie or something?" He put his hand on her knee and she let him.

"Okay, sure. We can do that, too."

Mark was okay to watch movies with, but he wasn't as good at it as Roman. For starters, he seemed to get irritated when she talked, even though she only said interesting and funny things. Why watch a movie in silence? Her and Roman ripped on movies all the time. She wondered how Roman watched movies with Queen Emma. It didn't matter though, because she never thought about them.

"It will be good to see everyone today," Mark said. "It's been a while."

"Yeah, almost three weeks."

"It's nice you dressed up for it. You look stunning, by the way. Gorgeous. I love that jacket."

"Oh." Vain's head, which had only now started to cool from the horrifying coffee ordering experience, lit all the way back up. He did that a lot, he'd say she was pretty, or try to kiss her. Sometimes she'd let him and sometimes she'd compliment him back. The whole thing was strange. Mark was a goof, saying those things. Still, he was willing to hang out with her, so that was enough.

To cover her nerves, she sipped at her coffee and looked around the shop. At least Mark had let them get a seat with a view of the doors. That was something she wasn't willing to negotiate on. If she couldn't see the exits, she wasn't staying inside.

This place really only had the one way in or out, the door by the front. A patio outside had a bunch of normal seats and was occupied by people out for casual Sunday dates, no different from her and Mark. One couple laughed and held hands. Another guy sat reading the paper. A third dude sipped his coffee and looked up.

Vain gasped.

Short brown hair. Average looking guy. But those ears. Cauliflower ears.

"Vain, are you okay? You're white as a ghost."

"There is a Wyatt on the patio." She examined the table for anything to use as a weapon. Plate with a bagel? No. Plastic butter knife? No. A server walked by and Vain plucked his sleeve. He stopped.

"Can I help you?"

"Bring me a mitten coffee, but as hot as you're allowed to make it. Scalding hot, please. Boiling. An entire pot of it."

"It's fine, we're okay." Mark shooed the server away. "What are you doing?"

"I'm going to throw a pot of coffee at the Wyatt. What else would I do with it? I guess I could smash this coffee mug over his head, but my feelings are really directing me to a scalding, and I don't want to limit my self-expression."

Mark had been teaching her about being more open with her emotions, and this felt appropriately in line with his direction.

"You can't rush up and attack him."

"First you tell me to be more open, now you don't want me to throw scalding hot pots of coffee at people. Which is it? Pick a lane."

"Are you even sure it's a Wyatt?"

Vain didn't bother to answer. Mark glanced to where she'd been looking and all traces of fun, flirty date-Mark vanished.

"We have to get out of here before he sees us."

"Not a single chance. We're three blocks from the restaurant. He's probably headed there now. I have to see what he's doing."

"We should grab the others."

"And lead him straight there? Are you nuts?"

"You just said—"

"I know what I said, Mark. There's a Wyatt sitting outside, drinking a coffee, probably planning something horrible, and I know you want to get Queen Emma so she can fix everything, but I'm following him. Keeping my friends safe is my job, not yours." She realized she was going at him a little hard and tried to take some of the sting out by rubbing his knee. "You were demoted, remember?" It was hard for her to think straight, and she was dizzy. A Wyatt. Here. This close.

"I'm not letting you attack a Wyatt in broad daylight. How is he even here? We closed the Portal."

"Maybe it's opened back up. Maybe he's a leftover. I don't know. That's the point. I don't know and I'm going to find out. We're three fucking blocks from the restaurant, Mark. Three blocks. He's in my home."

The Wyatt finished his coffee and threw a tip on the table. Vain stood, and Mark grabbed her arm.

"I can't talk you out of this, can I?"

"Nope."

He turned her towards him. "You listen to what I say, okay? We follow at a distance. We watch. We play this safe and find out what we can. We absolutely do not throw pots of coffee at him. Agreed?"

"Watch and look. That's all I said I was going to do." Her hands were clenched at her sides. There was no possibility a Wyatt meant anything good. And there was no way she was getting Emma, she'd rather be captured by an entire group of Wyatts than call Emma for help.

Six months. That's how long her freedom had lasted before the Hotel intruded again

Chapter 2: Emma is really good at art.

Emma could tell that it was time to get rid of energy when she dreamed about crushing people's heads. Six months since the incident at the Portal, and she still wasn't clear on the relationship between 'too much energy' and 'head crushing', but it existed, nonetheless.

Roman was still asleep, so she sat on the couch in the living room by herself. The Padlock rested on the table against the maybe-dangerous magic Doorknob she'd taken from the ruins of the warehouse.

"Who should keep the Padlock?" Vain had asked during that first week after the explosion, all those months ago.

Roman tried to play mediator, although he mostly made it worse.

"Emma," he said, earning a glare from Vain. "She's the only one who can get it back up to full power."

Emma kept quiet. If she said anything, Vain would feel under attack and dig in.

"I can dump energy into it as easily as she can," Vain said.

"Sure, but then you and I have to be tied at the hip, storing energy, dumping it in. It's basically like being back in the Hotel at that point, pouring ourselves into the Well."

"The last thing you'd want is to be attached to me." Vain said, and Emma winced, hoping Roman wouldn't make it worse.

"I don't mean that. I only meant we wouldn't have as much use for it."

Vain chewed on her bottom lip while Emma stared off into the distance, trying to look like she wasn't interested in the outcome.

"Fine," Vain said. "I don't need it anymore, anyway." She slid the Padlock over to Emma and folded her arms.

"I'll take care of it for you, Vain. If you ever want it back, you tell me and it's all yours." Emma made sure to use the word 'tell' instead of 'ask'.

Vain visibly relaxed, and the tension passed. "I know you will, Emma. I trust you."

So, the Padlock went home with her, a place to deposit her energy when her dreams turned weird. After six months, it was back in the lock position, a faint glow in the burnished gold base, and the word 'safe' clearly visible on the side.

No one knew that Emma had taken the Doorknob, the Device that powered the Portal. She wasn't even sure if Vain or Roman noticed, and she didn't know why she took it, only it felt wrong to leave it behind. Besides, it was broken anyway. A large crack ran through the center, and it couldn't be turned. With the Padlock filled, she had started dumping her excess into the cracked Doorknob. So far, there had been no change. She suspected it required significantly more energy to charge.

Today made day six of absorbing energy. Too much power meant less Emma. It was time to drop what she had collected. She'd feel normal afterwards, or as normal as she ever felt, and she and Roman could spend a stress-free day together without her bouncing off the walls or needing to jog in place every fifteen minutes. They were supposed to meet everyone for lunch today, and it would be nice to enjoy real food.

She picked up the Doorknob and cupped it in her hands. To deposit energy, she imagined a bridge between her brain and the Device. The pull started immediately, the Doorknob hungrily devouring what she provided. Lethargy overcame her as the power drained, slowly at first, but with increasing intensity. In less than a minute, she was empty. The Doorknob kept pulling, sucking at her like a baby on a breast, but she was becoming proficient at severing that link. If she left it open, she had no doubt the Doorknob would pull forever, and force her to take energy from the surrounding environment to stay alive. But before it could get to that point, she concentrated and broke the tie. She dropped the Doorknob on the floor, sagged over against the plush couch, and closed her eyes.

This was her favorite time. She couldn't so much as lift a feather right now with the power. Her body was scrubbed completely clean, and at least for a few hours she could pretend she was normal. Pretend like Vain hadn't come along and upended her entire life. But that was unfair. This wasn't entirely Vain's fault. Maybe seventy percent Vain, thirty percent life's vagaries.

Eighty percent Vain, tops.

She fell into a light, peaceful doze, and was enjoying a daydream about Roman with a perfectly uncrushed head, but was jarred awake by a loud click. She opened her eyes, and leaned over the couch.

The Doorknob. It moved. It had been facing the couch, now it wasn't. She scooped it up to examine it closer. What had she done?

"Is that the Doorknob?" Roman stood in the bedroom doorway, rubbing sleep out of his eyes.

Emma yelped and practically jumped three feet in the air while simultaneously trying not to look guilty. She coughed into her fist. "This? This is… an art project I'm working on. Yes. I do art now, it's a thing I do. And I don't like painting, I guess, so I do sculptures. Not sculptures I build, more like garbage I pick up off the ground and call art." Inwardly, she yelled at herself for being a moron. Art. That was the best she could come up with. Well, too late to turn back.

"You see Roman, art comes in many forms, and Andy Warhol said, 'art is anything you can get away with', and he made both soup and the Velvet Underground popular. Now, obviously, I don't think this doorknob is a soup can, but I do think that once I stick it on a platform, paint half black and half white and put a sign underneath that says, 'the only doorknob that turns is tolerance' then you'll see where I'm going. So, in conclusion, while this is certainly a doorknob, it's not the doorknob that opens inter-dimensional hell gates between Earth and a realm of impossible Hotels."

Emma kept her eyes as wide and innocent as they could go, convinced she'd nailed that one.

Roman rubbed his temples and smirked. He took a deep breath and walked over to take her in a giant hug. "It's reassuring to know that if you ever cheated on me, I'd find out in half a second. You are the worst liar I've ever met. It's adorable."

Well.

She pressed herself against his chest. Hugging your boyfriend was better than fighting with your boyfriend and hugging meant she wouldn't have to explain why she took the Doorknob in the first place.

The hug went on well past the point of acceptable hug-time, and Roman tried to extricate himself. She clung tighter. "No fighting," she said into his chest. "Only hugging. Only sweet, soothing hugging."

"Emma, come on." He pushed her away and held her by the shoulders. "I'm not mad at you. But that's obviously the Doorknob from the Portal. I thought it was destroyed when you blew it up, but I guess not. I'm glad you took it. Better we have it than let someone else stumble along and pick it up."

"I don't know why I didn't tell you. It was right there when we woke up. I didn't want to leave it behind." Now that he knew, she realized how desperate she'd been to talk to someone about this.

"I'm honestly not mad. Tell me what you've been doing."

"I dump energy into it. The Padlock is full, so I use the Doorknob instead."

"That seems dangerous."

"It's broken. Look at the crack, see?" She passed it to him so he could take a better look. "No matter how much I put in, it's still cracked, and it doesn't ever move or click alarmingly."

He raised his eyebrow, and she tried to look as cute as possible.

"How are your dreams?" he asked.

"Not great. Better after this."

"Any more about the Wyatts?"

Emma grimaced. In addition to head-crushing, she couldn't stop reliving the moment she killed those five Wyatts by slamming them together. She lost herself when she used the power, and it terrified her.

"None at all." No sense in getting him worried. Sure, there'd been some dreams, but whatever. It was only her brain working stuff out. As long as she didn't use the power, she'd having nothing to worry about.

Roman turned the Doorknob over. "We should show this to Vain and the group. They might have some thoughts."

"I don't know, Roman. What if Vain wants to do something Vain-like with it?"

He scratched his head. "I don't know what that means, exactly. It's not like she'd have any idea how to re-open the Portal. What about Charm? She knows more about Hotel stuff than anyone. Maybe she'll know how much energy you can safely put in it."

"Okay. You're right. I would like to hear Charm's ideas. We'll tell them today. In the meantime, I'm all energy-free and there's plenty of time before lunch."

"Plenty of time for what?"

She pushed him back towards the bedroom with one hand. "Other things."

Roman got a stupid grin and she felt pretty confident they weren't going to talk about the Doorknob anymore. She'd tell everyone in the afternoon, and that would be that.

Still, though. That click.

Chapter 3: Vain comes up with some neat code names.

They'd parked a few spots down from the shop, and Mark went to get the car while Vain craned her neck, trying to keep the Wyatt in sight. Crowds of irritating hipsters covered the streets, making her job harder. To her enormous relief, the Wyatt headed away from the restaurant.

Mark pulled up, and she hopped in the passenger seat. He had a worried expression on his face. Vain couldn't understand what he was worried about. They were trailing the Wyatt like pros.

"Do you think we should have code names?" Maybe that would help him get over whatever was bothering him.

"I honestly don't, Vain."

"There's not enough time to buy high-powered binoculars and some kind of walkie talkie thing where I talk into my wrist and you hear me, or where I touch my ear and somehow that works. All I can do is code names. Mine is HotPunch. You can be Beefslab."

"As soon as he gets to where he's going, we go back to the group. Agreed?"

"I don't agree, Beefslab. What if there's more? What if they have a second Portal? I'm going to figure this out."

"Vain—"

"Who?"

Mark took a deep breath through his nose. "HotPunch, this is a terrible idea. This is a Wyatt. We have to be careful."

"I'm being as careful as a kitten. Look, the stupid loser hasn't even turned to see if he's being followed."

"Most people don't check that."

"Are you serious? I've already checked like four times since we've been following him. Anyway, you do whatever you want, Beefslab.".

The Wyatt pulled out his keys and got into a car parked on the side of the road.

"Shoot. I bet they all work for Uber now," she said.

"They probably just own cars. Okay, we followed him. Satisfied? He's leaving."

"Why are you not more concerned about this? Aren't you the head of security or whatever? Secure something."

"I'm glad you asked. Security is more about—"

"He's getting away." She patted his hand. "Thank you for teaching me about security. That was a good talk."

Mark looked like he swallowed something, the way his face got all red, but he followed the Wyatt, which was all she cared about.

*

The Wyatt led them out of the city. After about half an hour, they got off the highway and on to less-traveled roads. Mark became much more cautious, letting the Wyatt get further ahead.

"This is getting nearly impossible," he said. "This area is all industrial. I won't be able to realistically follow him for much longer without being noticed."

As he said that, the Wyatt turned into a parking lot in front of a long, squat building that looked fairly abandoned. Mark drove past without slowing, but Vain got a good look at the area.

They drove around the corner and pulled over into a deserted loading bay. She opened the door.

"Where are you going?" Mark grabbed her.

"Closer."

"No. That's not what we agreed."

"Okay. Shit, there's a Wyatt behind us."

Mark turned and let go of her, and she hopped out of the car. He let loose with a few expletives, but Vain figured maybe he shouldn't have been the head of a security firm if he was so easily fooled.

She crept towards the Wyatt building and Mark caught up, looking angry enough to explode.

"Damnit, Vain." He leaned close to her ear.

"Who are you talking to? I don't understand. I'm HotPunch."

"I don't want to play, Vain. This is serious. Let me at least protect you if you're going to be this foolish."

Vain ignored a wave of irritation and deliberately held up her wrist to her mouth. "That's a ten-twenty, Beefslab."

Mark chewed on his cheek.

"Cautious. Okay?"

They crept across the cracked pavement, one agonizing step at a time, keeping low to the ground. Dilapidated cars and wooden transport pallets surrounded the building. They crouched towards the open window. Vain tried to listen for sounds coming from inside, but her heart was beating so hard that all she could hear was the thumping in her ears. Mark gestured for her to stay down and craned his neck to look inside. He peeked in for three heartbeats, then sat back down beside her.

"We have to leave. Now. Don't look inside."

If he was trying to reduce her interest, that sentence seemed to be specifically designed to do the opposite. She didn't bother to argue. Instead, she stood up so she could see inside while he pulled at her arm.

The interior of the warehouse had been converted into a barracks. It held a giant common area where at least a dozen Wyatts lounged; some having drinks, some playing cards, some laughing with each other. Several doors were situated around the room, presumably leading to living quarters. A Wyatt walked through one, rubbing a towel on a dish. A kitchen, maybe.

She dropped back beside Mark. "We need to get Emma and the Padlock."

"We are not blowing up the warehouse," Mark said. "We need to get out of here."

"What we need is a word for a group of Wyatts. I am going to suggest a douchebaggery. As in, there is a douchebaggery of Wyatts in this converted warehouse."

"Come on." Mark kept them crouched low, but pulled her away from the building. Her head spun with what she had seen. Wyatts. So many Wyatts. What would she even do about this? It stood to reason that Trick and Arthur had created multiple places for Wyatts to live and recover. It wasn't like a group of twenty or so duplicates could simply rent a hotel. This was a Wyatt nest.

She scurried across the pavement a step behind Mark. Stealthy running, as it turned out, was difficult, which was why she failed to notice the group of Wyatts standing between them and their car. Vain wasn't sure how they'd been discovered. It didn't matter. They were spotted right away, and the Wyatts yelled.

Mark didn't waste time with any cool slogans; he charged straight into the group.

She'd seen Mark fight before, but even she was stunned by the ferocity of his attack. He grabbed a Wyatt by the throat and threw him to the ground. Another got an elbow to the face. A third took a punch. Mark was a grain farmer, and the Wyatts were his chaff. Or, wait. The Wyatts were his wheat? Which was the one you threw away?

Even an angry Mark-outta-nowhere was not really a match against a douchebaggery of Wyatts, and they swarmed him. One punched him in the head and another dove at his legs. Vain needed to do something. She ran at the closest Wyatt and jumped on his back.

"Time to reap what I sow!" she yelled. That didn't make sense, but no time to course correct. She brought her elbow down on top of the Wyatt's skull. He reached up and pulled her forward, throwing her off his back and to the ground. She landed hard, the air exploding from her lungs. He kicked her in the ribs, making it worse. She couldn't breathe. She curled into a ball.

Mark was being brutally pummeled by several Wyatts, and she tried to reach him. A Wyatt kicked her in the back. This was not working at all. She needed help. She needed Emma. She needed a much better quip.

Something solid slammed into her head, knocking her

stupid.

Dizzy, barely conscious, and unable to defend herself, she couldn't stop them when they dragged her across the concrete towards the warehouse

<u>Chapter 4: Roman enjoys a sip of water for lunch.</u>

Periodically, the group met at Hush's restaurant for brunch. It was the only time Roman really saw the twins, somewhat because Hush was kind of a jerk, but also because… no. No, that was it. Blunt was a great guy, but his brother was challenging to be around.

Jerk or not, Hush was the only reason Roman had a life. The twins had more money than they knew what to do with, and Hush, to his credit, was not stingy. He bought the Hotel group everything they wanted, kept them clothed and fed, set them up with bank accounts and identities. Roman's new name was Dale Boringston and Hush refused to admit he'd done that on purpose. Regardless, any path they had towards a normal life was through Hush, insufferable asshole or not.

Brunch, for example. Hush loved meeting for brunch, despite the fact that half of them couldn't eat. Himself, Charm and Blunt were conduits; hyper efficient at extracting energy from consumed substances, meaning they could live off Tic Tacs. Emma likewise barely ate, as the energy she absorbed gave her everything she needed. But jerk or not, it was worth it to see his friends, to feel normal.

He hadn't seen Vain in a couple days now. Whenever Emma showed up, Vain always had something else going on. Training with Mark, or going on shopping trips with Charm, always something to pull her away. He understood it, but he didn't like it. Vain was unable to picture a world where Roman cared about both her and Emma at the same time. Even though he told her they'd always be friends, it simply didn't penetrate. He wasn't using the right words, but he wasn't sure how to get his point across. But he wasn't mad that she stayed away. If anything, he was touched. He knew Vain well enough to know that she didn't act like this out of disrespect. She did it to avoid sabotaging his relationship with Emma. That was Vain's way of giving him space to be happy. He'd tried to explain it to Emma, but she didn't buy it and thought he was inventing a generous interpretation. She thought Vain kind of sucked.

Friends were tricky.

Hush's restaurant was called The HBC Grill, and the twins lived in a converted apartment over the bar with Charm and Vain. Roman had moved into his own place, another gift from Hush. Vain was also irritated about that, as apparently she thought they would live together in some weird mash up of Friends and Three's Company that he couldn't quite figure out.

He and Emma strolled down the street arm in arm. Emma was laughing about some guy from her college who got into a debate with the professor about how in a universe where time did not travel towards entropy, there could be no such thing as free will. Roman was unclear on the relationship between free will and time, but Emma was almost doubled over as she told the story.

"He said a deontological view of morality implies the epistemic idea that free actions can't be determined, and the professor said, 'Epistemic? More like an epidemic. Of shoddy thinking.'" She slapped her leg and Roman reflected that Emma might not understand what an actual punch line was. But she was breathless with laughter, she was gorgeous, and she was hugging his arm. He adored her down to her bones and seeing her happy made him happy.

"I know some of those words." He gave Emma a thumbs up. She wiped a tear from her eye and hugged him affectionately.

They continued to stroll in companionable silence, both content in the moment. With Vain, he needed to be on at all times as she would keep up a constant stream of patter about whatever thought flittered through her head, usually some bonkers theory about movies she'd read on the internet. He didn't think he could handle hearing again how all the Tarantino movies took place in a shared universe.

Roman wondered how he should deal with the Doorknob problem. To keep the peace, he'd acted like it didn't bother him, but truth was, he didn't want Emma anywhere near it. If he had his way, he'd drop it in the middle of the ocean and forget it ever existed. The Doorknob, the Padlock, anything connected to the Hotel. He hated all of it.

They got to the restaurant and headed to their usual table at the back. Hush, Blunt and Charm were already there. He could tell from the expression on Charm's face that she was struggling to pay attention.

"He pulled out a Kermit the Frog knapsack," Hush finished saying as they approached. He laughed and slapped the table. Oh yes. Roman had heard this one before, several times. The guy Hush energy-manipulated to give over his most valuable possession.

Charm smiled politely. If Roman had already heard this story a half-dozen times, he imagined it could be well into the high twenties for her.

"What's the matter," Hush asked. "Why isn't anyone laughing?"

"Hi everyone," Roman said, saving Charm from having to answer.

"Dale Boringston." Hush grinned. "My man."

"Hi, Roman." Charm stood up with a smile on her face, but playfully rolled her eyes when only Roman could see her. They all exchanged hugs and handshakes, and it allowed him to feel like a normal person, if only for a second. Not like some kind of walking battery deposit.

Hush's plate overflowed with bacon, fresh fruit, eggs, and toast. Roman's mouth watered. Of all the things he missed, eating was close to the top.

"Is Vain not here yet?" he asked.

"No," Hush said. "And I have a bone to pick with her. She's stealing my bodyguard. I barely see Mark anymore. They're always off doing some stupid mission, as Vain calls it."

"Leave her be," Charm said. "I think they were playing date this morning, she seemed pretty dressed up. Maybe they got distracted."

"Regardless." Hush bit into a piece of bacon.

A server approached with a cart groaning under the weight of about two dozen bottles, all in various shapes and sizes. He unloaded the bounty on the table.

"What's all this?" Charm asked.

"I know you guys can't eat," Hush said around a mouth of toast, "so I went and bought a couple thousand dollars' worth of water from all over the world. This, for example." He held up a crystal-blue glass bottle that beaded with condensation. "This is filled with glacier water from the Arctic. And not the fake stuff. I literally paid people to fly to the artic and retrieve glacier water." He pointed to the bottle in front of Roman. "That one is infused with the petal of a flower that only grows for three weeks in the mountains of Japan. I've understood it tastes like subtlety." He shrugged, suddenly awkward. "I know it's not the same. It's the best I could think of. I wasn't sure what else to do." He turned back to his plate and scooped up a mouthful of scrambled eggs with the corner of his toast.

Emma smiled and thanked him. Hush might have even blushed a little. Blunt laughed with pure delight and poured himself a glass of clear liquid with flecks of gold floating in it.

"Look at me," he said. "I'm Oprah Winfrey."

They all laughed, and Roman was so glad to be there, glad to be smiling and laughing among friends, glad to be sitting beside his girlfriend. Everything would be perfect, if not for one thing.

"Seriously, where is Vain?"

"She's an adult woman, Roman." Emma said. "You don't need to baby her. Maybe she just forgot."

"Maybe." He took a sip of water. To Hush's credit, it did, in fact, taste like subtlety. "I'll check where she is, quick."

"How?" Charm asked.

"We have each other in find my phone." He waggled his phone at the group. Emma turned her head, but not before he caught her rolling her eyes.

"That's perfectly normal, Roman," Charm said. She glanced at Emma, who coughed and covered her mouth. Were they laughing at him? "Do you also have Emma in find your phone?"

"No, why would I have Emma? She doesn't need me checking on her. She's a grown woman." He poked at his phone while Emma and Charm burst out laughing, although Emma's laugh seemed a bit forced. He wasn't sure what was so funny. Vain was somewhere on the edge of the city, about thirty minutes from there. It was tough to tell, but it seemed to be an industrial area. He relayed this information to the group.

Emma shrugged. "I guess her thing with Mark is going on longer than she thought. Leave it be."

Roman couldn't drop it. "I'll send her a quick text. Just to ask where she is and if she's joining us."

Emma took his hand. "Roman, can you not? Please? If Vain is skipping lunch, I'm sure she has a good reason. Just be present with us, okay?"

Presumably, he had dated women before the Hotel nabbed him and wiped his memories, but without any specific recollection of the subtleties of dating, he didn't have a lot of experience to draw on. That said, he wasn't a complete idiot. This was an obvious and direct request from his girlfriend. He was worried about Vain, but he wasn't suicidal.

"Of course, Emma. No problem." He deliberately placed his phone on the table, then forced himself to smile and push thoughts of Vain into the background.

A few minutes passed with light chatter. Emma had turned away from him and was talking to Blunt. He found himself unable to follow the conversation, distracted by Vain's absence. Under the table, he bounced his knees up and down and resisted the urge to check his phone. Where was she?

His phone beeped. It had to be Vain. It had to. Everyone else he knew was there. He practically lunged across the table to pick it up. Emma's lips thinned into a straight line.

He read the message.

"What the hell?"

Chapter 5: Vain prefers Alexa.

The Wyatts dragged Vain into the warehouse. Although she wanted to fight back, the kick to her head had made her dizzy and weak, and the best she could do was groan. Not quite the heroic struggle the situation called for. Odd details stood out as she blinked with heavy eyes. The warehouse floor was gray linoleum and in need of a sweeping. Florescent lights buzzed in the ceiling above her, mingling with Wyatt voices. A single black sock under a wooden chair seemed both out of place and perfectly appropriate. She smelled bacon. They threw her against a wall between some shelves, and before she could move, tied her wrists behind her back. Mark landed with a thump beside her.

A Wyatt said, "Stay put, pretties, while we figure out the best way to hurt you."

They left Vain facing the wall with Mark pressed against her back. Neither of them moved as the Wyatt walked away.

"Easy." Mark's voice was barely above a whisper.

Dust tickled her nose. Her eyes struggled to focus.

"Are you okay?" she whispered.

"Yeah."

She tried to rotate herself into a more comfortable position while the Wyatts argued. Because they all had the same voice, it sounded like a single lunatic talking to himself.

"I say, kill them," one said. "They know where we are now."

"How would we get rid of the bodies? It's not like the old days, when we could murder our way out of problems and hop back to the Hotel."

"It was never murder. Murder is when you actively conspire to kill someone with poison or something."

"What about second degree-murder?"

"Isn't that called manslaughter?"

"I'd really like us to use the term person-slaughter."

The Wyatts groaned as one. A single Wyatt said, "If any of you watched that video, you'd know that male-gendered terms are the worst injustice we can do against women."

"Shut up. You're the worst Wyatt of all now, do you know that? You're even worse than the vegan Wyatt and the Wyatt that likes cycling."

"Why, because I worry about equality?"

"No, because I can think of at least thirty things that are worse for women than gender-specific terms, and I'm sick of you throwing this in our face because you watched one stupid video. You know what? Shut up, all of you. We are having this discussion. He's had this coming for a long time. This is happening."

Vain had never wanted to know how Wyatts behaved by themselves, but here she was, getting an up-close lesson. If she survived, she needed a good joke to tell Roman about this.

"Here we go," the angry Wyatt said. "Ready? Pay inequality. Sexual harassment. Tampons not covered by health care or widely available in public washrooms. Dresses without pockets. Jean sizes that make no sense. The entire run of Sex in the City. Virtually all rap music. Video game culture. Women's magazines."

As the Wyatts continued their weirdly knowledgeable debate about women's rights, Mark's hands groped at her back pocket. Apparently, this conversation fired him up.

"Not now," she snapped. "I don't want that."

"I'm trying to get your phone."

"Yes. That makes way more sense."

"Don't move." Something warm dripped into her ear, and she shook her head. Was that his blood? In the dim light between the shelves, she couldn't really see how badly they'd hurt him, but the fact that they'd hurt him at all made her hands clench in frustration.

He tugged at her pocket and her phone slipped out. With some more squirming and tugging, he managed to maneuver it close to her head using his knees. She fiddled so it was resting by her cheek.

"Are they moving?" A Wyatt voice penetrated through the monologue.

They froze. She stopped breathing.

"Nah. We nearly kicked that big bastard to death. Let's keep going. Jordan Peterson. The way woman's wrestling is booked. Funding for women's basketball. The entire film industry and its categorical rejection of women over thirty."

"Fucking Wyatts," she whispered.

"Can you unlock the phone?"

"I think so." She pecked at the phone with her nose, trying to unlock it.

"Why don't you have face recognition turned on?"

"I don't like my phone judging me. I need to put on lipstick before I text? Come on."

"That's not how... it doesn't matter. Is your code one, one, one, one? You need to change that."

"This is the exact correct time to have that conversation," she hissed.

"Text Roman to bring Emma and come save us. Actually, I don't care if he comes. We need Emma."

"Hey, Siri," Vain whispered at the phone. "Call Roman."

"Calling: Rome." Siri's robotic voice blared from the phone and Vain cringed. She stopped moving and waited for the Wyatts to come beat the crap out of them. Thankfully, they were still arguing and didn't hear.

"Don't call Rome. Turn your volume down."

"Turning down volume," whispered Siri. Better. Stupid phone robot.

"Roman." She spoke slowly, so stupid Siri would do better.

"Calling. Row Man's boating supplies." Vain hissed at Siri to hang up.

"Try again," Mark said, sounding frustrated. "You have to say text."

"Siri. Text Roman. Wyatts. Come rescue."

"Texting. Roman. Whites come stew."

"We're going to fucking die," Vain said.

<u>Chapter 6: Emma solves a puzzle.</u>

Emma tried not to grind her teeth while Roman continued to pay more attention to his stupid phone than to the people he was with. She didn't consider herself a jealous person, but it was difficult to watch her boyfriend fall to inattentive distraction because his waif-eyed, attention-needing friend with a surprisingly hot ass skipped out on breakfast.

Okay, maybe she was a tiny bit jealous.

Roman read the text out loud.

"Whites come stew." His mouth dropped open. "Jesus Christ. I think she and Mark are—"

The phone beeped again.

"Hold on, there's more. Whites everywhere. I hate you. Why at here." He frowned. "I think that last one is a question?"

"Is she being racist?" Blunt looked up from his investigation of a Tibetan water bottle called Serenity Now.

"I knew it," Hush said. "I knew she was racist. Remember that time she said she didn't like Black Panther? Vain likes every movie ever made."

"Vain isn't racist, Hush," Charm said. "Roman, put your phone away. I'm sure she's just playing a game with Mark. You know how she is."

"What was that last one?" Emma asked. Something about

those last few texts nagged at her. Emma had always been good at puzzles, and even though Vain irritated her, this seemed out of character. Her jokes were obscure, not nonsense, and it was strange for her to joke about doing something with Mark, despite what Roman thought. Vain could barely bring herself to touch him.

"Why at here." Roman read.

"And the other?"

"Whites everywhere."

"Is she telling us she's surrounded by white people?" Hush asked.

"Maybe she's buying a yacht?" Blunt said.

Hush slapped the table. "I specifically told her not to buy a yacht."

"Seriously?" Charm asked.

"Last week she wanted to start a crime-solving boat company. I'm not sure whether she wanted the boat itself to solve crimes or if she would only solve crimes related to boats. She also asked for money to buy an Aurora Supercomputer, so I suspect the first one."

"I don't think she's buying a boat." Roman frowned at the phone, worry painted on his face.

Emma bounced the words around, trying to figure what Vain was doing. It came to her in a flash, and the hair on the back of her neck stood up. Whites. Why at.

Wyatt.

Emma's heart lurched, and she jumped up, sending her chair crashing to the floor.

"You're not reading it right. Wyatts. She's saying Wyatts. Wyatts everywhere."

"Oh no," Blunt said. "And white come stew? Are they… are they touching her?" The big man clenched the bottle so hard that water sloshed out the side, on to the table.

"Wyatts. Come rescue," Charm's face drained of color. "Jesus Christ."

Hush dropped his fork with a loud clatter, the only sound in the otherwise stunned silence. Roman swayed in his chair and squeezed his phone like he could wring answers from it. "She's on the outskirts of town," he said. "Maybe the Wyatts took them there."

"We have to go," Emma said.

"I'm positive you're mistaken," Hush said. "Let me see your phone, Roman, you're doing it wrong. You probably have auto-translate on or something."

"I'm coming with you," Charm said.

"No, you're not." Emma shook her head. "If Vain and Mark are really fighting Wyatts, the fewer people I need to worry about, the better."

"Are you seriously going to do this?" Hush asked.

"Vain's in trouble," Blunt said. Uncharacteristically, he frowned at his brother. "We need to go help."

Hush sighed and wiped his mouth with his napkin. "We can take my car. We'll go together." He looked around the table at all the unfinished food. "Just once it would be great to get together without Vain ruining it."

"Yes, quite inconsiderate of her to get kidnapped by Wyatts." Roman flushed an angry red.

Hush held up his hands in supplication. "I'm just saying. And let's be honest. Knowing Vain, she followed one back to wherever he was going, then attacked him or something."

"You're not leaving me behind," Charm said. "Even if I hide in the car, I'm not staying here wondering if you're all going to survive."

"It's a thirty-minute drive," Roman said, tapping at his phone. "Twenty if we don't stop for lights."

Emma smiled. "How long if we fly?"

Chapter 7: Vain is irritated with Emma for blowing it.

Vain wondered if her phone's support network had an option for this. Something like 'if you are being kidnapped and are unable to get Siri to relay rescue instructions, press five'. For sure, she was not letting this drop. Maybe she'd write her member of congress. Start a letter campaign, something viral. People would rally behind her, surely she was not the only one who'd encountered this incredibly specific and personal problem.

"My hands are almost loose," Mark said.

She strained at the strips around her wrists and found that, without too much trouble, she could probably get herself free as well. Screw the phone. Roman was a smart guy, he'd figure it out. She half-regretted calling him. It wasn't like they were in that much trouble. There were only twenty or thirty Wyatts. Mark could probably take fifteen by himself.

"Okay." A Wyatt clapped his hands, and the room fell silent. "Conflating gender terms with extreme prejudicial treatment of women is short-sighted and insulting. That said, we can all work to watch our language. Agreed?"

The room murmured their agreement and Vain struggled to free her hands for the punching this escape would require. Before she could finish, footsteps echoed across the room.

"Grab Vain and the other one."

Before she could react, rough hands gripped her by the arms and hoisted her to her feet, pushing her towards the center of the room. A Wyatt ripped off her restraints and threw them onto a plush leather couch that squeaked as they landed. She rubbed at her wrists, trying not to let any of the fear she felt show. At least fifteen Wyatts stared down at them.

Now that she was off the floor, she could see clearly. Mark's face was an absolute mess, and she couldn't understand how he was conscious. To say his eye was swollen shut would be an understatement. It looked as if a grapefruit was buried under his face. His lips were puffy and cracked and his nose bent at a funny angle. Blood dripped over everything. They hadn't knocked him out; they'd kicked the fuck out of him.

"Oh no," she whispered.

Mark tried to smile, but his mouth was too wrecked to work. Vain glared at the Wyatts.

"I swear," she said through clenched teeth. "If it takes the rest of my life, I'm going to kill every single one of you."

"Not if we kill you first." A Wyatt stepped forward. He had a mustache, so she assumed he was the leader.

"You have something we want," Mustachio said. "The Portal."

"I don't have the Portal. We blew it up, remember? Were any of you there?"

"I was." A Wyatt near the back raised his hand. "It was terrifying. That redhead is the devil."

"Here's how this will work, Vain," said Mustachio. "We know all about you. Trick talked about you all the time. I mean, like, all the time. I can't emphasize enough how often he talked about you. He said you always had a plan. So. Here we are. Out with it."

Vain blinked. Interesting. She'd never tried this approach before, but what the hell. "Okay. Here's my plan. I was going to pretend to have a heart attack. Then, when you came to check on me, I was going to punch you in the dick. I figured that would create enough commotion to distract you."

"Not that." Mustachio waved her to silence. "Your plan to

re-open the Portal, you must have one. Tell us how to get back to the Hotel, or we're going to person-slaughter you." Several Wyatts nodded their approval and one murmured, 'inclusivity makes us all winners'.

"I'm not going to tell you how to get back to the Hotel," she said.

"But you do know how?"

The fact was, she had spent some time thinking about it. Sometimes she got bored and Mark and Roman weren't always around to entertain her. She'd spent a couple dozen nights working through exactly how she would re-activate the Portal. Not because she ever wanted to do it, but because the only way she could relax was with options. Like right now, for example. She had no options and did not feel super comfortable. But something would occur to her. It always did. Being in a room surrounded by Wyatts seemed hopeless, but she'd been in hopeless spots before.

"You're stalling," Mustachio said, quite accurately summing up the situation.

"Let's talk specifics. How do I know you won't kill me after I tell you?"

"We promise." Mustachio held up three fingers pressed together. "Scout's honor."

"Bruce Willis's daughter? Why would I care what she thinks about this? Do you know her? Can you ask her if her dad hates Tom Hanks? For the filming of Bonfire of the Vanities, I read—"

"I promise. That's what I'm saying."

"Not good enough. Prove to me you're on the level. Let Mark go."

"Mark?"

"The giant man beside me."

"Oh, is that his name? Trick called him The Monster That Walks. He wrote a ditty about him. Want to hear it?" Mustachio cleared his throat and recited in a sing-song voice, "He's a fat stupid loser, he's the Monster that Walks. A fat stupid loser, he's the Monster that Talks. He can't hear you cause his ears are full of c—"

"Let him go," Vain said. "If you do that, I'll tell you how to open the Portal."

"Not a chance," Mark murmured through his ruined mouth. "I'm not leaving you."

"Not a chance is right," Mustachio said. "You'd run to Emma, and she'd energy the hell out of us."

"Wait." Vain held up a finger. She looked over at the door on the opposite side of the room. The Wyatts turned their heads. No one spoke for a few moments. A single Wyatt coughed.

Nothing happened.

"Say that line again," Vain said.

"Which one?"

"About Emma."

"Emma would energy the crap out of us?"

"Ah-HA!" Vain pointed at the door again.

Nothing. Wasn't it just like stupid Emma to miss her entrance?

A single Wyatt pushed his way through the group to stand in front of her and Mark. This one seemed different. More irritated. He did not have a mustache. In fact, he looked like a plain, original Wyatt.

"Remember when Wyatts used to be threatening?" He looked around the room, shrugging. "Before we'd spend hours playing with our food? Remember when we used to just get shit done?"

He pulled a gun from behind his back and shot Mark in the leg.

The noise hit her skull like a thunderclap, and she screamed. Mark also screamed, although his cry was filled with pain and rage and agony. Thick, goopy blood poured from the wound. Mark choked back his cries behind gritted teeth and pressed his hands over the injury. Vain's ears whined in protest.

"Now," the plain Wyatt said. "These other Wyatts have lost some of their intensity. I have not. I've told them, when you start watching cooking shows, it's the first step towards going soft." He leaned forward in a sickening parody of intimacy. "That one back there likes cupcake wars."

Mark groaned as spurts of blood oozed through his fingers. Vain lunged forward to punch the Wyatt in the nuts. He easily caught her wrist and shoved her back against the couch.

"No more playing. Either you tell us right now how to re-open the Portal, or I'm going to kill you both. Three. Two. One." He pointed his gun at Vain's head.

"The Stone Arch Bridge!" Vain threw her hands in front of her face. "It's a bridge in downtown Minneapolis, it cuts across the Mississippi river. You know the one?" The bridge was where she and Mark first held hands five months ago. He had let his hand brush against hers, and even though it took all her courage, she didn't pull away. She didn't know what she was saying right now. It was too hard to think. Mark was shot, and she was surrounded by Wyatts, and this wasn't a game. She had been so stupid to follow them. So stupid. Why didn't she learn?

"There's a Device at the base of the bridge," she said. "It looks like a… a… window. Under the river. It goes to the Hotel. It's a back door."

"A back door to the Hotel embedded in a bridge that Trick never once mentioned to any of us?" The Wyatt tapped his chin with the barrel of his gun. "I don't believe you. But we'll check it out. If you're lying, I'll kill the Monster That Walks." The Wyatt reversed his grip on the gun and hit Mark across the face. Blood splattered onto the other side of the couch and he toppled over. Vain threw herself on top of him and held out her hand.

"Stop," Vain gasped. "Please, stop hitting him."

This wasn't funny. It wasn't a game. Why had she ever thought she could do this? Mark was going to die, and it would be her fault. Everything was her fault. She needed to take all of it back.

If she could manage to get a few Wyatts to leave, to follow her false trail to the bridge, that would be her chance. Obviously, she couldn't take on all of them, but half of them? Maybe. Maybe. A remote chance. A whisper of a prayer.

Plain Wyatt barked orders to the others; instructions to check out the bridge and to keep watch. Mark's breath rattled and blood bubbled on his lips. The pistol whip must have knocked him out. Blood pumped out of his upper leg, soaking the couch. She didn't know what to do.

A presence started to grow in her mind. A tickle, at first,

but as she concentrated on it, the sensation expanded. A comforting knot of soothing, safe protection, getting stronger and stronger.

Roman. She was feeling Roman. He was getting closer. He must have figured out her text message.

Vain didn't want Roman there. The Vain that sent that message was a stupid, selfish Vain; one that didn't think about things like Wyatts and guns and people getting hurt. She needed to figure out a way out of there before he arrived. He couldn't put himself in danger for her.

"Do any of you feel that? A pulling?" The plain Wyatt stared at the door and tapped his chin with his gun, a gesture that Vain found horrifying. The collected Wyatts murmured and shrugged.

Plain Wyatt turned towards the entrance "She's coming. Get ready."

Vain felt it, too. Barely there, hovering under the surface, but present, nonetheless. A tugging lethargy.

Emma.

Emma had finally arrived.

Chapter 8: Emma makes an entrance.

As it turned out, flying was impossible. Apparently, the energy she needed to pull was equivalent to the energy required to keep her suspended above the ground. Attempting it had been an embarrassing waste of three minutes.

Cars worked great.

Emma couldn't stop licking her lips. Everyone in the car was grim and serious. Hush cracked his knuckles against the steering wheel. Charm held Emma's hand and squeezed with enough force to hurt. Even Blunt, normally talkative and cheerful, wore a sour expression. None of them were prepared for a potential life and death showdown with however many Wyatts Vain had pissed off.

"Left here." Roman pointed at the upcoming intersection.

Two-way city roads gave way to narrow tracks shoehorned between squat warehouses surrounded by construction machinery. The occasional truck rolled past them, but otherwise the place was quiet and deserted.

Hush pulled into the back of an empty parking lot, some distance from a brown, corrugated-tiled warehouse. The only other vehicles were red SUVs; three of them. The place felt like a Wyatt den. He turned off the car and peered at her from the front seat.

"What's the plan?"

They all looked at her, waiting for her to do what she did when they broke the Portal. Become the Emma of death and destruction. But that Emma terrified her. That Emma would crush five bodies in the cruelest, most agonizing way possible. That Emma was uncontrollable.

"Can you yell at them to stop?" She licked her lips again.

Hush shrugged. "Why bother? It's faster for you to put them down."

"I don't want to hurt anyone," she whispered.

Crying before a violent faceoff with photocopied monsters didn't strike her as productive, so she blinked back the tears. Hush rubbed his face and ticked off points on his fingers.

"I have to be close enough for them to hear me, I need an instruction they'll all understand, and I need to be fast. I think I can get five of them." He exchanged a long look with his brother, then nodded. "Five."

"Can you put up a shield?" Roman asked. "The twins go in first, but with protection, so they don't get attacked. Does that work? Give them more time?"

"Yes." Emma wiped her cheek, her blinking strategy proving insufficient to the task of holding back tears. Energy pulsed all around her. So much of it. She could become the Emma of Death easily. Part of her wanted to. That was what terrified her.

"We'll be okay, Emma. Hush is really good at this." Blunt said.

Blunt was trying to reassure her, but Roman wasn't paying attention. His focus was on the building, seemingly unconcerned with what happened to Emma as long as Vain was safe.

Hush pointed at Roman. "When this is over, you need to have a talk with your idiot friend. No more of this bullshit. It's like she wants us in danger."

Roman nodded, his face wan and pale. Emma suspected he'd agree to anything if it meant saving his precious Vain faster. When this was over, he owed her a talk as well. They could discuss fun things like boundaries and why he sort of sucked when it came to Vain.

"Let's go," Hush said. "Charm, you stay in the car."

"No," Charm said.

She got out, accompanied by a curse from Hush. Emma followed and shielded her eyes from the glare of the sun off the pavement. It was barely noon. Who got into a Wyatt-fight before lunch?

In the months since the Portal, her control over energy-absorption had become flawless. While there wasn't any way to stop it from coming in, at least not completely, she could restrict where the energy came from. She almost never pulled from her friends anymore. Besides, there was more energy in things than there was in people. The car, the ground, the building; things with weight had the most energy. That said, she allowed herself to feel the presence of the Wyatts inside and tried to take a little of what she felt. Maybe it would make them sluggish. Anything to give them an advantage.

Hush led them to the side of the warehouse towards a faded steel door. He leaned forward and put his ear against the metal.

"I don't hear anything," he said. "I'll go in first and yell at everyone to get down. I'm not going to be specific, I'm going to throw it as wide as possible. I'll probably catch Vain and Mark too, but it should be okay. Blunt, you stay outside, alright?"

"I want to go with you," Blunt said.

"I need you out here, boss. I'm going to have to take almost everything from you. Sit down beside the building so you don't fall."

Blunt protested, but Hush took off his jacket, handed it to his brother and guided him down to the ground. "Wrap it around your head, so you don't bang it. Emma, are you ready? Can you put a shield on me?"

Emma nodded while her stomach clenched. Shields took a ton of energy. More energy meant less Emma. She needed to keep everyone safe, but she needed to keep herself safe, too. Even as the protective shield formed around him, she could sense her emotions diminishing. Things like her affection for Roman, her concern for her safety; they still existed, but were harder to pay attention to. She gestured for Hush to get moving.

"Three. Two. One." He slammed the door open with his shoulder and pushed through.

A dozen Wyatts faced the door, guns pointed. This wasn't the element of surprise, it was hardly a molecule. Somehow, the Wyatts were waiting for them. Had she tipped them off by leeching from them?

"Vain." Roman rushed forward, past Hush, past the only person with production.

Everything happened at once.

Before Hush could speak, the Wyatts opened fire. At the same time, Emma put shields on everyone, no longer caring what the power did to her. Roman dropped to the floor at the same time as Hush.

Vain threw herself at the Wyatt closest to the couch, and they both went down in a heap. Hush's lips moved, but Emma couldn't hear any words. The noise from the gunfire obliterated everything. Pinpricks tickled her chest where the bullets hit.

Emma fired an energy blast at a Wyatt, trying to disarm, not murder. It struck him with horrendous force, sending him flying towards the opposite end of the building. He collapsed in a ruined heap, coughing out thick gouts of blood. Too much. She had no fine control. It was like trying to do a root canal with a jackhammer.

Acrid gun smoke filled the air. Emma lashed out at another Wyatt, this time trying to pin him under energy. His legs collapsed at an unnatural angle, bones splintering out the sides. Blood exploded from his body under the weight. His head popped like a grape. The ground cracked underneath him. Too much. It was all too much.

The Emma of Death was taking over.

She fought against that Emma as hard as she fought against the Wyatts. She couldn't let herself go, couldn't surrender to the power. The anger terrified her, the pure rage that wanted to destroy those fucking Wyatts. Those miserable, piece of shit Wyatts. She caught another and slammed him into the ceiling. Too hard. He went right through, leaving behind dust and splintered beams of wood. Sunlight poured through the hole.

The Wyatts stopped shooting, and all of them started tripping over each other, trying to make it to the back exit. Emma could kill them all right now. She held up her fist.

"Stop," Charm screamed. "Emma, don't."

The older woman's voice got through, and Emma lowered her arm. Somebody was growling, a raw, hostile animal noise. It was her. Oh.

The Wyatts poured out the exit like water from a glass. The one wrestling with Vain gave her a punch to the head and scrambled to follow the group. In moments, the only Wyatts left were the two she'd killed. Gun smoke filled the room, making it hard to see. Emma stopped pulling energy and sank to her knees.

Vain screamed, a sound of raw, unhinged agony.

On her knees, she scrambled towards Roman, who hadn't moved since the whole thing began. As Emma came back to herself, she was able to care a little more about what that meant. Roman should be moving, he'd avoided the gun fire. Hadn't he?

Blood pooled beneath his body. Wailing and sobbing, Vain rolled him over. She had blood all over her hands and jacket. Roman didn't blink. Vain screamed again.

A single, dark bullet wound made a parody of a third eye, high up on his forehead. Vain cradled his head and rocked him back and forth, his blood soaking into her jeans. Emma took a step towards them.

"Stay away." Vain snarled at her, showing only teeth. "You don't get to touch him."

Vain hugged Roman's head and alternated between screaming and sobbing. Emma could only stare. She opened her mouth a few times. Nothing came out. Roman was shot. Her Roman. Not Vain's Roman. Hers. She crawled forward. Vain lashed out with her foot and glared at Emma with eyes that promised murder.

"No. This is your fault."

<u>Chapter 9: Vain looks for a joke.</u>

Charm wouldn't let Vain kill Roman.

Vain stretched, trying to work the ache out of her lower back. Hush had moved a cot into Roman's room so she'd have a place to rest, but after a week of restless sleep, her body was protesting.

The machines keeping Roman alive beeped and hummed and hummed and beeped. Even though she didn't know what they meant, Vain memorized the patterns. One emitted a sound every thirty-nine seconds. G-sharp. A second beeped once every four minutes, fifty-one seconds. Maybe a C. Vain wasn't great at music, but she hummed the scales between beeps and figured out their notes. It gave her something to do, and the noises reassured her. The noises meant Roman was still alive, even though the version of alive he was right now barely meant anything.

Vain had wanted to tape the Padlock to his hand and pull the plug. He'd die and the Padlock would bring him back, simple. Charm said without any brain activity, the Padlock had nothing to work with. Vain thought Charm was being awfully intricate in her explanation of how magical immortality Padlocks worked, but the older woman was adamant. The Padlock had nothing to save.

Vain couldn't feel him anymore. She'd never had a moment without him in her head, not that she could remember.

He'd been with her since the first days of the Hotel, but now, his presence was extinguished. She'd felt it go during the gunfight at the warehouse. It was like getting a limb severed. Its absence ached. She didn't feel like Vain anymore. Not without Roman. She'd never considered how much she'd come to rely on that feeling. The single point of pressure in her brain that meant him.

A tube down his throat breathed for him. IVs attached to his arms helped him drink. Look, Roman, she'd joked in the early days, you're so lazy. You barely need to do anything anymore. They said he couldn't hear; that his brain wasn't working, but they were wrong. Of course he heard her. And Roman liked jokes, so she told him jokes all the time. All the ones she could think of.

A blind man walks into a bar. And a table. And a chair.

What's orange and sounds like a parrot? A carrot.

Why can't you tell puns to kleptomaniacs? They take things literally.

They weren't very funny, so Roman didn't laugh. She needed to try harder, that was all. If she found the best joke in the world, it would get through to him and he'd laugh. He'd be okay and she would feel him in her brain again and everything would be perfect. Laughter was the best medicine. The doctors did not agree with her and said 'no, laughter is not the best medicine, in fact, it's not medicine at all. Medicine is the best medicine'. Doctors didn't know everything. They didn't know what it was like to love someone so much that when they were gone, even blinking became a confusing chore.

Hush, as he did, threw money at the problem. He flew in doctors from everywhere, all of whom told the same story. Roman was brain dead. Not dead-dead, but brain dead, which was like a single step above dead-dead. But Vain wouldn't give up. She'd find the joke to bring him back. Thinking of jokes and timing beeps kept her busy. It kept her from thinking about other things, like the sequence of events that led to Roman being in that room.

"Knock, knock." Charm poked her head through the door, carrying two steaming mugs.

Vain leapt up from the couch. "Do you have a new joke?" Knock-knock jokes were all generally terrible, except for the one about the interrupting cow. But it was so great of Charm to try to help. She was a good friend.

For some strange reason, Charm's eyes filled with tears, and her frown became so pronounced that it looked like her lips were sliding off her face.

"No, honey." Her voice was soft and sad. "I don't have a joke. I was just coming into the room."

"Okay," Vain said. "But if you think of a new joke you need to tell me."

"I will." Charm pressed a mug of something hot into Vain's hands. Soup, maybe. When had Vain last eaten? Yesterday or a week ago. It didn't matter.

"How are you?"

"I'm peachy," Vain said. "My head has zero bullets in it."

"You've been in here awhile." Charm rubbed her back.

"He's getting better, Charm. Yesterday, or maybe the day before, the g-sharp beep went off after thirty-five seconds instead of thirty-nine. That's a four second beep improvement. I told Hush to call the doctor and tell him. Did he do that?"

"He did. The doctor said that doesn't mean anything."

"It does mean something. It's ten percent better. We need new doctors." Vain put her eyes on the monitor, on the floor, on the tacky wallpaper, anywhere that wasn't on poor Roman's pale and broken face.

"There aren't any more. We've had them all in and they've all said the same thing."

Vain sat on the couch and held her mug of soup. She blew on it. Her stomach rumbled, but she ignored it.

"Emma would like to see Roman," Charm said.

Not that again.

"No. She can't come in here."

"It's not fair to keep her out, Vain."

"Fair?" Vain slammed the mug down on the table beside the bed. Hot soup sloshed over the side and burned her hand. She hardly noticed. "What's fair is that Emma should have put up a shield. What's fair is that Emma could have killed all the Wyatts with her mind and stopped everything before it started. What's fair is that Emma should be the one lying in a bed attached to machines that keep her alive with beeping." Vain was yelling at the end. But she wasn't mad. She wasn't. She was simply telling the facts, and some facts need to be told at maximum volume. That's all.

Down near the bottom of Vain, near the place she almost never ventured, a tiny shred of a plan had started to form. The barest whisper. Did that theoretical plan require Emma to be slightly off-balance and malleable? Maybe. Did keeping her away from Roman encourage that mental state? Also maybe. Normal Vain plans weren't ordinarily that ruthless, but this was a pretty insane Vain plan. Way crazier than blowing up the Portal. And besides, she was right. It was all Emma's fault.

"No." Charm picked up Vain's hands. "You don't get to do this, Vain. I know you're aching. But Emma gets to see Roman and you're not allowed to stop her anymore. You haven't left this room for a solid week. Roman isn't going anywhere. What about Mark? You haven't even visited him."

"Mark is fine." Vain waved her hand.

Charm bit off her words one at a time. "Mark might never walk again. He has a severe concussion. He was beaten nearly to death. Mark is not fine, and it's beyond selfish that you haven't gone to visit him. He's asking about you."

"Emma should visit Mark, then."

"That's enough." Charm stood and put her finger right in Vain's face. What the hell was happening? "You're coming with me, young lady. You stink and you need to sleep. You're being incredibly selfish by keeping Emma away. It's a horrible, horrible thing you're doing. Emma has been a ruin for the past week and I won't have it anymore. This won't do."

"None of you know." Vain turned away, showing Charm her back. "You don't know what this is like."

The sound of labored breathing floated over her shoulder. Not the counter-yell that Vain expected. She let the moment sit for a few heartbeats before turning her head.

Charm's face was a mottled purple. Her lips had vanished and her nostrils were the size of quarters. With a deliberate intensity, Charm spoke, her voice barely above a whisper.

"You don't ever get to say that to me. Not you. Not after Patience. I know you're in agony, so I will not let this damage us.

But you don't say that again. Not once."

A small ferret had seemingly made its way into Vain's stomach and was chewing her from the inside. She was hollowed out and raw. But Charm's words had stung, and Vain considered a reality, for a moment, where Emma loved Roman as much as she did. It was impossible, though. No one loved him like her. So, she opened her mouth to yell some good counter arguments.

She erupted into tears and fell into Charm's embrace.

"He nuh-nuh-nuh-needs me. I cuh-can't leave. What if I luh-luh-leave and he… and he…"

She couldn't make herself finish. Big, ugly sobs ripped through her body, and Charm wrapped her up and took all her pain and whispered "shh, shh, shh" and rubbed her back and even though none of it helped, it all helped.

It took five thirty-nine-second beep cycles for Vain's crying to stop, and through the whole thing, Charm gathered up all the pieces that fell out and tried to hold her together. Vain could not consider a life without Roman, but if Emma came in and said goodbye, that's what it would mean. As long as Vain didn't leave that room, the beeps would change, she would find a joke, and Roman would be okay. He'd be hers again.

Instead, Charm continued to hug and soothe her, and before Vain even knew what was happening, she was being pulled away from her couch and towards the door. Vain didn't want to go, but she allowed herself to be led.

"He'll die if I leave," she whispered. There. Her biggest fear, ever, said out loud. The words were out.

"He won't," Charm said.

"Do you promise?" Vain needed something to cling to.

Charm nodded. "He'll be waiting for you. I promise."

It wasn't enough, but it would have to be enough. Vain cried into the other woman's shoulder as they walked out the door.

Outside, Emma waited.

Vain couldn't bring herself to look at her. Time for that after. Emma was the reason Roman was dead. Certainly not Vain. Part of Vain remembered she was the one who went after the Wyatts in the first place, but if she followed that thought to its logical conclusion it meant Roman was dead because of her, and she knew if she allowed herself even a single second in that dark place, she'd never get out. No, better to stick with rage and blame.

Emma reached out to pat her on the shoulder, but Vain flinched further into Charm's hug.

"Don't touch me," she murmured.

Charm whispered something about time that Vain didn't catch. Probably exchanging notes on theoretical physics or something. Emma was such a huge nerd for that sort of thing.

She let the older woman lead her away and tried not to think about Roman.

Chapter 10: Emma confesses to biting her nails.

Visiting Roman didn't help.

The tube forced down his throat, held in place by careless tape, caused Emma to experience an off-kilter dizziness that left her gasping, and she fell into the chair beside his bed. With cautious movements, she picked up his hand, held it against her cheek, and tried to feel some warmth, but only cold and pallid flesh touched her. She kissed his hand anyway, letting her lips linger on his palm, the salt from her tears mixing with the taste of his skin.

She stayed with him for two hours, saying goodbye one memory at a time. The time she showed him the top of the Empire State Building. Rollerblading around the lakes that dotted Minneapolis like water droplets. Feeling like an enormous loser for rollerblading. Laughing at a joke he told about penguins. His lopsided grin that made her stomach lurch in a way she never tired of. Soft nighttime kisses and whispered secrets. Her confusing boyfriend with no past and a psychotic best friend; gone, maybe because of her. She cried it all out, enough so that a damp spot formed on his shoulder. It didn't help.

Before leaving, she opened the window to let some of the stale air out, and reached into the bag she'd brought. Inside, a small, stuffed bear with dark brown fur peered out. A silly thing, but she couldn't stand to leave him with only machines and tubes. He liked company, her Roman. He'd always been a social guy, happiest around people. She tucked the toy under his arm, the image crippling what remained of her brittle heart, and gave him a final kiss on the forehead, on the side that was unmarred by a bullet hole.

The bullet hole that was there because she'd been too afraid to use her powers.

Tears pouring down her face, she left the room and shut the door behind her.

*

The next day, Emma decided to leave. What was even holding her there? She liked Charm well enough, but Hush was a bit difficult to be around and Vain was... Vain. On a good day, they barely had anything to talk about. Now, it was intolerable. She'd said her goodbyes. The next step was to find herself a magnificent therapist and devote the next couple years or so to avoiding suicidal depression. It might throw her studies off, but she could hardly bring herself to care about graduating anymore. She was honestly debating moving back in with her mom.

Emma's brain played a memory on a loop, picked seemingly at random. It was from about two months ago. She and Roman had been cuddling on the couch, talking about nothing, listening to music. An incredibly obscure song from a band named Archers of Loaf played; a song called Web in Front. The introduction was quite distinct, five sharp hits of a snare drum. Roman got this funny look on his face after the first hit and sat up. Under his breath, he started to sing along.

He'd obviously heard the song before. It was like that, sometimes. The Hotel's memory-wipe let bits and pieces through. She rubbed his back as he listened, happy to share his wonder.

"I remember camping," he said, when it ended. He gazed into the distance, almost talking to himself. "Or being outside, anyway. A huge fire. I was drinking a beer. Drunk, maybe, or at least buzzed. The sparks from the logs looked like fireflies and the air was cold. This song was playing. I remember liking this song. I remember the moment."

He turned to her, an expression of innocent wonder on his

face, and she drowned in that wonder. His first reaction to the memory wasn't bitterness that they'd taken something from him, it was joy that he got it back. In that single look, she realized she could fall towards his gravity forever, and never tire of finding life with him. Of finding memories.

She shook her head, and returned to the present. This hurt too much. This would never not hurt. She was sick of crying. She would never stop crying.

As she finished packing her small travel bag, the door opened with a single knock, and Vain poked her head in. Emma's stomach clenched and her heart lurched, but she tried to ignore the feeling and concentrated on folding her blouse. Her hands shook and somehow she couldn't make the arms match up, so she settled for wadding it up into a ball and stuffing it into the corner of the bag.

Vain crept in the room on silent feet and shut the door behind her. There wasn't anything about this upcoming conversation that Emma wanted to deal with. She knew what was coming. Vain leaned against the wall and held out one hand like she wanted Emma to genuflect.

"Did I ever tell you about the time a Wyatt ripped out my fingernail?"

Okay, maybe Emma did not know what was coming. What was this?

"This one," Vain continued. "Usually, when I didn't give energy for the Well they'd just beat on me, but one of the Wyatts wanted to try something new, so they ripped my fingernail out. They weren't good at it. I think the Wyatts are effective thugs, but they're not that bright and it's pretty obvious they weren't great at torture." Vain's mouth coalesced into a parody of a smile. "They botched it. Hurt worse than just about anything. The entire nail didn't even come off at once, so they had to hack the rest away with a knife. Look."

She pushed off the wall, showing Emma her hand. Emma didn't want to look, but Vain put her finger into Emma's face.

"It's funny, you'd think it would be more vivid. The torture. But somehow, it's all slushy. You know when you have a dream, something totally mundane, and then you're not sure if the dream happened? It's a bit like that."

"Okay," Emma said. "I'm glad it doesn't haunt you."

"No scars, right?"

"I guess so."

"I read about de-nailing. That's what the procedure is called. De-nailing. Normally, your fingernails don't grow back properly because of the trauma, but mine are great. Check it out."

"I get it, Vain, you have nice fingernails. I bite mine so I can't really do much with them. When I was fifteen, I got fake nails, but then I couldn't use a phone. What's your point? What do you want?"

Vain forced herself between Emma and the bed. They were almost the same size, but Emma had a few inches on the other woman. She suspected that irritated Vain, and so she lifted her chin a little.

"They healed me. In the Hotel. No matter what they did to me, they healed it."

Emma waited for Vain to say more, but she only stared with wet eyes, unblinking, as was her way. Her Jedi mind trick, as she called it. Emma sighed and wiped her cheeks. Vain exhausted her.

"I'm leaving, Vain. I'm going back to Boston." She stepped around Vain towards the bed, picked up another shirt, and stuffed it in her bag. There wasn't much else to say, and she didn't have the patience for Vain's stupid games.

"We can heal him, Emma."

Emma stopped, shirt halfway folded in her hands. Her heart constricted. She couldn't lift her eyes from the bed. Images flashed before her. Roman breathing through a tube. Roman's face when he heard a stupid song that reminded him of camping. Roman's head surrounded by blood. Roman when he looked at her.

Vain continued, throwing words like knives.

"The Hotel has healers. They could fix anything. Bruises. Broken bones. My nails." Vain paused, and the only sound in the room was Emma's breathing. She knew what came next.

"A bullet to the head."

The suitcase blurred through the tears that collected in

Emma's eyes. She didn't want to be there anymore, in that strange world with powers and crazy people and schemes and plans. She missed her life of books and school, where her greatest concern was passing a test. A few tears dripped onto her shirt. Roman laughing at a joke. His fingers running through her hair. The bear she'd left under his arm. Shared moments, whispered secrets.

"Leave me alone, Vain. Please."

Vain grabbed her forearm and pulled. Emma was forced to lift her head to look at the other woman, who glared at her with manic intensity.

"This is your fault," Vain hissed. "You have to make it right."

"Is it?" Emma didn't want to have that conversation, and also very much wanted to have that conversation. "Why did you follow the Wyatts?"

Vain chewed at her lips, but didn't answer. Emma continued.

"You did what you always do, Vain. You thought it was funny. Or I don't know, maybe you thought you were actually helping us. Intentions don't matter. Roman would still be alive today if you had left them alone. You know it, I know it and, I think if Roman was awake, he'd say the same thing. It's Patience all over again. You loaded the gun, left it lying around, then blamed other people for firing it. You leave ruin in your wake."

Emma never let her voice go above a steady monotone. If she started yelling, she'd never stop. Vain took the entire speech without moving, but the blood drained from her face and she swayed on her feet. She didn't release her grip on Emma's forearm. A single, fat tear rolled down her cheek. She stared at Emma without blinking.

"I saw you take the Doorknob."

This woman. Christ, she was relentless. Emma could never win. She could say the most horrible things she could imagine, and Vain would keep coming at her.

Emma shook her head. "What, do you think I can re-power it? It's too deep. I've been dumping into it for six months."

"I know how to do it."

Emma wrestled her arm from Vain's grip and turned away

to stare out the window. She'd done it again. Somehow, Vain had gathered Emma into her plan. Somehow, she'd turned the conversation to what she wanted done, even after Emma threw everything at her. Silence was the only weapon she had left. She needed to get out of that room.

"I know I killed him." Vain's voice floated over her shoulder. It was soft and exhausted and broken. "I know. You killed him too. You did. We're together in this. And even though I've made the worst mistake of my life, I realized something. Closing the Portal wasn't enough. As long as Arthur is alive, as long as the Hotel exists, they'll never stop coming after us."

"That's always your line. Fear. Intimidation. You've been singing the same song for months."

"You're too powerful to leave alone."

"You can't know that," Emma said.

On the sidewalk below, people rushed with their heads down, eager to get to wherever they were going. Emma was eager to get somewhere too, except she didn't know where she wanted to be. She only knew it was not in this room with this woman. The weight of tension was becoming untenable.

"How would we even do it?" she said. She hadn't known she was going to ask that. Roman singing a song. Roman touching her wrist. Roman's weight on her body, gasping together.

"The same way we did the Padlock. Immense amounts of power."

"The Padlock nearly killed me."

"You're stronger now. You can handle more."

Emma turned towards Vain. "I lose myself."

"I know you do."

She waited for Vain to tell a joke, or say some insensitive barb or some irritating reference that would allow Emma to get mad. This quiet, measured conversation was confusing. Vain was talking to her like a real person.

"What if I can't come back?"

"I'll keep you here."

Emma saw two paths before her. In one, she walked out of that room and never returned. In that path, Emma could lead a normal life. Treat that thing of hers like a manageable disease. Get a degree. Have a career. Normal life things. In the other, a desperate plan with little hope of succeeding took her further into a world where the rules were made up and the game show host was crazy. Path one would see her travel with guilt for the rest of her life. Path two would have her life shortened to remove that guilt.

Roman, broken, and within her power to heal.

Roman, telling her he loved her.

"We would need a huge source of power," she said, and realized she was trapped.

Vain reached out. "I have one."

Emma swallowed and took a step down the second path.

Chapter 11: Vain knows a lot of different dance moves.

"I'm sure you're wondering why I've called you all here," Vain said, delighted to be able to use that sentence. It was almost as good as 'no time to explain' or 'I think you're gonna wanna see this'.

She'd gathered the group in the living room. Hush, as usual, lounged against the pool table, more out of a desire to look cool as opposed to any real comfort, Vain suspected. Blunt took his spot by the mahogany bar, while Charm and Emma sat on the leather couches that puffed air every time anyone sat on them. Emma rolled a drink in her hands, keeping her eyes on the floor.

Getting Emma onside had been the hardest thing Vain had ever done, and even now, her hands itched to slap the lips right off Emma's stupid face. Talking to her with measured restraint had been brutal, but Vain knew it was the only way to get her support. Also, there had been at least four times through that whole conversation where she could have interjected with a Fast and the Furious reference, so keeping her mouth shut represented a demonstration of incredible self-control.

"Hurry up, Vain." Hush threw a pool ball from hand to hand, a move that only increased her already overpowering irritation.

Everything Hush did was annoying, but this was specifically annoying, and it was throwing off her concentration. She'd debated how to tell them about her awesome plan and decided that since they all trusted her implicitly now, the best way would be to hit them with it.

"As you know, we're going to re-open the Portal and kidnap a healer from the Hotel."

There was a moment of incredulous silence before the room exploded.

Charm leapt off the couch like something bit her ass. Hush's face turned red and he yelled something about 'crazy' and a word that sounded an awful lot like 'rich', so something about his money. Blunt buried his head in his hands. She'd expected applause, and maybe even high fives, so their reaction was a touch unexpected. This was why she didn't tell people her plans. So much drama.

"You want to re-open the Portal?" Charm said.

"That's right. Emma thinks she can do it, easily." Vain nodded.

Emma choked on her drink mid-sip. "A more accurate way to frame our discussion would be to say that Emma has no idea if this will work and thinks it might kill her. But sure. Easily. That's what that word means."

"No," Hush said. "Not a chance."

"Which healer were you thinking?" Charm asked.

"Flute," Vain said.

Blunt made a see-saw motion with this hand. "Flute maybe doesn't like you."

"That's not true." Vain walked over and tapped Blunt on the nose. "Everyone likes me."

She wasn't trying to be funny, but the group laughed at her comment for some reason.

Charm ran her fingers through her hair. "We open the Portal, waltz in, steal a Utility with her Conduit, and waltz right back out? All without anyone noticing us? It's bonkers. It will never work."

"I'm trying to learn to take feedback, and I agree that if we are going to dance towards the Hotel, waltzing would not be a good dance to select. I'll put that one up on the whiteboard." Vain realized she did not have a whiteboard.

"Vain, that's not what I meant."

"The running man could work, or maybe the moonwalk if we did it fast enough. Personally, I believe dancing is not a great move, but Mark says there are no bad ideas in brainstorming." Vain did not recall Charm being that bad at planning, but also she was doing a really good job at modifying her ideas based on feedback. Mark told her to work on that. But thinking about Mark hurt, so she pushed him out of her mind. She still hadn't visited him.

"Not going to happen," Hush said. "Is anyone listening to me?"

"Even if we could open the Portal," Charm continued, "and even if we could make it to Flute, she'd never leave. She loves it there."

"She would if we told her Roman was in trouble, and we get her Handcuff off." Vain wriggled her wrist. "She liked Roman a lot. But you're right, that by itself isn't enough. We'd need someone who was good at convincing people. Someone with an abundance of, oh I don't know, Charm?"

"Me?" Blunt pointed at himself.

"I think she means me, big boy." Charm sank back to the couch.

Vain thought it was going pretty well. The group was basically one hundred percent on side and now it was down to dull, sticky details, most of which could be worked out on the fly. Perfect.

"That's enough planning." She clapped her hands. "Let's go."

"What?" Emma said. "Go where? I'm still not even clear what your entire idea is."

"Open the Portal. Jump through. Steal Flute. Run back. Maybe dance moves to satisfy Charm." Vain gestured at the older woman. "Are you stuck on what happens after Roman is awake? I don't know, we'll probably hug or something? How are you not getting this? Do you need it spelled out in a formal report with bullet-points and an executive summary?" Vain felt that represented a fairly pedantic level of planning but was willing to cut Emma some slack.

"I'm not supporting any of this," Hush said. "You're nuts."

"We should think this through." Charm stood up and rubbed Vain on the shoulder. "I know you're hurting over Roman, sweetie, but not like this. We escaped the Hotel once and it nearly killed us. Now you want us to go back? Emma hasn't even agreed to this."

"I have," Emma said.

The group quieted and looked at Emma, who continued.

"I don't understand much anymore." She played with her hands as she talked, keeping her eyes downward. "None of what we can do makes sense and it violates several immutable laws of physics. I used to like physics. Now it makes me nauseous. It's been a rough few months." She laughed, a flimsy sound on the edge of tears. "I know this, though. If it were any of us on that bed, Roman would do whatever was needed to save us and you all know it. So I'm going to help Vain, even though her idea is dumb and unworkable and will probably get us both killed."

Vain squawked in protest. Emma continued.

"If none of you want to help, that's fine. But we're doing it anyway. I love Roman and I want him back."

"You can do this without us." Hush pushed himself away from the pool table to pace the room. "I don't give a shit that both of you have unresolved guilt in getting Roman killed. My hands are clean. Vain should have never gone near the Wyatts in the first place. This is finished. Blunt and I are both out."

"I'm in," Blunt said.

Hush turned to his brother, a frown on his face.

Blunt held up his hands. "I know I don't normally get involved in the planning," he said. "But Roman is my friend and we would still be in the Hotel if it weren't for him. Vain's plans are scary and weird but without her, we have nothing. And besides, it would be good to get more people out. We left so many behind. I think about them, sometimes, and how we got out and they didn't. It's not fair."

"I couldn't get everyone, Blunt" Vain said. "I tried to come up with a plan for that. I couldn't make it work. But I tried."

Blunt gave her a soft smile. "I know you did."

"We've got a good thing here, boss," Hush said. "I don't want to wreck that."

"How is it a good thing if our friends aren't here to share it with us?"

Hush opened and closed his mouth a few times. Finally, he said, "You sure, buddy?"

His mouth a grim line of determination, Blunt nodded. Vain resisted the urge to shoot a glare at stupid, stupid Hush. For a guy with a name like that he sure did talk a lot.

"What's the plan, Vain?" Charm turned to her with weary eyes. "Please nothing about exploding."

"It's like exploding in reverse."

"An implosion?" Emma asked.

"Plodes can't im, silly, they only ex." Vain thought Emma was smarter than that. "Anyhow, we have some advantages we can use. The Hotel will not be expecting us to re-open the Portal, so they won't be guarding it. Once we go through, Charm and I sprint to the lower level where Flute lives." Vain emphasized the word sprint and looked directly at Charm while she said it.

For some reason, Charm sighed. "There's no way for us to make it without being seen."

"Utilities walk around the Hotel all the time." Vain shrugged. "We'll get a fake pair of handcuffs. Oh! We can wear a disguise. I have this insane sombrero that would work."

"We don't need a disguise," Charm said.

Vain wasn't sure how fun hats could make a plan worse, but she wanted to get through the rest while she had their attention. She hadn't even told them the best part.

"Emma will create a distraction," Vain continued.

Emma looked at her with weary exhaustion. "How will I do that, exactly?"

"You're going to come with us, but head to the back. You're going to break the Well."

If Vain thought the group was agitated before, they were nuclear now. Emma almost passed out, and Charm was right behind her. God, next time she'd bring a fainting couch. Hush was yelling something about how her plans were mazy or hazy, but

Vain couldn't be bothered to listen. She let them bleat it out for a minute before sharply bringing her hands together.

"Emma will break the Well," she said loudly enough to get their attention. "Or at least try. I don't think you can actually destroy it, but I think she can break the levers we held when we poured our power in. The distraction will give us time to get Flute. Then we all meet up, run out, and shut the door behind us. It will work because no one will be expecting this. For all we know, Arthur is off adventuring in a different world somewhere. Where else would he be?"

"I liked your plans better when I didn't know them." Charm closed her eyes and leaned back.

"Where am I going to find enough energy to power the Doorknob?" Emma asked. "You still haven't explained that. I'd need something massive to pull from. Something enormous."

Vain smiled.

Chapter 12: Emma didn't think a hat was necessary.

Emma rubbed her forehead and tried not to think about what they were going to do. Vain knew she'd need energy for this to work, and the Capella Tower in downtown Minneapolis was the largest building in the city core. More weight meant more energy, and a giant skyscraper made sense. The fact that the plan had a shred of logic behind it did not reassure her.

The lobby was a circular monstrosity of hubris and windows, all arranged to be as disorienting as possible. It was the type of place where the answer to any question about why the architecture looked like that was 'because it can'. Shoppers and sightseers crisscrossed the polished-marble floors, none of them paying any attention to the group as Hush went to the security guards at the front.

"Once we get to the conference room Hush rented, we'll get started," Vain said.

It was unlike her to repeat herself or even give them a single detail, so Emma assumed she was nervous. She kept cracking her knuckles and glaring at any men with mustaches.

None of them were handling the pressure very well. Charm kept playing with her hair, and Blunt couldn't stop giggling. Emma, for her part, felt sick. Hot, gassy burps bubbled up from her stomach, and her mouth was a sandy cave. Part of her wanted to run to the washroom, crawl out a window, and leave them all behind. Then quit school, change her name, and move to Montreal to become the bass player in an indie band called something absurd like Precious Smoke and The Hangovers.

But that was silly. For one, she'd be a rhythm guitarist.

"Let's go." Hush came back, holding up a key card. He wore about ten thousand dollars of suit, reasoning that the more money he covered himself with, the less likely building security would bother them.

The conference rooms at the back of the building made the perfect spot to set up the Portal without being disturbed. The group walked past an elevator bank and down a long, elegantly carpeted hallway. They followed the signs to "conference room H" and Hush carded the door open. Vain pushed in, jogged her way to a stage at the far end of the enormous space, and cupped her hands around her mouth.

"Smallest room you could get?"

"Only room I could get," Hush said. "Blunt, lock the doors. Let's set up on the stage."

The group got to work while Emma focused on not throwing up. How much energy would it take to recharge the Portal? She rested her hand against the wall and closed her eyes, trying to determine how much energy ran through the building. Lots, it seemed. Power dripped through the interior, through the steel and concrete, through the wires and plaster, and thrummed underneath her hand. There was plenty there for the taking. An ocean's worth.

Vain snapped her fingers, startling Emma out of her reverie.

"How long do you think it will take?" Vain asked.

"I have no idea," Emma replied.

"Remember to protect yourself." Charm said. "Like we talked about."

Emma nodded. When she'd repowered the Padlock all those months ago, it had almost killed her. Too much energy flowing through her body. Charm theorized that Emma could move the energy from one place to another without absorbing it first. Like mentally creating a tube or something. Because, sure. An invisible gas siphon, why not? Science openly wept whenever she did her thing, but she was learning to ignore that.

"Let's get started," Vain said. "Once it's open, we go as fast as we can. The Hotel is five hundred yards from the Portal. Charm and I grab Flute, Emma mucks with the Well. Nice and easy. The whole operation will take five minutes. Bippity boppity boo."

Emma couldn't stop gnawing on her nails. All three of them wore cheap, plastic handcuffs so they'd look like residents of the Hotel. Vain was positive the Portal would be unguarded. In fact, their entire plan relied on that single assumption that they had literally no way to test or validate. If they were wrong, they'd be done before they started.

In her pocket, Emma wrapped her hand around the fully powered Padlock. It vibrated almost imperceptibly. Before she could change her mind, she thrust it at Vain.

"Take this. Just in case. I can protect myself."

Vain stared at the Padlock on Emma's outstretched palm for several moments before slowly extending her hand to pick it up. "Thank you, Emma."

Emma looked at the group one final time. Pretty high odds that re-powering the Doorknob would kill her. Even with Charm's advice, she wasn't sure she could pull that much energy without being burnt to a crisp. Still. Roman, smiling. She should have protected him. She needed to be brave now, because of her cowardice before.

She climbed on the stage and set the Doorknob down in the center. The group watched her from the floor and she thought about bowing or flourishing. After all, wasn't that the thing to do before performing magic?

"I'm starting," she said.

She imagined a funnel above the Doorknob with tendrils reaching out to the building. It took about a minute to fix it in place and connect everything together. It wasn't as if she could see the things she created, but somehow that wasn't a problem.

At first, nothing happened, but soon she had a steady stream of energy running from the building to the Doorknob, none of it going directly through her. Charm had been right, it was possible to channel without using her own body as the conduit. It wasn't perfect though, and some amounts leaked through her, making her bones grind together. Worse, even the act of channeling the energy caused her to float further away from herself, and opened the door to that other Emma.

"Everyone should stand back."

"Not a chance." Charm climbed up and squeezed her hand. "We're right here with you."

Emma gave her a grateful smile and closed her eyes.

The power contained in the building, in the ground, even in the ambient air was limitless, and she poured it all through the funnel. Slowly, at first, then with increasing intensity.

"It's happening," Vain said. "Can you feel it?"

Emma ignored her and clenched her teeth. Her muscles trembled. This was more than she'd done with the Padlock. Maybe more than when she blew up the Portal. Endless amounts. Waves of hot, sizzling power crackled around them, heating the air. Sweat trickled down her back and a weight settled on her, like a trench coat filled with mercury. And still she pulled. Charm's sweaty hand squeezed hers, and she clung to it like a life preserver, glad for the tether to something solid.

Emma opened her eyes. On stage, the Doorknob glowed, and a horrible whining noise came from every direction. The sound of bending metal and twisting iron. Of ruin. Of collapse.

"The building," Hush panted, trying to look everywhere at once. "She's pulling the building inward. Christ alive. Can you feel that?" He had to raise his voice to be heard over the terrible, low groaning that filled the auditorium.

The steel complained, tortured by the pressure Emma brought to bear. She strained with her labor, past the point of caring about damage, either to herself or to the structure. The Doorknob needed power, and Emma wanted to provide it.

The windows of the sound room cracked, then exploded. Blunt screamed as shards of glass pelted him. The Doorknob was almost impossible to look at, it glowed so brightly.

And still, Emma pulled.

The amount she was handling was awe-inspiring. Her knees trembled with the strain, but she wanted more. What could she do with that much power? Anything. She could do anything. More; she was everything. Why had she been scared? With that much control, she would never have to be afraid again.

The groaning reached a crescendo, a twisted scream of scraping metal that blocked out all other sounds. A crack appeared along the wall and spiderwebbed its way to the ceiling. Dust fell like gossamer webs on their heads. An alarm sounded, a piercing wail that filled the air, adding to the cacophony. The floor trembled under her feet. Hush was right. She was pulling the building down. She was doing that. Her. The pull. The power, the power, the power.

The Doorknob gave a final, explosive burst of light. With an audible click that was somehow louder than the crying of the building, it jumped like a flea and turned.

In that turning, the Portal emerged.

It took shape, a giant haze of purple light contained within a fifteen-foot-high black wooden frame, the Portal only visible and glowing on one side. The sound of a million voices screaming emerged, like the universe was protesting the unnatural act. Hush was knocked off his feet by the force that sent him tumbling to the ground with his brother. Charm was pulled from Emma's grip, landing hard and skidding across the stage.

The Portal was open.

"Emma, stop! You have to stop!" Vain clambered to her feet. Emma wondered if she could crush the other woman's skull. It would be so easy. Fun, too. Her head would pop, then no more Vain. Delicious.

"Emma, come back to us. Please." Charm pulled Emma forward so their heads were touching, her sticky breath hot against Emma's cheek. "That's enough, sweetie. You can stop now."

"No." Emma tried to pull back.

White dust from the breaking ceiling covered them like snow. Emma considered snapping every single bone in Charm's body. But Charm didn't let go, and she kissed Emma on the cheek, and put her lips close to Emma's ear.

"Come back, dear one. We love you. For Roman."

The name penetrated through the power. Roman. Yes. She had to let go.

With a violent wrench, Emma cut off the energy. On knees that twanged like plucked guitar strings, she fell onto her bum with a thud. She couldn't even make herself blink.

Vain stood in front of the Portal, white dust from the ceiling covering her hair. Hush and Blunt were staring at Emma with horrified eyes. The alarm blared in the background and even though the terrible groaning had stopped, the building seemed less stable, somehow. A tremor shook the ground, and they all yelped. Emma sucked air in huge gulps, trying to chase away the dizziness.

"Let's never do that again," Hush whispered.

"We don't have to. We control the Portal now." Vain pumped a fist in the air. "Everyone okay? Charm? Emma? You good?"

Emma didn't trust herself to speak, so she only nodded. She let her head hang between her knees and spit onto the stage. Charm rubbed her back.

She had nearly killed them. Even now, she could remember what it felt like, how badly she'd wanted to do it. But she hadn't. That was the important thing. She'd resisted, and the Portal was open. No one needed to know how close she had come to losing everything.

"This is it," Vain said. "In and out, ten minutes, tops."

"Hurry," Hush said. "They're probably going to evacuate the building." People were yelling outside and sirens were getting nearer. "She nearly brought the whole thing down on top of us."

Vain helped her to her feet. "You did real good, Emma. Can you do this next part?"

"Maybe she should hang back," Charm said.

"I'm fine." Emma pushed Charm away and straightened. "Let's get this over with. For Roman."

"For Roman." Vain nodded.

"For all of us," Charm said. "God help us."

The three of them held hands and stepped through the Portal.

Chapter 13: Flute enjoyed the original Matrix.

Flute struggled with the arpeggio that had escaped her for days or minutes or years. Wind instruments were tricky, and the clarinet even more so. Her mouth would not form the right shape, and an army of notes died against her lippy barricade. Sunrise, bless his heart, did not comment on her labors, and kept his nose buried in his book. Asimov, maybe.

Mozart watched her halted progress from his permanent spot on her window, his poster covering the entire pane of glass. Flute didn't enjoy seeing the red, lighting-striated sky above the Hotel. It never changed, and thinking about what existed beyond its borders gave her a headache. Thinking about almost everything gave her a headache, but that was part of living in the Hotel. Instead, she poured her energy into music, the same way she poured her energy into the Well.

All the furniture in her room sat flush against the walls so she'd have a spot to rehearse. Instruments lay scattered across the floor. At the far end, a giant canopy bed doubled as a fort for when she and Sunrise watched movies.

Their rooms connected through a single door, but they kept it open all the time. His room mirrored hers, although he paid less attention to the décor. She couldn't recall the last time she'd been apart from Sunrise. Some nights, after a tough session of putting energy in the Well, he'd curl up beside her in the canopy bed. He'd stroke her hair and cuddle her close as they both waited for the tremors to subside.

Once, they'd asked a Wyatt to knock down the wall between their rooms, but the Wyatt asked if he looked like Mike Holmes, a reference neither Flute nor Sunrise understood. They didn't push further, though; it had taken most of their courage to even speak to him. Nothing good came from pushing a Wyatt.

A discordant note emerged from the clarinet, and she threw the stupid thing on the ground.

"This sucks. Let's go to the music room. I want to play the harp."

Sunrise nodded and bookmarked his page. He brushed his scraggly black hair back off his forehead and rolled out of bed. He wore loose-fitting jeans and a nondescript sweatshirt. He liked to wear baggy clothes so no one would laugh at him. Flute told him, over and over, no one in the Hotel would laugh, but he wouldn't listen. If anyone even dared mock him, she'd do something vicious. Punch them in the nose, maybe.

The Hotel had plenty of amenities to keep them entertained. Sunrise mostly read sci-fi and cozy mysteries, but the music room was Flute's favorite spot. It contained every type of instrument imaginable. Pianos, guitars, drums; even something called a cello horn. It was completely ridiculous, entirely unplayable, and she loved it.

Flute loved everything about the Hotel, except for minor annoyances like the sky, the lack of time, the headaches when she tried to remember her past, the terrible agony of giving energy into the Well, and the clarinet. The Hotel was great.

Her wrist itched, and she adjusted her bracelet. Every guest of the Hotel wore one, a signifier that they were special. Chosen. The simple act of touching it calmed her thoughts and smoothed the wrinkles on her forehead. What had she been thinking about? Oh, yes. The music room.

The absence of memory bothered some pairs. Sometimes, she and Sunrise would pick at the faint threads of recollection that remained, traces of traces of traces of what their lives had been. But dark and cold thoughts would emerge, and Flute suspected that whatever her life had been before the Hotel, she was better off here. Here, she was someone. Here, she was Flute, and kind of a big deal. If she snapped her fingers, not that she ever would, a Jane would come running. If she told Trick she wanted more of anything, he'd make it happen. No other pairs gave energy like she and Sunrise. Not even close.

As they got ready, Flute kept up an idle stream of chatter. Sunrise didn't talk much, so she had to do most of the work. She didn't mind.

"Can you put the room sign up?" She pointed to the stack of door hangers on the corner desk. "A Jane can clean up while we're gone. Put in a request for dinner too. What should we have?"

Sunrise rubbed his chin. "Thai."

"Okay. Want to grab a movie?"

"Pauly Shore Matrix."

Flute sighed, but nodded. Sunrise loved the Matrix movies, and the Hotel had access to versions from other timelines where Keanu Reeves didn't star in the main role. His favorite was one where Pauly Shore played Neo and Jason Alexander played Morpheus. It was unwatchable garbage, but it made him happy.

The Janes were counterpoints to the Wyatts. Where the Wyatts acted as security, the Janes kept the Hotel running. Each Jane was a quiet, tiny woman in her late forties, with sad eyes and long, frizzy hair. All the pairs loved the Janes as much as they hated the Wyatts. Sometimes, Flute would wonder about where they came from, and how the Hotel functioned, but Sunrise would shrug and go back to his book. He was right; thinking about it spun her in circles. The Hotel simply was.

As they readied to leave, a knock interrupted them. Probably a Jane, coming to check on them. She opened the door and gasped.

Trick.

He smiled at her, flanked by a Wyatt and a Jane. The Wyatt stood there with crossed arms, looking menacing.

"Trick," Flute stammered. "What are you doing here?" She smoothed down her long, black hair. Oh my, was she wearing a t-shirt? Oh no, was that her underwear in the corner? Oh gosh, how many days since she'd changed?

"Do you mind if we come in?" Trick asked.

Flute backed away from the door and gestured them inside, kicking a tambourine into a pile of dirty socks. Sunrise stood straighter and dusted crumbs from some historical meal off his sweatshirt. His scarlet face beamed out a nervous smile. Her own head practically radiated heat, and sweat already pooled in her lower back.

"Thanks," Trick said. He motioned for the Wyatt to stay outside, but the Jane followed him. "Listen, I'm sorry to bug you both. Were you going to the music room?"

Flute nodded, not trusting herself to speak. Trick. In her room.

"I won't be long," he continued. "I'm visiting all the pairs, making sure you're okay. Since the Portal closed, things have been uneven."

"That horrible woman," Flute said.

Vain. She caused all those problems; she and those pairs she escaped with. She left the safety of the Hotel, and then ruined it for the rest of them by closing the Portal. Flute didn't understand what the Portal did because that was Trick business, but if he didn't like it, then neither did she.

Because of how wonky time was, Flute didn't perfectly remember what had happened, but could conjure up an image of Vain; sharp, angry features and a pointy nose. Too bad Roman got stuck with her. Most of the pairs felt sorry for him. Flute assumed she'd kidnapped Charm and Patience and the twins. They were, likewise, wonderful. Well, Blunt was, anyway.

"Beaches?" Sunrise asked.

Trick shook his head. "Sorry, my man. No more off-Hotel trips until we get this business sorted out. That's what I wanted to talk about." He leaned against the dresser with folded arms, and Flute swore she saw his muscles bunch under his shirt. It was too hard to focus.

"You two are the best we have," Trick continued. He smiled at Flute and her knees trembled. "Easily our best producers, by a long shot. You keep the Well full, and I want to tell you how appreciated you are. Arthur agrees."

Flute stammered and blushed, and Sunrise silently stammered and blushed. This was maybe the greatest day of her life, although she had no reasonable way to evaluate that metric. Her wrist itched.

"Okay." She tried not to swoon. "Tell me. I'm ready."

Trick stopped for a beat. "Sorry? Ready for what?"

"For you to tell me how appreciated I am. Wait. Jane, can you get a camera? Sunrise, come stand beside me. Oh, your hair." She licked her palm and fussed at him.

"Are you... like you want me to literally tell you?"

"Yes, that'd be great." She finished with Sunshine's hair and frowned at the Jane who hadn't found a camera.

Sunrise put his arm around her and flashed the peace sign at Trick, who sighed and pinched his nose.

"Flute and Sunrise, I appreciate you."

She squealed and fanned herself. Trick wore a half-smile and shared a glance with the Wyatt.

"I have something for you." He snapped his fingers at the Jane who pulled a record out of her bag and handed it to him. "Flute, this is for you. A token of our appreciation, for all the splendid work you've been doing. You two are the real heroes here. Thank you."

Flute clutched at her gift with greedy hands. She'd never gotten a present from Trick before. She barely even cared what it was.

The cover showed a black-and-white picture of a waterfall, with the word "Unmaker" superimposed over the top. At the bottom was the band name—Joy Division.

"What?" she breathed. She flipped it over to look at the production notes. Nineteen eighty-two. "Trick, what is this? Joy Division only made two records. Are these outtakes?"

"No. We found a world where Ian Curtis didn't kill himself. They still broke up, after, but you're holding a piece of music that literally no one from your earth has ever heard. Joy Division's third record."

Flute tried to talk, but no sound came out of her mouth. Joy Division was her favorite band, ever, ever. How did Trick even know? And to do this for her—her!—was beyond considerate. Perhaps the nicest thing anyone had ever done for her.

"Trick." She didn't trust herself to look him in the eye, or she'd start crying. "Thank you so much. I don't know what to say."

Trick turned to Sunrise. "We've got one for you too, big guy. The last three books in Wheel of Time, written by Robert Jordan." The Jane handed over three books the size of dictionaries and Sunrise's head turned hot red.

Trick tucked one finger under Flute's chin to force her to look at him.

"Just keep doing what you're doing. We'll get the Portal fixed and everything will be back to normal. Remember, the Janes are here if you need anything. You're a good girl."

He left the room with a wave, the Jane trailing behind. Flute's heart thumped a rapid staccato in her chest. She sat on the edge of the bed and fanned herself with the new record.

"Jordan." Sunrise hugged the books to his chest. "Music room canceled?"

Flute nodded. She wanted to listen to music, lay on the bed, and daydream. Sunrise had already hopped back under the covers and was handling the books with reverence, like they were some holy artefacts. Maybe, for him, they were.

Flute sighed and hugged the record to her chest. Nothing could spoil her mood. The Hotel was the best place ever.

Chapter 14: Trick knows a lot about electricity.

"Oh Trick, thank you for the record, I loooove you." The Wyatt made kissing noises and spoke in an absurd falsetto.

Trick sighed and swatted his hand away. "Stop it."

Normally, the Wyatts' games didn't bother him, but he wasn't in the mood for it, and he walked towards the main lobby in dour silence. Being in the Hotel scraped at his psyche, and with the Portal shut down, he had no relief. Sure, he could still visit worlds they'd already been to, but most of them sucked, and without the Padlock to keep him safe, traveling to a new world wasn't something he was interested in attempting. No Portal. No Padlock. No idea how to fix anything. What a mess.

"She's a looker, that one," the Wyatt said.

"Don't touch her," Trick snapped. "You know the rules."

"I'm only making conversation, boss. Where was she from again?"

"Hawaii. No hands on the pairs, clear?"

"Sure, Trick. Sure." The Wyatt held up his hands in supplication. "Besides, it wasn't me asking. It was Wyatt eight hundred and six."

"Don't you have better names for each other?"

"There's only so many ways to screw around with the name Wyatt. Wyatt, Wy, Wat-wat, Att, Atty, Watty, Wat-what, At-why, Whywhy, Watson, Will, Water, Wickershank—"

"One of you is nicknamed Wickershank?"

"Yeah. You know him? He's got a lazy eye from where Wyattson punched him."

Trick rubbed the bridge of his nose. "It is impossible for me to express how profoundly I don't care about any of this. Don't touch the pairs, we're losing enough as it is. Speaking of, how many have we lost since the Portal closed?"

"Four, I think. Maybe five. I'm not sure."

"Five." Trick tried not to let anything show on his face. The Wyatts pounced on weakness, and the only way to keep even a bare semblance of control over them was to never break. But hell, five. That left them with about a hundred pairs and no chance to grab new ones because the only place they could get them from was the solitary world through the Portal.

His temples throbbed and he cracked his knuckles. Pumping energy into the Well wasn't easy, and pair burnout was a real issue. Either the Utility or Conduit could have the ability fried out of them. It happened to one in four. Pairs like Flute and Sunrise were critical. They didn't burn out, ever, and right now Trick needed all the energy he could get. On top of that, it seemed the Wyatts were becoming bored and restless. Another thing to worry about. He'd need to talk to Arthur about it. The Wyatts listened to Arthur.

He strode down the narrow hallway towards the lobby, the gold and red wallpaper pattern giving him a slight headache. The carpet was a stomach-churning puce-yellow, although the last time he'd been there, it had been green. Nobody lived in that section except Flute and Sunrise, so there weren't any other doors. But if he moved in new pairs, a new room would appear. Why? Because the Hotel always changed. It flexed.

A series of brass lamps hanging high up on the walls cast gloomy shadows across the carpet. One had a burned-out bulb. He stopped beneath it, squinting upwards. He flicked at it, but it didn't respond.

"Hmph."

"What?" asked the Wyatt.

"This bulb is burned out."

He flicked the lightbulb again, trying to coax a reaction. A cold sliver of dread made its way into his stomach. He'd never seen a broken lightbulb in the Hotel. Not once. He had a horrible suspicion of what that meant.

"You want a Jane to look at the lightbulb?" the Wyatt asked.

"The lightbulb is a metaphor, Wyatt. Do you know what a metaphor is?"

"Sure. It's the guy who stabs the bulls."

Trick stared at the Wyatt for timeless seconds. "No. It's not that. Do you believe there's physical wiring in the walls, done to code? That we pay a company to provide us with electricity? Nothing exists here, this is all conceptual. There's no filament in that bulb, no tungsten to heat. Do you see?"

"You're smart about lightbulbs, boss. That's great."

"I'm smart about everything. That's not the point. The point is the lightbulb doesn't exist. Why isn't it working?"

The Wyatt shrugged, clearly having lost interest in the conversation.

Trick turned from the offensive light fixture and continued towards the lobby. The hallway from the living quarters opened into the foyer of the Hotel. At present, an enormous crystal chandelier the size of a truck hung above the floor. Elegant couches and chairs provided comfortable places to sit and chat. It was an effort not to notice the surroundings. The lobby changed every time he entered it, which he found disorienting. Prior to visiting Flute, it had looked like an old-timey Western saloon, complete with player piano and beer-soaked wooden benches. He'd never seen the same configuration twice.

The Well loomed at him from the back of the lobby, the only thing in that place that never changed. A circular stone wall, fifteen feet in diameter, surrounded its cavernous hole. Silver handles protruded from the side, the metal scuffed and tarnished from being gripped thousands of times. The Well never moved; never so much as wavered. All the pairs avoided looking at it.

Now that he was playing closer attention, was some of the chandelier crystal cracked? Was that a creak he heard when he walked across the floor? Was the paint chipping?

"Trick?" A pair approached him and the Wyatt, each jostling to hide behind the other. Used, the Utility, was an older man with thinning hair. His Conduit, Frail, was a younger man with dour eyes and dark hair.

"What is it, Used?"

"Um, Frail was wondering—"

Frail elbowed Used in the ribs.

"Frail and I were wondering if we could have a break from maybe going to the Well? Um, Frail says—"

Another elbow to the ribs.

"I mean, we think we're both pretty tired after the last one and I know it makes you mad if we don't do it, but I'm not sure we have much left and it wouldn't be much of a break, only like one cycle."

The Wyatt crossed his arms. "No breaks. Beat it."

Used flicked terrified eyes between Trick and the Wyatt. Those two weren't great producers, and while Trick didn't want to lose even a fraction of energy, he wanted to lose another set of pairs even less. But Arthur's instructions to the Wyatts were clear. Keep the pairs producing energy and do whatever is necessary. Sometimes they could go a bit far. Like with Vain. Regardless, he couldn't show weakness in front of the Wyatt.

"Tell you what, Used. If you and Frail manage to find someone to take your spot and do two shifts, you can get a break."

"What?" Used said. "No one is going to do two. Not for us."

The Wyatt cracked his knuckles. "We can provide some encouragement, if you're feeling tired."

Used and Frail almost fainted. "No, that's great. We're good. Never mind, and forget we even asked. See you soon. Bye."

Before Trick could say anything else, they scampered off and up the stairs to the second floor. Was that rust on the banister?

"I'm going to grab a few Wyatts and visit them, I think," the Wyatt said.

"Don't. You get to touch them if they don't produce. That's the only time. I'll tell Arthur."

"I'll tell Arthur," the Wyatt muttered under his breath.

"Do we have a problem, Wyatt?" Trick stepped closer to the bigger man, his blood pounding in his ears. Never show weakness in front of a Wyatt. Never. Not once.

The Wyatt stared down at him and Trick concentrated on not swallowing.

After an uncomfortable number of moments, the Wyatt finally took a step back. "No problem, Trick. No problem at all. If we're all done here, I'm going to get a scotch."

"The Wyatts are drinking now? Really?"

"Yeah. We're bored."

To call this a shit show would undersell the inherent qualities in both shit and shows. Drunk Wyatts, burnt out bulbs; this place was going to hell. Trick hadn't been paying enough attention. He thought this day couldn't get any worse but the lack of time in this stupid place made sentences like that pointless. He woke up and went to bed. He did things and then did other things. He'd been awake for twenty minutes or fifteen years. Who could even tell? Arthur created watches that helped stabilize time, but they were poor imitations of the real thing.

Oddly, he found himself thinking of Vain, which he'd been doing more frequently since she closed the Portal. He'd be doing something, and an image of her pretty face and enormous eyes would swim into view. Going after her and Roman had been both completely necessary and a wonderful distraction from the mundane, if somewhat terrifying, routine of managing the Hotel. Even though some parts had gotten a bit crazy, it had been better than staying there. What would she do in their place? Quip and punch the Wyatt in the dick. She was so great. If he ever got the Portal fixed, he should see if she wanted to team up or something. Maybe he could strand them on a world for a month or two.

The Wyatt tapped him on the shoulder. "Have we always had a pulsing beam of purple light out front?"

"What?"

Trick peered out the front window, shielding his eyes. The Wyatt was right; a purple light pulsed in the garden before settling into a steady glow. Only one thing had been purple in the garden.

"The Portal." He pressed his face against the glass. "The Portal is open. How?"

"Is this a lightbulb question again?"

"Get the pairs to their rooms. All of them. No one in or out. Got it?"

"Can I use some encouragement?"

"No." Trick grabbed a passing Jane. "Jane, the Wyatts are going to need help escorting the pairs to their rooms. There's something going on. Make sure they're all safe. Can you do that?"

"Yes, Mr. Trick." The Jane scurried away to start rounding up pairs, resulting in good-natured groans as they got off the couches and let themselves get ushered back to their rooms.

"Grab a couple of sober Wyatts and wait for me here. Don't go near the Portal until I'm back."

"Where are you going?"

"To talk to Arthur."

Trick left the Wyatt where he was and ran up the stairs. Arthur's rooms were on the top floor, but given how funky space was in the Hotel, that could mean one flight or fifteen. As he made his way up, he tried to understand what an activated Portal could mean. Arthur couldn't have done it. He'd tried to fix it, but it required too much energy. Pulling that much would have probably killed him, and without the Padlock to bring him back, he wasn't willing to risk it.

It was a bit of a pickle. They needed the Portal open to get energy for the Well, but opening the Portal would take all the energy they had. He could almost laugh. Vain, for all her idiotic ideas, actually crippled the Hotel, probably more than she ever imagined doing.

Vain.

She could have opened the Portal from her side. The explanation made sense. Emma, maybe, could have done it. Trick suspected she was more powerful than Arthur. Much more. For whatever reason, she must have opened the Portal.

A cold drop of sweat rolled down his back. Seeing Arthur wasn't something he enjoyed during good times. Nothing that had happened since the Padlock went missing had been good.

After a few flights, he reached the top floor and stepped into the cold and featureless entrance that led to Arthur's room. His shoes clacked loudly on the marble floors. He paused a moment to collect himself and to smooth his hair back. As he tucked in his shirt, a tile by the door caught his eye.

A crack ran through the center.

Before he could wonder about what that meant, Arthur's voice came from inside.

"What do you want, Trick?"

Trick swallowed and pushed the doors open.

Cold and dusty air wafted out of the dim room. Paraphernalia from Arthur's trips decorated the walls; items that didn't exist in their world. A poster from some soda company called Slurm. A weird object that looked like a thin hand vacuum with a glowing green tube sticking out of it. A blue and white hat with a pine tree logo. Hanging from the ceiling was a robot corpse that looked exactly like Abraham Lincoln from that horrible world that was exclusively populated by robots that looked like Abraham Lincoln. Somehow, the rooms they occupied never changed; only the building. Arthur said it was due to their personal signatures being imprinted on the space.

Arthur lounged on a couch, the wire-rimmed glasses he normally wore sitting carelessly on his chest.

"What?" Arthur snapped without preamble.

"Sorry to bother you. I need—"

"Then don't."

"I only meant that there's something happening."

"Something is always happening, Trick. We're in a timeless Hotel, not a void. Are you here to give me an update on the Utilities?"

Trick blinked, not sure at first what Arthur was referring to, but then it came to him. Two Conduits had burned out, leaving them with two Utilities. Arthur wanted to try to connect them.

"I don't think that's something we'll ever work out, Arthur. The last time we tried a Utility-to-Utility pairing, it nearly killed all of us. The backlash wave of energy it created was—"

"Problematic, yes. Did you go to that world I suggested?"

"I did, Arthur. But even in a timeline where Einstein and Stephen Hawking are best friends, they had no idea what I was referring to. This is magic, not science. We can't pair the Utilities."

"Then why are you here? Was a Wyatt mean again? A Jane got confused? Where's my Padlock?"

"I still haven't—"

"I know you haven't. Is this all you came to tell me? That you're still incompetent? I don't need daily updates for that."

"No, I—"

"Spit it out. Get to the point."

"The Portal is—"

"Closed, yes. Okay, so you did simply come here to remind me how staggeringly ineffectual you are. Thanks for the update. You may leave now. Have a Jane bring me up some orange juice in about half an hour."

Trick couldn't handle this anymore. "The Portal is open," he blurted.

"What?"

"The Portal is open. The light. In the garden. I saw it and so did a Wyatt."

Arthur stood up and put on his glasses. "Why am I only now hearing about this?"

"I tried to tell you. You kept—"

"Asking questions to hurry you along. You blather, Trick. That's your problem. One of. So you saw a light out front of my Hotel and decided it must mean the Portal." Arthur gestured and floated a glass from across the room that he caught in his hand. The hairs on Trick's arm stood up.

"What else could it be, Arthur? We can go look on the balcony."

"So help me Trick, if this is another one of your idiotic pranks, I will peel a portion of your skin off. Think closely before we go any further. Think very closely."

It was an effort to keep his face neutral. Never show weakness. Not in front of the Wyatts, not in front of Arthur. "I'm not playing a prank. I'll show you."

"By all means. Please do." Arthur gestured and Trick gathered the detritus of his dignity and headed towards the balcony.

Arthur threw an arm around his shoulder, and said, "It's all teasing, Trick. You take things so seriously. Laugh a little."

Trick forced a smile on to his face. "Sure Arthur. It's all fun and games."

"That's right. Something to entertain us while you dither and flail for solutions to our problems. You know how hard I work to keep this place running. It can't always be me all the time."

The balcony gave them a panoramic view of the Hotel grounds. From that high up, the edge of the rock the Hotel floated on was clearly visible, and Trick's stomach lurched. Once, a long time ago, before the Handcuffs, a Utility and Conduit jumped off the rock. They didn't drop. They floated.

No single place in the Hotel gave Trick as much mental vertigo as the balcony. From the outside, the Hotel was two stories tall. This balcony was at least twenty stories off the ground. Stupid magic architecture.

Arthur shoved Trick aside and leaned over the edge of the railing. The Portal was clearly open. It stuck out vividly against the faded pink sky.

"My Portal," Arthur said. "How?"

"I think it's Vain," Trick said.

"There's nothing Vain about the Portal. It's a required piece of equipment, integral to the functioning of this establishment. The music room? Now that's vanity."

"No, I mean I think Vain opened the Portal."

Arthur squinted at him. "Is Vain an idiotic name you've given to one of them?"

"Yes. She's the one that stole your Padlock, remember?"

"Do tell." Arthur drummed his fingers on the balcony. "How did she open the Portal?"

"I think Emma did it. The other one I told you about. The one who's like you."

"Another one of your failures. Yes, I remember. Why? To attack us?"

"I have no idea."

"Of course you don't."

"I told the Wyatts to meet us by the front doors."

"If it really is them, I'm taking my Padlock back."

"Don't kill Vain," Trick said. Fast. Too fast. He needed to be careful. "She might be able to tell us something. Give us information."

"I can't see what information she'd have that would be of any use to me."

"We won't know if she's dead."

"And you're still pushing this idea that Emma can help us?" Arthur chewed on the word help.

"I do. She might be able to come up with a solution. Something. I don't know."

"Fine. Let's go visit this Vain of yours."

Trick nodded and didn't swallow. Vain was back.

Chapter 15: Vain suggests a new haircut for Emma.

Vain hopped through the Portal, and millions of honeybees kissed her skin. Eternity stretched to its breaking point, a humbling expanse of forever that reminded her of how much of her life she'd wasted. It took both one second and a million hours; then she was through.

The Portal opened into a waypoint; a stone cavern with low ceilings illuminated by soft white light that bled from the rocks. She'd defeated Trick there before Emma blew it up, but no signs of their battle remained. Vain expected rubble and debris. They had, after all, blown it up. But the stone rocks and floor were unmarred by scorch blasts.

"Well, that's disappointing." She blew an errant bang from her forehead.

Emma's frisbee-wide eyes shimmered with tears. Charm groaned and rubbed her hands together. They did not look like a cool trio of super badass warriors; they looked like scared and helpless people.

Time to rally the troops.

"Every great group of heroes follow a pattern," she said. "Charlie's Angels. The Three Musketeers. Three's Company. Most of the Ghostbusters. There's the brawn, the brains, and the beauty. Obviously, I'm the brains. I could be all three, but that would be greedy. Charm, you're the beauty. Emma, that leaves you as the brawn. There. Nothing to worry about, anymore."

Neither woman applauded her fantastic role-setting. If anything, it was almost like they weren't paying attention to her, but that wasn't possible. Obviously, they were missing something. Had she not been clear about their roles? Did she get the order wrong?

"That's not even close to what I am worried about," Charm said.

Vain motioned at the door. "It's a straight sprint from the gardens to the Hotel." She held up her wrist and jangled the plastic handcuff. "These will help us fit in. If we see a Wyatt, play it cool and stupid."

"I'm so scared." Charm licked her lips. "I don't want to go back."

"We can do this." Vain tried to look confident. Her own stomach was only so unsettled because she hadn't been eating much. No other reason she could think of.

"Let's get this over with," Emma said.

"If we're captured, don't tell them anything. They can only kill us once and I'm sure it will be quick." She tapped her chin. "Unless they torture us. Which they almost certainly will. Do either of you want tips for getting through torture?"

"Please stop talking," Emma said. "We're wasting time."

Vain shrugged and took their hands in hers. Time to get going.

The first step, as Vain had learned was the case with steps towards time-refracted magic hotels on the corner of space and nowhere, took a second or forever. More bees kissed her skin, then her foot came down on solid ground.

Red, lightning-streaked skies. The smell of nothing. Lush green bushes that stood out against the jagged, barren landscape. Time no longer making any sense, and her memories colliding into themselves, making rational thought ten times harder. And, of course, the ever-changing magic Hotel loomed at them in the distance.

Home.

"Oh my heavens." Emma breathed. Her eyes were teacups,

and she covered her mouth. "It's real. I always intellectually believed it, but it's not the same."

"Real like a housewife," Vain said. "No time for sightseeing, though. We need to move."

Emma turned in a circle, taking everything in. "This place is a disaster. I can barely think. If I don't make it out, can one of you tell my mom? I guess you'll have to make up a story or you'll be arrested for murder, but is that okay? I don't know why we didn't talk about this before."

"No one's dying today, honey." Charm gave Emma a quick hug. "In and out. Right Vain?"

"Right. But if we do die, I have something I need you both to know."

Emma and Charm nodded, giving her their full attention.

"I preferred the third Nightmare on Elm Street to the original. I'm sorry I never told you that before."

Charm blew a huge breath out of her nose, and Emma rolled her eyes for some reason. But she also wore a small smile.

"Thank you for telling us that, Vain. I unironically like Justin Bieber. I think he's cute. Please don't tell anyone."

"I cheat when I do crosswords," Charm said.

Emma half-laughed, half-sobbed, and hugged Charm. It made sense that something like crossword puzzle cheating would bother Emma. It was courageous of Charm to admit that, even though Vain didn't quite see the big deal.

Behind them, the Portal glowed an angry, visible purple. Super visible, if Vain was being honest. Like 'visible from a couple hundred miles away' visible. Shit.

"I don't remember it being this ostentatious," Vain said. "We have to be really fast, I think. They're going to see this. Emma, are you okay with your muckity-muck power or whatever? Does thinking about math help?"

"Yeah. There's a lot of it here, but I'm holding it back. It's okay. I can do this."

They got moving.

Gravel-paved paths weaved through the topiary like twisted snakes. Vain couldn't understand how the grass grew there, but nowhere else on that stupid, floating rock. Benches lined the pathways, some covered in spilled water bottles or discarded books, as if people had dropped everything before leaving. They ran for long enough that a stitch settled into Vain's side.

"Too long." Charm skidded to a halt and bent over to catch her breath. "It's all too long. We've been in this garden for weeks. We're going to die in here."

"It's been three seconds, tops," Emma said. "What are you talking about?"

"Don't think about time." Vain pushed them forward. "It screws you up. Don't worry about before and after. There's only now. Keep your mind on the mission. We're almost there."

Behind them, the Portal's ominous purple glow reflected against the backdrop of the faded-red sky. She no longer had any reasonable expectation of getting in and out unnoticed. Arthur couldn't miss that. But they had to keep going.

"When we get to Flute, you do all the talking," Vain said to Charm. "She likes me a lot, but it's better that you convince her."

"What am I supposed to say?"

"I don't know, Charm," Vain emphasized the older woman's name. "If only you had some defining characteristic to use in this exact scenario."

"What if she won't come?"

Vain held up her fist. "Plan B."

Even by her standards, walking through the front door was too reckless. She turned down a path that ran perpendicular to the Hotel. Hopefully, they could use a side door, although the way the Hotel fluctuated, nothing was certain. Currently, it looked like a rustic lodge, complete with dirty windows and foliage crawling up the eaves. No matter what form the Hotel took, it always appeared malignant, and Vain could not shake the feeling that it knew they were intruding.

The path took them to a break in the bushes and a sharp turn that led to a side door. With renewed energy, they gave a last push of speed and burst from the garden. Her plans were as spectacular as she thought.

The door opened, and a Wyatt stepped out, putting a cigarette in his mouth.

Vain braked hard, and Charm and Emma ran into her

back. Charm held up her wrist.

"We're pairs. Don't hurt us."

The Wyatt regarded them with a bored expression. "Get back to your rooms, ladies. Trick called for a lockdown. Didn't the Janes tell you?"

Besides the cigarette that now dangled from his mouth, this Wyatt held a bottle of whiskey and swayed on his feet. A day's growth of stubble covered his cheeks. Vain didn't know the Wyatts drank professionally, but this one seemed loopy. He squinted at the group for several moments, then his eyes widened.

"You." He pointed at her. "You kidnapped me after the fight in the abandoned parking lot. You're Fame."

"Vain." She threw herself at the Wyatt, expecting to catch him off guard, but he dodged and she sailed past, skidding across the gritty pavement before slamming up against the side of the building.

The Wyatt threw his whiskey bottle at Emma, hitting her in the head with a grotesque thunk. She dropped to her knees with a startled cry, hands going to her face. He rushed forward and spin-kicked Charm in the chest, sending her flying. Vain shook her head. Drunken, spin kicking Wyatts were not something she imagined she'd need to prepare for.

Time to try something different; a move that had never failed her, not counting the several other times when it had not worked. She ran at the Wyatt again, but this time jumped on his back and wrapped her legs around his waist. He yelled and tried to shake her off, but she held tight. Time to end it.

"Yaa!" She twisted the Wyatts neck with a single, jerking movement.

"Oww, shit, my epiglottis," the Wyatt howled. "Did you just try to break my neck?"

"That works in movies." Vain panted, clinging to his back as he swung her about. "Do Wyatts have robot bones?"

The Wyatt elbowed her in the ribs, sending the air out of her lungs with a whoosh. She held fast and bit him on the temple. His hair tasted like soap.

"Get off me, you stupid bitch." He yanked her forward, sending her somersaulting through the air to land beside Charm with a bone-jarring thud. A sharp pain flashed from her elbow to her shoulder, and she moaned. The Wyatt kicked her in the skull and everything went blurry.

Through the haze, she saw Emma sit up, cradling her head while blood poured through her fingers. The Wyatt hurled himself at her, connecting with tremendous force. He pinned her shoulders under his knees and wrapped his giant hands around her throat. Emma yelled and bucked her hips, but he was too big. His shoulder muscles bunched as he squeezed her neck. He was strangling her. Christ, he was going to kill her.

Vain tried to get to her feet, but the ground rocked like a boat in a tempest, and she couldn't seem to get her legs steady. Beneath the Wyatt, Emma's beet-red face turned to her, pleading, her eyes bulging from their sockets. Vain needed to do something. Emma was going to die. She needed to—

The Wyatt released Emma, his arms pulled outwards. He struggled against whatever was happening. "What the fuck?"

As if being picked up by an invisible hand, he raised up and hovered above the ground, legs kicking in the empty air. Emma sat up, coughing, glaring murder at him. Her red hair fell over her face, mixing with the blood that poured from her forehead. When she wiped it, she held her hand up as if it wasn't even part of her body. Like she was examining a distasteful insect. With a contemptuous gesture, she flung the Wyatt against the building. He thudded against the side and slid to the ground, unconscious.

Charm helped Vain up and they leaned on each other for support. Blood covered Emma's face. Hell. A single, drunken Wyatt did that. They were supposed to be the ones with superpowers.

"That worked great," Vain said, trying to rally. "Next time, let's not get our asses kicked that badly."

Something grabbed her by the neck and lifted her off the ground. She had no idea where this new attack was coming from. The vice-like pressure on her throat was smothering, and she gasped and spat while trying to take a breath. Her feet dangled below her.

Emma held out her hand like she was clutching an invisible cup. She grinned at Vain.

"I never liked you," she said, "not really. I pretended to, because I pretend to like everyone, but honestly? I think you're kind of an asshole."

Emma closed her hand into a fist, crushing Vain's windpipe. Vain scratched and clawed at the invisible pressure on her neck, trying to do something, anything, to stop it.

"Emma, stop!" Charm stumbled towards Emma and spun her around. "Fight it! You're killing her!"

The sight of her friends faded and a rushing noise filled her ears, like the ocean was right beside her. Even kicking her legs took too much energy. What was she trying to do again? Oh, right. Breathe. Her chest screamed for oxygen. Fire filled her lungs. She was so tired. More tired than she'd ever been. Darkness took over her vision, and the ocean noise became softer. So this was how she died.

The pressure on her neck vanished with a pop, and she collapsed. She took the largest single breath she'd ever taken in her entire life, a sucking inhalation of air that tasted sweeter than any drink she'd ever had. That, followed by coughing and choking. Every gasp was agony. Every gasp was paradise. As more breaths followed, her vision returned.

Emma had tried to kill her.

Charm had Emma wrapped in a hug, her eyes wide and wild. Emma sobbed into her shoulder, the blood from her forehead staining Charm's shirt, clinging to her like a life preserver.

"I'm sorry. I'm sorry. I didn't mean to."

On her hands and knees, Vain coughed and spat into the dusty ground. Her neck was on fire. With trembling hands, she prodded the skin and was rewarded with a fresh wave of pain.

"We have to leave, Vain," Charm said over Emma's crying. "I hate your plans so much. I'm sorry, but I do. This is horrible. We're going to die."

"Not leaving," Vain coughed. She could barely talk. "Flute."

Emma pushed herself away from Charm and hugged Vain. Tears cut clean paths through her blood-soaked cheeks. It took all of Vain's self-control to not punch her.

"I can't do this," Emma said. "I have to get out of here."

Vain groaned and gnashed her teeth. With a sinking heart, she realized they were right. It would never work. Emma was too dangerous. Bringing her had been a terrible idea, the only poorly thought-out element in her otherwise spectacular plan.

"Charm, get Flute." It hurt to talk. "Emma. Me. Portal. Home."

"You're leaving me here?" Charm said. "Why me?"

"Flute. Hates. Me." It was hard to admit, but now wasn't the time for heroics. "Won't come. If. Me."

"Christ on a cracker," Charm said.

"I ruined this," Emma wailed. "I'm sorry."

Vain took Emma's hand and gave Charm a shove towards the Hotel. "Only hope. Charm." Her throat screamed at her, saying no more talking. Even breathing hurt.

Emma squeezed Vain's hand hard enough to make her bones grind together. Charm stared at them both with terrified eyes.

"Please. Roman," Vain croaked.

A loudspeaker hissed to life, and whining feedback filled the air. Charm gasped and clapped her hands over her ears. A Wyatt started speaking with a slurred voice.

"Attention. Is this working? I didn't know this existed. Has this always been here? This rules. Sibilance. Sibilance. Check this out."

The Hotel had a loudspeaker system now? Vain groaned. This day-slash-eternity kept getting worse and worse.

"My name is Wyatt, and I cannot lie. You other fellas might deny. When a girl walks in with a— hey, stop." Sounds of slapping hands and scuffles came out of the speaker, followed by the high-pitched whine of feedback. A more sober Wyatt voice spoke.

"This is not a drill. The Hotel is under lockdown. All pairs are confined to their rooms until further notice."

The loudspeaker gave a final buzz and clicked off. Vain couldn't even tell where it was coming from.

Charm took a deep breath and set her jaw.

"Keep the Portal open." She pointed at Vain. "Promise?"

"Pinky swear," Vain said. She held up her pinky, but

Charm grabbed both her and Emma in a rough embrace.

"Love you," Vain croaked. "Careful."

"I'll be back with Flute," Charm said.

She spun and ran towards the Hotel by herself, the bravest thing Vain had ever seen someone do. Emma dropped Vain's hand and squeezed the sides of her head like she was trying to make it pop.

"Don't try to kill me again, okay? That sucked." Vain coughed.

They stumbled back towards the Portal. Vain only hoped they'd make it in time.

Chapter 16: Flute doesn't like jewelry.

Flute tried to ignore the Wyatts wrestling for control of the loudspeaker system she hadn't been aware existed up until that moment. Each time she thought they were done, it would whine to life, and they'd continue entertaining themselves.

"This emergency broadcast system is for emergencies only. And broadcasts, I suppose."

A blare of feedback was followed by punching sounds. A drunker Wyatt said, "There once was a girl from the cities. She had the biggest set of—"

More scuffling followed, then the loudspeaker went silent. Flute rolled her eyes and tried to focus on the music from her record. Sunrise sat beside her on the bed, reading his book, but she could tell his heart wasn't in it.

"Has this happened before?" she asked.

Sunrise shrugged. Sunrise had a few dozen shrugs, and they were all expressive. That one meant 'I'm not sure what's happening, but it's okay because we're together'.

"I wonder if the Hotel's under attack or something? What would even attack it?"

Sunrise did a different type of shrug, one with more left shoulder. This one meant, 'your questions are worrying me, Flute, and I wish you'd stop asking.'

On good days she could coax dozens of words from him, but not now. Disgruntled, she rolled off the bed and peeled back the poster covering the window. Nothing looked different outside. Same red sky, same endless void surrounding the Hotel. Boring.

"I'm going to poke my head out," she said. "I want to see what's happening."

"Don't," Sunrise said.

"The Janes wouldn't let anything bad happen. I'm only peeking down the hallway. Maybe we're getting some new pairs, that would be fun." New faces were always nice, although she wasn't sure why it required a lockdown. But that was Trick and Arthur business.

Thinking always turned her head to jelly. Something about the way time worked made it difficult to string together thoughts. In a more loquacious moment, Sunrise had reasoned that memory was a physical act, and physical acts required time to work. The lack created a temporal chasm; without the connective material, memory stopped functioning. Flute had frowned in thoughtful attentiveness, but couldn't understand a thing he was saying. He was great for trying to explain it, though.

Whatever the reason, attempts to recall the past made her eyes water and her skull pound. So she really didn't know if this had happened before. Either way, it was something new; something different to take away the crushing tedium of the endless present. Maybe even a fun adventure. She'd always wanted one of those.

Flute opened the door. A Jane leaned against the opposite wall with her hands on her hips.

"Stay in your room, Flute," said the Jane. "Whatever's happening, it's trouble."

"Do you know what's going on?" Flute tried to peer past, but the Jane stepped forward, creating a barricade with her body.

"Nothing that involves us. The Wyatts are a kicked-over beehive and Trick is with Arthur."

The Jane tucked an errant strand of hair back under her bandana and Flute used the opportunity to scoot under her arm. A person ran down the hallway towards her room, arms pumping. Not a Wyatt, not a Jane, not someone Flute recognized.

Was someone coming for her? Was someone trying to attack her and Sunrise? That would explain the announcements and how everyone was so worked up.

Flute's breath seized, and she toppled backward, sending both her and the Jane to the floor. Sunrise hopped from the bed to help them up. Flute kicked at the door, trying to close it, stomach clenched in fear.

A woman appeared in the doorway, breathing hard and holding her side. Flute yelped and tried to scramble behind the Jane. The newcomer looked familiar; long brown hair with streaks of gray peeking out at the roots and happy, smiling eyes, although they weren't smiling now.

"Charm?" Sunrise blurted. Flute squinted.

"Charm?" She untangled herself from the Jane. "Why are you here? You died. Days ago? Years?"

"Hello, Flute." Charm leaned over to catch her breath. "Hi everyone. Wait, why would I be dead?"

"Trick said Vain killed you when she escaped and ruined everything."

"Vain what?" Charm shook her head. "There's no time for this. Flute, you have to come with us. Roman needs your help. I'm sorry to be so abrupt but there's actually no time to explain. Vain would love that I said that."

Flute couldn't make sense of this new, confusing adventure. Charm was alive? Roman needed help?

The Jane positioned herself between Flute and Charm. "Get out of here. I'll get a Wyatt. I swear I will." Sunrise, brave soul that he was, also stepped forward.

"Let me explain," Charm said.

"Why did you even come back?" the Jane said. "Who are you kidnapping now?"

Charm recoiled. "We didn't take anyone, Jane. We left on purpose."

"You can't have this one."

"I told you. Roman is hurt. He needs her help."

"Find someone else."

"Get out of my way. Flute is the only one who can do this. Why do you even care?"

"We protect the pairs," the Jane said. "It's who we are."

Charm inhaled through her nose and stepped eye to eye with the Jane. Flute held her breath. "You're the seventh Jane." Charm reached out and brushed the top of the Jane's ear with her fingertip. "You have this scar from where a Wyatt cuffed you."

The Jane flinched from Charm's touch and flicked her ear like she was swatting a fly.

"You can choose who you are," Charm said. "Let me pass. Leaving should be Flute's choice, not yours. You don't get to make that decision for her."

The Jane looked like she was going to argue, but continued to rub at her ear. She wasn't getting out of the way. Charm had said Flute was needed. Being needed was even better than an adventure, so Flute pushed her way forward and jutted out her chin. "Let her talk."

It was two against one and the Jane gawped, unable to respond. She backed away, sniveling, and ran from the room.

"I think she's going to tell on us," Charm said.

"How are you alive?" Flute asked. "Trick told us Vain killed you and Patience."

Charm shook her head. "Vain didn't kill Patience, the Wyatts did."

"We had a funeral for her."

"Oh." Charm put her hand to her chest. "You did?"

Flute nodded. "Ever sang a song. Do you remember him? He has a beautiful voice, he's paired with Noble. I played guitar. It was lovely. I cried a little."

"I wish I could have seen that. You can tell me about it later. I need your help, Flute. Roman is hurt. Badly."

"Leave the Hotel?" Flute reached out to grab Sunrise. "We couldn't ever."

"Stay," Sunrise agreed.

"Oh crap, right. The Handcuffs. How Vain was able to think around them to plan an escape, I'll never understand. Sheer stubborn insanity, that one. Flute, give me your wrist. We don't have much time. I think the Jane is going to get a Wyatt."

"No." Flute pulled her hand behind her back. This was too much adventure. Way too much. Her Handcuff burned against her skin and her chest constricted. She wished she'd never sent the Jane away. "I want you to leave."

Charm reached forward and grabbed her wrist. Flute tried to wrestle free, but Charm's grip was too strong. She pulled Flute to the ground and pinned her hand. Sunrise jumped in to help.

"Stop fighting me!" Charm yelled.

Sunrise howled and bit Charm on the shoulder. Charm screamed in pain, but didn't release Flute's arm. The three fought and scrambled, and somehow, Flute took an elbow to the temple. Charm managed to kick Sunrise in the knee, causing him to clutch his leg in pain. He reached up and pulled the Robert Jordan book off the bed and hurled it at Charm. It thudded off her chest.

Charm howled and dove on top of Flute, flattening her to the ground. She grasped the silver Handcuff Flute had worn for so long, and pushed at the edges with two fingers. With an audible click, it opened and fell off.

They all sat there, tangled up in each other's arms, panting heavily. Flute raised her wrist to her eyes. Her bare wrist. The weight was gone.

In an instant, everything changed.

Moments shuffled through her mind, the images coming lightning-fast, but with new clarity. The torture they endured, the Wyatts assaulting them, the agony of the Well. They were objects. Things to be used. The smug way Trick laughed and placated her with records, as if that excused an eternity of misery. The covers came off and she could see.

"I'm a prisoner."

She had to get out of there. Of course she did. How had she ever thought otherwise?

"Do Sunrise next," she said.

Sunrise had huddled up against the bed, holding his hands behind his back, horror written across his features. Charm reached out for his wrist, but he wouldn't let her near him.

"It's okay, Sunrise," Flute said. "I promise. Believe me."

Sunrise gave her a pleading look, but Flute held firm and motioned at him to give Charm his wrist. After a moment, he sighed and handed his arm over.

"Patience figured this out," Charm said as she worked.

"She examined the Handcuffs at the Well, in those seconds when we regained our powers. Patience could see things. There's a hidden clasp. Almost impossible to recognize but... ah, there we go."

Once more, Charm pressed with two fingers and the Handcuff clicked open and fell off Sunrise's wrist.

At first, he didn't react. He went statue-still, his chest rising and falling in agitation. Flute rubbed his arm, but he didn't even acknowledge her presence.

He screamed.

Flute shushed him and tried to settle him down, but he stormed away, knocking over the table beside the bed and throwing the lamp at the mirror. He followed that by punching the wall, and for good measure, he kicked the dresser. Flute understood his reaction and let him destroy the room. Spent, he dropped to his knees, chest heaving with exertion.

"Feel better?" Flute rubbed his shoulders, and he looked at her with soaking eyes.

"Fuckers," he said.

"We have to go," Charm said. "Vain and Emma should already be back at the Portal."

"Vain? Vain is here?" Although the rational part of her mind understood she'd been manipulated, the name provoked a tremor in Flute. It was a name to whisper when the Wyatts or Janes weren't listening. The one who escaped. The one who ruined everything.

Flute and Sunrise exchanged a long look. How did he feel about this adventure? She could still feel the phantom weight of the Handcuff and she absently rubbed her wrist. They'd never put it on her again. But going without him simply wasn't an option.

"Let's go," Sunrise said.

Charm gave them a weary thumbs up and stuck her head out into the hallway. "This way," she said. "We'll go out the side exit. We have to move as fast as we can."

"Wait." Flute took a final look around the room she'd spent an eternity in. She couldn't stop rubbing her wrist. Impulsively, she ran to the dresser Sunrise had knocked over, and picked up her record. She turned it over in her hands and brought it down on her knee, snapping it in half. The broken pieces fell to the floor.

"I'm ready."

Chapter 17: Emma remembers her kindergarten teacher.

Emma had tried to kill Vain.

Not hurt her, not attack her, she'd straight up tried to murder her. They had no idea how close she had come; how difficult it had been to pull herself back and regain control. It was getting worse. Now, it seemed even a trickle of the power caused her to be overwhelmed by anger and fury, by a rage that threatened to consume everything. She needed to fight harder, that's all there was to it. Fight against the rage and somehow find calm and peace.

She let Vain pull her along. If she opened her eyes, she'd see the horrible black and blue bruises that surrounded Vain's neck like a parody of a Christmas wreath; see the damage she'd done to her sort-of friend. The memory already haunted her; a ghost in her attic, rattling chains of remorse.

Coming here had been a horrible idea. Attack the Well? Why had she let herself be talked into that? What did she even think she was going to do? Vain's plans never worked out, and Emma was always the collateral damage. When Vain taught Emma to use her powers, they blew up a gas station. When she convinced Emma to fight Trick and the Wyatts at the abandoned parking lot, her fingernails fell out. God, she'd created a platform across two buildings so they could sneak out the window. The expression went 'fool me once, shame on you, fool me twice, shame on me'. What was the expression for 'fool me half a dozen times'?

Now everything rested on poor, brave Charm. If she could get Flute, this disaster could still be salvaged. But Emma's part in the adventure was done. There was simply too much power in the Hotel. Eddies and currents swirled around her, and it took all her control to keep them from overwhelming her.

Long ago, she'd gone swimming in the ocean. Signs covered the beach, warning of undertow; but Emma had been young, and her friends had been doing it, and she wanted to fit in. With a fluttering heart, she'd stepped into the water, feeling the pull of the waves sucking at her legs and body. She believed herself safe if she kept her feet planted, but a single wrong step took away that tenuous security and before she could blink, the current had whipped her fifty feet from the shore.

The next ten minutes had been spent on some of the most terrifying swimming of her life, and wait, why in the hell was she thinking about a ten-year-old memory? What was even wrong with her? She was running through a different dimension, after almost killing her friend, and she was worried about swimming. The Hotel was to blame. It made concentration a million times harder. Random, disjoined ideas pinballed through her brain.

"Shit," Vain said.

Emma snapped back to attention, surprised they'd already crossed the broad expanse between the Hotel and the garden. The trip seemed faster this time, but Emma was already learning how useless any measurement of time was.

"What?" she asked.

"Look." Vain pointed. "At the Portal. People."

"Who?" Emma squinted across the distance. They weren't far away. A couple dozen more steps and they'd crest the slight incline and be in sight of the people guarding the Portal. "Wyatts?"

Vain's voice was crushed rocks, gravel rubbing on gravel. "Worse."

Emma looked closer. One man, with his full lips and model's face, was familiar. Trick. The man who had her kidnapped, and who sort of tortured her boyfriend with a fake testicle-eating rodent. Another man stood beside him; one Emma hadn't seen before.

"Who is that?" she asked.

Vain spat into the dirt.

"Arthur."

Emma's heart entertained itself by performing what seemed to be the entire opening routine of Riverdance. She gasped and clutched her chest. Her legs were damp string.

Whatever she expected from Arthur, this wasn't it. He didn't wear a black cloak or radiate the full weight of all of humanity's evil; he looked like a bank manager. Thin wire glasses perched on an upturned nose beneath thinning black hair. He had a mustache, for goodness' sake.

"He looks like a kindergarten teacher," Emma said.

"He looks nothing like Arnold Schwarzenegger," Vain said.

Emma checked off 'incomprehensible, baffling reference' in her Vain bingo card for about the fiftieth time. She'd need to tell Charm. They both were struggling to get the spot for normal, human joke.

"What do we do?"

Arthur was a person she'd heard so much about; a being of incomprehensible power. And here he stood, half a football field away.

Vain rubbed her neck and grimaced. "Have to lure them away." She pulled the Padlock out of her pocket and wiggled it. "I have something they want."

"You said Arthur was all-powerful. How are we going to stop him?"

"Not me." Vain poked her in the chest. "You."

Emma blew a strand of hair out of her eyes with an annoyed puff. "How?"

"Dunno. Can you beat him?"

That was the question, the one Emma had been avoiding thinking about since she set foot on that bizarre floating rock. Could she take Arthur in a showdown? She closed her eyes and probed with her mind, letting her senses expand. Power radiated from him, there was no question. Not Hotel amounts, not Portal amounts, but enough. But... could Emma summon more?

"Well?" Vain gave her a nudge.

"Maybe. I'm not sure. Are we going to split up?"

"We need to pull them from the Portal, so Charm has a clear path. It's the only thing that matters."

"What good does it do to save Roman if we die in the process?"

"What good does it do to live if Roman's not around?" Vain cracked her knuckles. "Do whatever you want, Emma. I'm going. I owe him for… everything. I owe him for everything."

Vain stopped rubbing her neck and glared at Arthur and Trick with enough intensity to start a fire. If Emma did nothing, Vain would get captured, Arthur would get the Padlock, Roman would still be in a coma, and everything would have been pointless.

"Charm's right. Your plans are terrible." She took a deep breath. "Let's go attack Arthur."

Chapter 18: Vain's insults need a little work.

Vain ignored the way her heart slammed against her chest, ignored the hot, angry burn surrounding her neck, and ignored Emma's quite saucy remarks about her flawless plans.

Sure, it had some wrinkles. Why had Arthur shown up? He should be mucking about in the multi-verse or whatever he did to pass what passed for time. Didn't he have any hobbies?

Her plan was turning out to be way more complicated than she'd intended. She wished it were more like Ocean's Eleven. Now that was a straightforward plan. Hire a bunch of people, fit a contortionist into a box, get out, boom. She bet George Clooney couldn't pull off a Flute Heist. Besides, Emma was hardly a Brad Pitt-like sidekick.

"You're barely Matt Damon," she said, in case Emma worried that Vain expected her to do something Matt Damon-like.

"What?" Emma frowned. Fifty percent of their interaction was Emma struggling to understand simple sentences. She didn't have that problem with Charm. When it all ended, Vain would visit Emma's fancy college to figure out why it made her dumber.

Vain gave her neck one final rub and took Emma's hand. Even though she was weird and not great at jokes, and she'd tried to kill her not moments ago, Emma was still sort of her friend. A friend that was stealing her other friend, leaving her with fewer friends, but still a friend. Relationships were tricky.

"Are you ready?"

"Ready."

Emma's eyes were wide and worried, so Vain tried to put on a sideways smile that would hide the gnawing horror in her stomach. One of them needed to be brave.

Every breath sent a furious rush of pain through her neck, and she couldn't stop opening and closing her free hand. Emma squeezed her other with enough force to make her wince, but Vain didn't ask her to stop. At least Emma had wiped the blood off her forehead, but the welt from the whiskey bottle still looked nasty.

Arthur and Trick watched them approach while a single Wyatt leaned against the Portal, looking bored. Trick wasn't bored. His mouth hung open in shock, and he didn't even glance at Emma. Stupid, irritating, beautiful Trick. And finally, she'd see Arthur up close. Her nemesis. Face to face. She'd never talked to him before, but there he was. Her legs were shaking. Probably something to do with the altitude of floating rock Hotels.

They stopped five feet away from the Portal. Arthur raised a single eyebrow, taking them both in. Vain tried to swallow.

"Hello, Arthur," she said.

Arthur gave her a lazy look up and down, and Vain pulled her jacket closed.

"Is this the one?" he asked Trick. "Emma?"

"No," Trick said. "Emma is the other one. This is Vain."

"I can see you didn't name her that for her looks."

Heat rushed to Vain's face and she blurted, "He should have named me Padlock-stealing Magoo for all the hot, sexy Padlock-stealing I did."

She'd never felt this small in her entire life, and she struggled against the gross feeling of insignificance that bubbled up from somewhere deep in her stomach. He didn't know who she was. She'd stolen his Padlock, broken his Portal, crippled his operation, and he didn't even know what she looked like.

"Where's Roman?" Trick asked. "Why is it just the two of you? Why did you even come back here? Did you do this?" He waved at the Portal.

"You've asked me a lot of questions." Vain could hardly

make her mouth work, it was so dry. "I will answer them sequentially, but the answer is the same to all of them, and it's suck it." Stalling for time was always a great technique, but she had no idea what to do next.

Arthur winked. "Goodbye, Padlock-stealing Magoo."

His entire demeanor changed, from casual guy having a chat to ruthless murderer. The way his face transformed was startling. His lips curled back in a snarl and his eyes flashed with hatred. A single pulsing vein throbbed in his forehead. He raised his hands, palms up, then made a pushing gesture towards her, and Trick yelled "No! We agreed! Not her!"

Emma staggered back and shot out her arm across Vain's chest. Her knees buckled and a small, meagre whimper escaped her lips. The grass beside them smoked and blackened. The air itself had weight and mountains of pressure crashed around her.

Arthur's murderous gaze shifted to Emma and the two locked eyes. The hair on Emma's forearms was standing up.

"Emma?" Vain whispered.

"He is attempting to crush you with power," Emma's jaw clenched. Her hand in front of Vain's chest shook with exertion and the cut above her eye dripped a single line of blood down her check. "I am preventing it. Barely."

Vain had no idea how to react to that statement. Emma and Arthur waged a silent battle across five feet of space.

"Run," Emma said.

Emma seemed to lash out with an energy strike against Arthur. He deflected it, but the shock wave sent Vain tumbling backwards. Once she stopped rolling, she staggered to her feet. Her body was already such a horrific mess of bruises that the fresh, new pain hardly registered.

Arthur struck with the power, and it was Emma's turn to deflect. Whatever Emma did, it sort of worked, except Vain was once again hammered by residual energy waves and thrown a half dozen feet away.

"Run," Emma said again. "I'll handle Arthur."

"You miserable bitch," Arthur snarled. "How dare you? Trick, get me my Padlock from Magoo. Emma and I are going to have a talk. It seems she wants to learn a lesson."

Trick nodded and approached with his hands out, like she was a skittish calf. "Easy does it," he murmured. "Don't run, Vain. Let this happen. You don't have the full story."

"Go get them, babe," Vain shouted. Emma glared at her, and Vain swallowed. She gave Arthur the finger. "Hey dicktits. Suck your Padlock."

She waggled the Device at him one last time for good measure, then ran towards the Hotel.

"There's nowhere to go." Trick yelled.

Well, that wasn't true.

She could think of one place to go.

<u>Chapter 19: Flute really likes lemonade.</u>

Flute followed Charm out of her room, stepping across the threshold that marked her as being someone's property to being her own person. To signify the moment, she stomped her foot and paused, wondering if the Hotel would react.

The Hotel did not.

The hallway remained confusing and off-putting. This version presented as a hospital, complete with gleaming metal tiles on the wall, and faded, aqua-blue tiling on the floor. Nicotine lights cast a jaundiced yellow glow on everything. This Hotel seemed bitter.

Perhaps it was reacting, after all.

No matter how hard she tried, she couldn't stop rubbing her wrist. The Handcuff had been part of her wardrobe for eternities and her unadorned arm looked wrong. How much of her behavior had it been controlling? Did she even enjoy music? Or Sunrise?

Speaking of her devoted friend, his hands were so deep in his pockets it was as if his arms ended at his elbows. A muscle in his cheek twitched and his shoulders were bunched around his ears. Poor thing, he was terrified. Flute hitched up her pants and harrumphed. Personality-controlling bracelet and evil forever

Hotels notwithstanding, she couldn't let him face it alone. Not while she drew breath.

She linked her arm with his and said, "Take us out of here, Charm. We're both ready. Together." The relieved look Sunrise gave her made her fears vanish. He was still her best friend, Handcuff or not.

Charm motioned them to silence, trying to look in every direction at once. She walked in a bent-over crouch, like she was afraid of mortar shells or something.

"Should we run?" Flute didn't want to interrupt their getaway and obviously Charm was the expert in all things escaping-related, but this slow, cautious crawl forward seemed excessive.

"The Wyatts," Charm whispered. "I don't want to run into one by accident."

That made sense. Flute shrugged and followed in an uncomfortable crouch, with Sunrise also doing his best to scootch. The hallway continued for longer than made sense, with only the sound of their footfalls on the tile floor working to separate the moments. Before she could ask how many weeks they'd been walking, it abruptly ended at a set of glass doors with thick, black trim. A buzzing neon sign read, 'Charm necklace'.

"Why would it say that?" Flute whispered. "Does it know who you are?"

"This place is terrible," Charm said, but Flute noticed she didn't look at the sign. "Let's get out of here."

They stumbled outside, and Charm spun in a circle with frantic motions of her head. She hugged the wall and ducked. Flute and Sunrise waited politely. Perhaps Charm was not the master escapist Flute believed her to be.

Flute tapped her on the shoulder. "May we run now, please? I don't see any Wyatts."

"Okay. We can do this. Okay. We'll run. Ready?" Before Flute could nod or agree, Charm took off at a dead sprint towards the garden. She realized the other woman was completely terrified out of her wits, and the understanding caused Flute's knees to shake. They were escaping the Hotel. This was really happening. A fun adventure, to be sure, but also one where if she was caught, she'd have to answer to the Wyatts. Or even worse, Trick.

Flute took Sunrise by the hand and tried to put on a confident smile.

"Ready?"

Sunrise nodded and they got moving.

For a woman of her age, Charm had wheels. Flute had to half-drag Sunrise who was more of the 'quiet as a' kind as opposed to the 'fast as a' kind. But he was giving it everything.

Without the influence of the Handcuff, emotions churned in her brain like the mashed potatoes the Janes made special just for her; with cream cheese added to give them a zip. Even recalling the Janes dropped her down a rabbit hole of confusing and erratic memories, so instead of thinking, she concentrated on the slap of her feet on the ground, the rush of the wind in her face, and the abundant green of the garden against the light red sky. In front of her, Charm pumped her elbows, an Olympic sprinter sighting the finish line, and something about the absurdity of the escape, the sheer and utter stupidity of it, gave Flute the giggles. This wasn't even a fancy plan where they drugged the Wyatts or created disguises to gain a secret key; no, just straight-up open the door and run.

Although she could hardly get enough air in her lungs, she couldn't help it; her giggles turned into laughs. She'd been so gullible. They put an actual handcuff on her wrist, and somehow she thought they were her friends? How had she not seen any of it? They may as well have slapped a stamp on her forehead: dimwit. That was how little they worried about their perfect, placid prisoners. Shame gurgled through Flute's body, starting in her feet, bubbling through her chest, and settling on her head. She wanted to curl up and die.

As fast as it came, her frivolous mood shattered, and she started crying. She stumbled to a halt, unable to go any further. Sobs wracked her body and she clutched herself tight.

Sunrise, also crying now, took her in a powerful hug, his wet cheeks rubbing against hers. She leaned on his body and sobbed on his shoulder, taking strength, as she always did, from her most wonderful friend.

"It will pass," Charm said between gasps. "It's the Handcuffs. Everything they've kept suppressed is coming to the surface. Don't watch any sad movies for at least a week, and weirdly, stay away from lemonade. I'm sorry, but we need to keep running."

"Are there movies on the outside?" Flute wiped her nose.

Sunrise liked movies so much. He leaned forward to hear the answer. Charm gave her a quick hug and a megawatt smile that Flute remembered.

"There's everything outside, Honey. I'll show you. Both you and Sunrise. First, we've got to get out."

With a final, hiccupy sob, Flute got herself moving again.

Behind a crest in the hill, the Portal loomed, unfortunately blocked by people. Wyatts and Arthur and Trick, oh my. Perhaps Charm's plan included them; so far, nothing about their escape was going how she would have guessed. And look, there was Vain, although her hair was shorter and black now. Unconsciously, Flute raised her hand to her own hair. She couldn't remember ever having a haircut. Or cutting her fingernails. Or shaving.

Trembles coursed through her body. That place kept them static. Pairs would never die as long as they stayed there, not from natural causes, but they'd never live either.

Charm pulled them down behind a bush where they could remain hidden and watch.

Vain said something Flute couldn't hear and ran towards the Hotel with Trick chasing after her. Arthur and the other woman, Emma, hammered each other with the power, neither able to get the upper hand, but each time they struck a concussive detonation rang through the garden.

Flute couldn't believe someone was challenging Arthur. More than any of the revelations, that shook her. Arthur's mastery and dominance were so ingrained in her head that it was hard to watch. It was like looking at someone try to fight God. She actually flinched when Emma landed a blow that staggered Arthur back. Sunrise groaned.

Arthur lashed out with a thunderous blast that knocked Emma off her feet, sending her sailing through the air. Charm gasped. Emma, however, appeared unhurt. She got up and struck back, creating another one of those shock waves. Flute ducked. It was getting tougher to see as they were angling away from the

Portal, but as near as Flute could tell, Emma looked extremely pissed off.

Flute found herself silently cheering the other woman. To her surprise, she wanted to see Emma kick Arthur's ass, and now that they were this close to their destination, Flute could hardly make herself wait. Maybe there was something she could do to help Emma. Create a distraction, maybe? As soon as the thought came, it vanished. All Flute would do putting herself between those two was get herself killed. It still galled her to not be able to help.

"Even," Sunrise said.

"Totally," Flute agreed. "She's holding her own against Arthur. How is that even possible?"

"She's Emma," said Charm, "And she kicks all the asses."

Arthur ran towards Emma, away from the Portal, and their fight continued into the garden.

"Come on." Charm pulled them up from behind the bush. "This is as good a chance as we're going to get."

They ran across the lawn towards freedom. Flute had never been that close to the Portal before. Trick and the Wyatts told everyone to stay away, so they did. The Handcuffs worked better than guards or warning signs.

A single Wyatt stood in front of the Portal. Charm skidded to a halt and, before Flute could even register what was happening, Sunrise threw himself forward in a ferocious tackle. It took the Wyatt by surprise and knocked him out of the way, clearing a path. Sunrise gave Flute a thumbs up.

"Escape."

It was happening. What an adventure this was turning out to be.

With Sunrise and Charm by her side, Flute stepped into the Portal.

Chapter 20: Emma has a friendly chat.

Arthur's attack sent Emma hurtling through the air, and she covered herself with a protective membrane seconds before landing deep in the garden. No sign of Vain.

In her previous twenty-eight years of life, her number of near-death experiences had been zero, unless she counted that time an ostrich pecked her shoulder at the zoo. In the six months since meeting Vain, this was about the fourth or fifth time someone had attempted to murder her. The fact that she couldn't immediately summon the exact number was the most alarming part. Barely escaping death was not something she wanted to become more skilled at.

Arthur appeared through the bushes, and she lashed out with a blind shot of energy that hit him in the chest. It didn't send him flying, but he grunted. She stood up to press the attack, hardly even aware of what she was doing. Most of it was going on instinct.

The Hotel overflowed with energy, and she drank it all in, letting it fill her up and push away the fear. A blank numbness took over, the one that meant she was becoming Emma of Death. And even faced with the possibility of serious injury or death by Arthur's hands, she still fought against it, trying to keep some semblance of herself. Even as she lashed out with the power, she still held back. What other choice did she have? If she gave herself over to that other self, she'd be lost forever.

She was readying herself to attack again when Arthur put up his hands.

"Wait. Stop. I don't want to fight."

Emma titled her head, confusion replacing anger.

"This is a trick."

Arthur approached with caution. He wasn't attacking her with energy. "It's not a trick. I had to defend myself. You attacked me."

Emma lowered her hands. The stunning accusation startled her enough that the power drained from her body. "What? I did not. You attacked me first."

"No, I attacked Vain. It had nothing to do with you."

"It has everything to do with me! It's the same exact thing."

"I'm sorry, I didn't realize you were married."

"Are you equating protecting my friend from being murdered with marriage? I don't think that's a wedding vow. At best, it's a weird interpretation of until death do us part."

"Enough." Arthur made a chopping motion. "Let's agree for the moment we won't attack each other. Deal?"

"Sure." Emma kept the power at the ready in case he tried something. What now? Should she try to escape? Arthur smoothed back his hair and dusted some dirt from his shirt.

"Trick told me you were powerful, but I had no idea. I'm impressed."

"Super."

"That was a compliment."

"Okay."

Arthur frowned. "Not that talkative, I see. Are you not that bright?"

"I'm standing only feet away from the person who had me kidnapped and tried to kill me."

"Semantics."

"That's not what that word means. Saying 'semantics' doesn't negate earlier sentences. It's like saying 'no offense' before you call someone ugly. And speaking of that, I can't believe you said that about Vain. I'm not sure how things work here in Hotel Land, but back on the Earth I come from, we treat women with respect. Okay, that's mostly a complete lie. We treat women terribly, but we at least pretend that we don't. Which… now that I say it out loud is probably worse."

Arthur interrupted. "I have no idea what you're talking about and I don't care."

"I want to go home."

"We're past that point. Why did you come here?"

As they talked, Emma inched closer to the pathway that led back to the Portal. Maybe she could distract him and run, or something. "I don't think I need to tell you that."

"It's not a matter of need, it's a matter of want. I want you to tell me, so you will."

"Is this where you say we can do this the hard way or the easy way and then you make fire appear or something?" Emma had no idea what she was saying. A hollow pit had formed in her chest, and she couldn't stop rubbing her hands on her jeans. She only knew that if they were talking, they weren't fighting, and she was moving herself closer to an escape route.

"You must have had some reason. Trick theorized you wanted to steal something from me. Is that it? You're coming to take what's mine? Again? And stop inching closer to the Portal. I can see what you're doing, I'm not an idiot."

Emma stopped in mid-step. Arthur continued.

"How about this. I'll tell you what I want and then you tell me what you're doing here. Nothing could be fairer than that."

"A fair."

"What?"

"A county fair is fairer than that. It's fairer than anything. Ha. Don't attack me again." She swallowed.

"You really are an imbecile." Arthur wiped his glasses on his shirt in a movement that appeared entirely affected. "Let's cut to it. What do you think we do here, Emma? What's my master plan? Why don't we start there?"

What had Vain told her about Arthur? Crappy, jerk, mean, monster, loser. She'd been non-specific on what he was trying to accomplish.

121 | Michael James

"Generalized evil." That sounded right.

"You believe I created all this and sacrificed several of my lives for generalized, unfocused evil?" He shook his head and sighed. "That's stultiloquence. Let me show you what I'm doing."

"Feels like you're patting yourself on the back for fitting stultiloquence into a sentence."

Arthur frowned, and she wondered if she was brave or psychotic. Both, probably. He spoke in a voice that was frozen ice.

"The only reason I haven't killed you is because Trick believes you can help me. I'm not entirely convinced, but he's been adamant, so I'm willing to entertain this notion. The moment I no longer believe that to be true is the moment you die. Do you understand what I'm telling you?"

"Yes." She did.

"You have no idea what is going on here. None whatsoever. There is a specific problem that all of this addresses. There is a possibility that you can help me fix that problem. That is what I want from you."

"But I don't want to help you. I want to go home."

"You should have thought of that before you came here. Your turn. Why did you open the Portal?"

Emma frantically scrambled for a lie and said the first thing that popped into her head. "I wanted to learn more about my powers and so I came here to see what I could discover."

"Uh-huh." Arthur didn't quite roll his eyes at her, but it was close.

"How do you want me to help you?"

"I'm going to show you the truth of this place. It will make this easier to understand. I have the feeling I need to take it slow."

"And after that, if I'm not interested in helping you, will you let me go?"

He smiled. "Sure."

He was lying, and she knew it. She was lying, and he knew it. How wonderful. They were both lying to each other, and she realized how bad she was at showdowns with supervillains. Through this entire exchange, he'd insulted and threatened her about ten times, and the best she'd managed was a single half-step towards the portal. But lying or not, she didn't want to have superpowered fights, either. And as long as they were talking, they weren't fighting.

"Okay. Show me."

Chapter 21: Vain pushes a bunch of buttons.

Vain sprinted towards the Hotel through the lush topiary of the garden with Trick hot on her heels. Although Vain believed herself to be talented in several disciplines such as planning, joke-telling, and, thanks to Mark, ninja-fighting, she never considered herself a gifted sprinter. That was why she never wore a skirt, even though she liked to look at pretty pictures on the internet and dream. Skirts were for girls, and she was a warrior, and holy shit, why on earth was she thinking about skirts?

That was the problem with the Hotel, it mucked up your thoughts. Eighty percent of her awesome escape plan had been getting her head to work right, and she forgot how hard it was to maintain any semblance of coherence in that awful place. It played with you, screwed with your emotions. She needed to focus.

The entrance was a giant revolving door, and she put her shoulder to the glass, trying to press her way through. She stumbled out the other side into a garish lobby, complete with blood-red chandeliers that held candles instead of light bulbs. Silver-trimmed banners hung from stone walls. Smoke from three giant hearths filled the air, burning her lungs and aggravating her poor, tender throat. Thick, oaken tables with long, wooden benches completed the fantasy look.

Huh. A Game of Thrones thing. That was certainly new.

Did the Hotel get Netflix somehow?

Three Janes looked up from polishing the tables and squeaked in surprise.

"Hello, Janes." Vain slid to a stop in front of them, breathing heavily. She only had moments before Trick caught up to her. Apparently, he was also not great at running. "Which way to the Elevator?" Talking still bothered her, but some of the pain was starting to fade.

The Janes stared at her in horror, one going so far as to cover a gasp with her hands. Vain found them to be a timid, pointless lot, and even though she didn't wish them any specific harm, she also wanted to slap them silly basically all the time.

"Which way," she said again, through clenched teeth. Trick would be there any second. She clapped her hands.

"That way," one yelped and pointed over her shoulder.

"Stop her!" Trick burst through the doors, now giant steel monstrosities, and pointed at her. Thankfully, he didn't have any Wyatts with him.

"I was never here," she said to the Janes, before sprinting off towards the door they had pointed at. Trick could completely see what direction she was running, so it's not like the Janes could help cover her tracks, but old escaping habits die hard.

A Wyatt came out the door she was running at, and rather than slow down, she dropped and slid across the cold, polished stone floor. Miraculously, she sailed between his legs and on her way through, thrust upwards to punch him square in the dick.

It was probably the coolest thing she'd ever done in her life.

The Wyatt howled and fell to the ground, cupping his groin. Vain skidded to a halt in front of a second Wyatt and leaped to her feet. She put her fists up, ready to fight.

"Ha." The Wyatt slapped his thigh. "That was awesome. Dude, she totally bagged you."

"Right?" Vain wondered if they should high five.

The totally bagged Wyatt mewled in agreement.

"Grab her, you morons!" Trick yelled. He stumbled over a wooden bench.

Before the Wyatt could break their shaky truce, she did it

first and kicked him in the knee. Mark said the knee hurt worse than the balls.

"Arg!" The Wyatt fell to the ground.

She vaulted over his back, another cool move, and kept running towards the door. Christ, she was absolutely killing it. She hit it high with her shoulder, expecting it to lead into a hallway. It did not. Instead, it opened to a deep, spiraling staircase that she immediately fell down.

Although time did not work right in the Hotel, gravity functioned fine. She tumbled forward, her shoulder banging into something, then her hip. She wasn't sure which way was up, only that up was in every direction, and the stairs were seemingly made of jagged rocks. She covered her head and hoped for the best.

After several disorienting and painful moments, she came to a stop at the bottom of the stairs. Her entire body hurt, and hot moisture trickled down her cheek. She was in a long, imposing hallway with orange fluorescent lighting embedded in the ceiling. With a groan, she rolled over and got to her knees. Blood dripped from her head.

Shit, maybe her plans were terrible. Roman really owed her for this.

She took a couple lurching steps before her knee gave out, causing her to slam against the wall. Using it as leverage to hold herself up, she slid forward, not daring to look back. A careless wipe took care of the blood dripping into her eyes.

"Vain, are you okay?" Trick called down from the top of the stairs. "That was a brutal fall."

Even though he couldn't see it, she gave him the finger and continued her lurching, half-walking gait down the narrow hallway. At the end, a door made entirely of garish bronze waited. Presumably, the entrance to the Elevator.

This time, she approached with caution in case Arthur made the door open to a bottomless pit filled with scorpions or something. Honestly, who would put a stairway right there? He was a psychopath.

Behind her, Trick's footsteps echoed against the granite walls, a staccato click clack click that meant he would soon catch her. When she'd run away from Arthur, her idea hadn't extended beyond playing keep-away with the Padlock. But now that she was that close to the Elevator, she knew what she had to do. All that mattered was Roman.

She entered an enormous circular room with high walls that went up for fifty feet at least, another architectural impossibility she tried not to think about. White pillars of chalky marble stretched to the roof, lined with gold and red trim. Dust floated through the air.

In the middle of the opposite wall stood the Elevator.

Like everything else in that insult to good taste, it was garish and ostentatious; gold-trimmed and covered in a spidery molding. Favoring her sore leg, Vain limped towards it and rested a hand against the grating.

It did not hum with otherworldly power, and she felt a moment of disappointment.

She pulled the door open and poked her head inside. It looked like an ordinary elevator, except for the glowing, circular buttons that covered the walls from floor to ceiling. The buttons were covered in letters, strange symbols, words, and in one instance, something that appeared to be a picture of Martha Stewart giving her the finger.

"Vain, that's enough."

She whirled, and there was Trick, walking towards her with his hands out, showing that he wasn't holding anything. For once, he didn't look smug or happy or any of the asshole expressions she normally associated with him. He looked worried.

"Give me the Padlock, okay? Just… give it to me. Stop running. Stop fighting. I can talk to Arthur. I can get you out of this."

She took a step back, almost into the Elevator. "Why would you help me? You suck. You're my nemesis."

"I'm not. I can help you."

Her neck screamed at her. Her knee throbbed. The hot blood had dried on her face, making it feel like she was wearing a second skin. She withdrew the Padlock from her pocket with a shaking hand and held it out flat in her palm. As always, it hummed with stored energy. So much death and destruction for this little thing.

"Why doesn't he just make a new one?"

"He can't."

Trick took a step closer, cornering her, cutting off her exits. She had nowhere to go. If she backed up any further, she'd be in the Elevator. Trick held out his hands like he was settling a dangerous animal.

Every part of Vain ached. She was so tired. She hoped Charm managed to convince Flute to come. It was looking increasingly likely Vain would never get to know how the story ended. But she'd pretend everything worked. Roman would be fine and he and Emma could get married and talk about books and tape measures and laundry detergent or whatever it was they did together.

She stepped into the Elevator.

"Vain, get out of there." Trick crossed the room, but didn't follow her inside. "It's over. Stop this."

Vain thought about Roman.

None of the buttons made sense, but they must have been how you got to other worlds. Arthur should have left instructions. Because she had no better ideas, she found a section of buttons that were letters and punched in R-O-M-A-N.

"I can't let you do this." Trick stepped into the Elevator as Vain finished entering the sequence.

The buttons glowed with fevered intensity. He grabbed her wrist and tried to wrest the Padlock from her fist. She struggled and jerked her arm away, falling against the back wall. The doors started to slide shut. Her stomach clenched. He hadn't noticed. A tear rolled down her cheek. She thought about Roman's smile.

"Hey, Trick," she said. "What's it called when you put a cow in an elevator?"

"I don't—"

"Raising the steaks."

The doors shut with a ding. Trick realized what had happened, and he spun, trying to pry them back open. He banged on them as the entire Elevator started to vibrate. Vain looked at the Padlock in her hands and held on to Roman's smile.

The Elevator traveled.

Time and space stopped having any meaning. She expanded to fill everything. Her bones stretched and her blood turned to rubber. Breathing was impossible. Everything was impossible. An incredible pressure smothered her, and she curled up into a ball. From a million miles away, Trick screamed.

It lasted forever and it lasted a single second.

With a loud, cheerful ding, the Elevator stopped, and everything returned to normal. The doors opened to a snow-covered field in bright, blinding daylight. It looked like farmland. In the distance, she could make out a barn.

Trick groaned and rubbed his face. Vain would get one shot at this. Arthur couldn't make two Padlocks. He had no way of knowing what combination of buttons she'd pressed.

She lunged at Trick and pushed him out the door. He was caught off guard and stumbled into the snow onto his back. A single button, larger than the others, read "close".

She hit the button with the palm of her hand and dove out of the Elevator, landing on Trick with a thud. Too late, he realized what she'd done. Much too late. He couldn't get to his feet.

Behind them, the Elevator doors closed. They glowed for a moment before fading to nothing. Once they vanished, it was just her and Trick, alone in a snow-covered field.

He pushed her off him and lunged at the spot where the Elevator used to be, but there was nothing there. She'd done it. They were trapped there with no way back.

Trick dropped to his knees and screamed; a cry of pure anger and frustration.

Vain smiled.

Her plans were fantastic.

Chapter 22: Trick doesn't like tasers.

Trick gaped at Vain while she performed an awkward dance that consisted of limping in a circle while smacking her ass and pointing.

"Suck it," she sang. "I beat you."

She waggled her finger in his face, and he swatted it away.

"Stop it." He blew into his hands. Not only had she stranded them who knows where, it was freezing.

Neither of them was dressed for that. She wore jeans and a tank top under a leather jacket, and he was in pants and a sports coat over a button-down shirt. Her lips were starting to turn purplish-blue and crystal air puffed from her mouth with every exclamation.

"Suck it," she reminded him.

He ignored her and scanned the horizon, trying to think of what to do next. They appeared to be in a field, barricaded by thick forest on three sides. The sun beamed at them through a cloudless sky, although it was too cold for any real heat. In the distance, a series of flat buildings, barns and farmhouses, completed the view.

"That way," he said. "We need to get out of this cold."

Vain held up her fists, ready to box. She took a couple of exploratory shadow punches before facing him.

"What are you doing?" he asked.

"We are going to fight." She appeared confused.

"Why would we do that?"

Instead of answering, she flicked a jab at his head, which he easily dodged. He backed away from her, keeping his guard up.

"I'm going to kick your ass." She swung at him again.

"Why?"

"Because, we're enemies." Another punch followed that he slapped away.

"We were enemies," he clarified. "You've murdered us both. I don't care about that anymore. Why would I want to fight you? I want to get out of the cold and not die. You can follow or not, it makes no difference to me."

He turned to the farmhouse. The ankle-deep snow filled his shoes, and his feet were already going numb.

A scream from behind was all the warning he received before a Vain-sized body hurled itself on his back, knocking him to the ground.

"Snice to meet you!" She rubbed his face into the snow.

Sputtering, he rolled over and bucked her off. She launched a kick at his head. Somehow he was the violent one?

"Snice?"

"You know. Like 'nice', except I pushed you into snow, so—"

"I understand. I don't care. We're going to die of exposure. You're already turning blue. I'll make you a deal. We'll get to the building over there, then you can beat me up all you want, okay?"

"P-p-promise?" she said through chattering teeth.

"Sure."

"M-maybe those people will help." She pointed at a spot over his shoulder.

Trick groaned and turned around. Sure enough, a group of people headed towards them from the direction of the buildings. About five, although it was hard to tell from that distance.

"Run."

"Hey!" Vain jumped up and down and waved her hands. "Over here!"

"Get down you stupid idiot." He scanned the edge of the forest to figure out which way offered the fastest escape.

"They can help us."

"They're going to kill us."

The group, alerted by Vain's idiotic screaming, broke into a trot towards them. One carried a rifle. Of course they did.

"Why would you think they're going to kill us?"

"They're always going to kill us," he said. "Look. Are you able to accept, even for a fraction of a second, that you don't know everything? That maybe, just maybe, you don't have all the information and you should listen to other people before doing something?"

She bit her lip and hugged herself. Frosty air misted from her nose. "Nope."

Trick punched the air.

"You stupid f—"

"Here they come." Vain waved her arms again.

Trick didn't want Vain to die, but he also didn't want himself to die. And he would for certain die if he stayed there.

"I don't have time to explain."

"You wasted explaining time saying you don't have time to explain."

Trick choked back anger. "You are so frustrating."

"Better hurry." She pointed at the approaching people. "You know how many explaining seconds you've wasted? Buckle up cause it's ten."

"Most of the worlds the Elevator takes us to are horrible. It's always werewolves or monsters or killer viruses or aliens or whatever. They're not all like that, but the majority are. These people will almost certainly be hostile. You can stay here or you can come with me. Do not tell me to—"

"Suck it," she said.

Trick threw his hands up, finished with trying. But where could he even run? Whatever this world was, it was guaranteed to be terrible. And with the Elevator closed, there was no way to get back to the Hotel, unless Arthur miraculously, and against all possible odds, happened to press the same sequence of buttons Vain did. The only other way out was—"Do you still have the Padlock?"

"You're damn right I do, and you're never getting it back."

Vain had a lot of unresolved animosity towards something, making it difficult to have a conversation with her. In other circumstances he might have found it charming, but under the current conditions, it was all he could do to keep himself from yelling at her. It was like talking to a small child. A small, stupid child.

Before he could make another plea, a gunshot sounded, and a patch of ground exploded at his feet, sending dirt and snow into the air.

"Are they shooting at us?" Vain asked.

"They are shooting at us," Trick said. "We have to run."

"I'm not going anywhere with you."

The group of strangers approached, and his heart dropped at the sight of them. Long, unkempt beards. Clothes that looked like they were other sets of clothes just sewn together. One had a bone in her hair. Nothing screamed 'post-apocalyptic psychopath' like wearing bones. They were grimy and had the look of people whose favorite joke was a person getting hit with a rock.

Vain stepped forward and held up her hand. "Hello," she said. "My name is Vain. I come in peace."

Trick sighed as a man pulled something from beneath his jacket that was actually curtains arranged into the shape of a jacket. The rectangular and black object had the distinct look of a fully functioning taser.

"Hey, what are you—" was as far as Vain got before he pointed the fully functioning taser at her and tased her.

Trick put his hands in the air. "If I surrender now, is there any chance I can avoid being tased?"

The man grinned at him with an expression that held zero humor.

"Vain sucks, like, so much," was Trick's final, pithy thought as a couple thousand volts of
electricity charged through him.

Chapter 23: Flute and Hush work together perfectly.

Flute dropped out of the Portal and fell to her knees. The concept of time followed, and seconds became seconds again. Exhilaration and nausea washed over her in equal parts, and she couldn't stand through the dizziness.

She knelt on a stage in what appeared to be a giant auditorium. An alarm wailed in C sharp, two sharp staccato bursts followed by a legato. Wah-wah waaaahh. Two men she recognized ran to help Charm to her feet.

"Blunt?" She rubbed her eyes.

"Flute!" The big man clapped and helped her up before turning to Sunrise and embracing him in a giant hug. Sunrise seemed flustered, but returned the gesture, blushing straight through to his roots.

"Where are the others?" Flute tried to remember who this other person was. Hush? It was Hush. Now that she was outside, all her memories of the Hotel collapsed into a single moment; a single, confusing moment that lasted all of forever or barely a minute. If pressed at gunpoint, she could not say with any confidence how long she'd been in there for.

"Still inside," Charm said, leaning against the wall. "How long were we in there for? Days? A month? It must have been at least a month. Why are we still in the conference center?"

"It's been like four minutes," Hush said. "They're evacuating the building. I think Emma caused an earthquake. Or broke the supports that hold up the building. I don't know, I'm not an engineer. People have been coming in, non-stop. What do you mean, 'still inside'?"

"They needed to lure Arthur and Trick away from the Portal so we could get out."

"Arthur was there?" Hush clenched his teeth. "Vain is wrong about everything."

Flute couldn't get her bearings. A grinding noise filled the air, blending with the blaring alarm, a loud and grating sound like two pieces of steel rubbing together.

"What is that?" She clapped her hands over her ears.

"Two pieces of steel rubbing together," Hush said. "We need to get out of here."

The doors at the opposite end of the room burst open and a man wearing a maroon jacket burst in holding a walkie-talkie.

"Everyone out of the building. Now," he said. Flute was having enormous amounts of difficulty following along with the action. She reached for Sunrise, who took her hand and shrugged. That shrug meant 'I am quite scared Flute, but I am also glad we are scared together'.

"Leave us alone," Hush said. The man's face went slack, and he left the room. "I don't think that's going to last long. I didn't hit him with much. We have to get out of here."

Charm kicked at the giant glowing Portal. It didn't move. On this side it looked different, more like a plain, if excessively large, door, albeit one that held a glowing purple nimbus in its frame. She ran her fingers down the side of the jamb, surprised to find it was ordinary wood, although she wasn't sure what she'd expected. It easily stood fifteen feet high and six feet wide. The frame itself was at least a foot. Not a single nail or seam marred the finish.

"Can we move it?" Blunt grasped the doorframe close to the bottom and heaved. Hush screamed at him, but it was too late. The Portal swayed and tipped over, falling off the side of the stage. Sunrise jumped out of the way to avoid being crushed. It hit the ground with a thunderous crash.

"Stop!" Hush yelled.

"Broken?" Sunrise asked.

"Whoops," Blunt said.

Flute could tell it was not broken; the Portal side faced towards the ground and the purple glow poured out from underneath. The side facing upwards looked like an everyday black door, although it had no doorknob. It rested, half on, half-off the stage. Flute wondered if that would also turn the waypoint room sideways. She had precious little exposure to how magic Portals worked.

An entire chunk of ceiling fell behind them, landing on the ground with an explosive crash, causing her to flinch in surprise. The alarm blared incessantly. Blunt and Hush argued about what to do with the Portal, with Blunt suggesting that they hire a crane while Hush loudly explained that didn't make any sense and also did Blunt know how much cranes cost and finally, where was he even supposed to find a crane-rental place, assuming such a thing even existed.

This was the worst escape ever. Honestly. How did they manage it the first time?

"I bet we can move the Portal ourselves," she said.

No one paid any attention to her. She hopped off the stage and began to pull and tug at the side of the Portal, trying to get it upright. Sunrise saw what she was doing and moved in to help. The Portal was heavy, but not unmovably so. Presumably, the purple nimbus had no weight, a fact that simultaneously made perfect sense to Flute while making absolutely no sense at all. Charm ran over, and between the three of them, they managed to get the Portal standing back up, now off the stage.

Hush watched what they were doing and snapped his fingers.

"I know. We can drag it out ourselves."

Flute looked around, wondering if language worked differently there.

Charm snorted and put her hand on Flute's shoulder. "You've been Hushsplained, honey. Get used to it."

"Is the outside all words crammed together and ignoring people?" Flute didn't want to appear foolish. "I'm excitified to be here."

Hush took out his phone, dialed a number, and said, "It's Hush. I need a truck brought to the plaza. Meet us out front. It's going to be brutal to get through because I think they're evacuating the building. You have to hurry. We're going to be moving something heavy."

The man in the maroon jacket burst back into the room.

"You have to… wait. Have I done this already?"

"Tell me your name," Hush said, focusing.

"Ernie."

"Ernie, I need you to bring me at least two other people. Can you do that?"

"I can," Ernie said, and ran from the room.

"Okay," Hush said. "When Ernie gets back, we'll haul it out of here, then drive it back to the restaurant."

"How are we going to get it out the door?" Flute asked. "It's fifteen feet tall. And not that I'm complaining, but are you making this up as you go? Because I suspect that good plans do not normally invent themselves in real time. If you need help, I can give you notes."

Sunrise shushed her while Hush ignored her well-intended suggestion.

Continuing his transparently slapdash plan, Hush directed them to drag the several-hundred-pound Portal a few feet closer to the doors that it pretty obviously wasn't going to fit through, a point that seemed to bother no one else except her. Ernie appeared again, this time with two other people: a big guy with a bushy beard and a smaller man with a wrinkled face and a huge nose. They all wore maroon jackets and Flute found the similarity of the outfits comforting.

"All three of you, do what we say," Hush ordered. "Help us move this giant Portal."

"Am I allowed to complain?" the smaller man asked.

"Sure, man, whatever."

"I don't get paid enough for this," he said. Flute waited for further clarification, but that was the extent of his dissatisfaction.

With the help of the additional hands, they dragged the Portal forward an inch at a time. By now Flute barely even paid attention to the siren that hadn't stopped its bleating since the moment she left the Hotel. The outside world was a strange and cacophonous place.

"It's not going to fit," Charm said, and before Flute could jump in with a well-placed 'I told you so', Hush said, "Tip it on its side."

"Will that also tip the way station?" Flute asked.

"Do I look like an expert in Portal technology?"

"You don't," Ernie said, then laughed. "I don't even know what a Portal is. What the fuck is this thing? Wait. I mean that seriously. What is happening right now? We have to evacuate."

"Do what I tell you and stop worrying," Hush said.

Blunt collapsed to one knee.

"Hush, you're pulling too much from him." Charm said.

"Everyone needs to shut up and let me think. Blunt, are you okay? You, there. Tall beardo. What's your name?"

"Micky."

"And you?" he barked at the smaller man.

"Ron."

"Knock the Portal over."

Micky didn't wait for further instructions. He rammed the doorframe with his considerable bearded bulk. Almost in slow motion, the entire thing fell, Portal side first, right at Charm.

She had time to scream and brace for impact before it slammed on top of her, and now the Portal faced the carpet and Charm was nowhere to be seen.

"Pick it up! Pick it up! You idiots!" Hush hopped around the edges of the doorframe while Sunrise tried to support Blunt back up to his feet. Flute had never felt so useless in her entire life, but also, she couldn't think of a time where she'd ever been more irritated. Had Hush always been this much of a dunderhead?

The men strained and managed to get the Portal hoisted back up the right way. There was no sign of Charm.

"Drag the Portal, like parallel to the ground. Gently tip it on its side so it's resting lengthwise." she said. All the men looked at her with vapid o-mouths as the siren wailed in the background.

Oh my gosh.

"Enough." She clapped her hands together, making them

jump. "Ernie and Micky, you get the front. Hush and Ron, you push from the back. We'll tilt the Portal on its side and get it through the door that way. Sunrise, you help Blunt."

"What about Charm?" Hush asked.

Flute bit back her irritation. There was something uniquely annoying about people expecting you to have all the answers when they didn't, and you were the only one thinking.

"She'll be safe in the transition place until she pops out," Flute said. "Come on now. I'm all done with this escape. Move it, people."

The hypnotized men looked at Hush and she wondered if there was a metaphor in that, but she was too strung out to care. This had been the longest, most confusing day of her life, and she didn't know why the rules of this escape meant dragging a mystery portal through a door and moving it somewhere else, and she didn't care. She wanted to get to wherever she was supposed to be, chill out with Sunrise, and maybe unpack the last epoch she'd spent in captivity.

The men finally got going, dragging the tipped-over Portal through the doorway. Why did it need to be fifteen feet tall, anyway?

Once they cleared the door, they were in a long, beige-carpeted hallway with benches against the wall. Plenty of room to drag the Portal, but which way?

"How do we get to... wherever Hush wants us to get to?" she asked.

"The front," Hush said.

"What's happening? Am I at work?" Ron leaned against the wall with his hand on his forehead.

"Keep doing what I tell you," Hush said. Blunt groaned and sagged against Sunrise, who was struggling to keep him upright.

"Faster," Flute said. "Let's drag this massive thing out the front of the building then."

Ernie spat on his hands and Charm fell out of the Portal, coming to rest in a ball by Flute's feet. She screamed a few times, looked around at where she was, then screamed once more for good measure and then a final time after that.

She hugged herself and said, "I want it on record how horrible this plan is. The rescue. Getting out of here. All of it. I fell sideways, but then landed on my feet. Do you know how disorienting that is?"

Flute hauled her off the ground while Ernie and the crew struggled with the Portal, dragging it towards a set of closed doors at the end of the hallway.

"I poked my head back into the Hotel," Charm said. "Still no sign of Emma and Vain."

The corner of the doorway ripped a deep welt in the carpet as they dragged it along the hallway. Hush sent Ernie ahead to check out the situation in the lobby, a mediocre show of foresight that Flute supposed represented an improvement. She continued to push the stupid Portal.

Ernie came back from his mission, flushed and out of breath.

"It's a madhouse out front, the lobby is packed. Only a quarter of the building has left. Whatever we're doing with this terrifying hell-door, we'll need to get past a mob."

"We need to clear a path," Hush said. "What's the best way to get everyone out of our way?"

"Bomb threat?" said Ron.

"Too noisy," said Micky. "It would create panic."

"Wait." Flute straightened and let go of the Portal. "When you brought the Portal here, what was your original plan to get it out?"

Hush opened and closed his mouth a few times and Flute sighed, hoping to contain the world's frustration in the noise. By the look on Hush's face, she nailed it. She turned to Sunrise and threw her arms up in frustration.

"Sunrise, help."

Sunrise tapped his head and said, "Idea."

"Oh, good." Sunrise always had great ideas once she pulled them out of him. She turned to her work crew.

"Ron, get the doors."

"Then we pull the hell-gate through?" Ernie asked.

"It's not a hell-gate. It's a Portal to a Hotel on the outskirts of time where horrible duplicate monsters force people into crippling labour for eternity in service to a madman who lives above everyone in his, oh I see your point, yes, it's a hell-gate."

"Get ready," Ron said.

With a final heave, he pushed open the doors into bedlam.

Chapter 24: Vain does not get the chance to explain how names work.

Vain regained consciousness somewhere that smelled like a pigpen, her face covered in dirt and hay.

Mark's self-defence lessons had covered a wide number of topics, and he spent a whole day on 'Slowly and Alertly Regaining Consciousness After Capture' or SARCAC, as he called it, even though she begged him not to.

She did what he'd taught her, controlling her breathing and opening her eyes a slit, barely enough to let any light in. The stench of rotten meat assaulted her, coppery and rancid, and she needed to take shallow breaths through her mouth to stop from gagging. A collar around her neck, connected to a thick and rusty chain, secured her to a black metal ring protruding from the wall. Matted straw covered the floor, and a waist-high wooden gate barricaded the enclosure. A trough at the back completed the look.

Definitely a pigpen.

Realizing her captors were not around, she opened her eyes fully. The enclosure was in a barn with high ceilings supported by criss-crossing beams. Enough light peeked through the cracks between the wooden boards that she could make out her surroundings.

She'd never visited Mark.

Why would she think of that now? Was it because she was using his techniques to get her bearings? She ignored the hot, sticky guilt over how she'd treated him that filled her stomach. Charm told her he was alive, and they didn't have to amputate the leg, so it wasn't like he was in mortal danger. But he was her friend, and she'd never visited him. Too worried about Roman. But leaving Roman wasn't really an alternative she could have explored. Would Mark be mad?

She gave the chain an experimental tug. There didn't seem to be a lot of give. Pulling harder, she checked whether there was any possibility to yank it from the wall, but it held fast. What a total disaster. Trapped in a pigpen, in a barn, chained to the wall.

Also, super freezing.

The barn offered scant protection from the cold and her breath came out in frozen puffs. A tiny brazier on the other side of the gate let off some amount of heat and was probably the only reason she wasn't entirely frozen to death.

Trick lay curled up beside her, still somehow looking stupidly gorgeous even while unconscious. She had no idea how he did it, and for about the millionth time, she thought about how unfair it was to make men that beautiful. How was a girl expected to think and plan with that around? Mark was a decent-looking guy, but Trick made him look like King Ugly, Lord of Repulsive.

Trick groaned loudly, and she considered telling him she was a better waker-upper than he was. It gave her small comfort. Instead, she kicked him in the elbow. He yelped.

"Shush," she said, and kicked him again, prompting another yelp. "You're so bad at this. Wake up better and more quietly." She kicked him a third time.

"Vain?" He pushed himself to a kneeling position and squinted, trying to figure out what was going on.

"You're terrible at SARCAC."

"Are you trying to say sarcasm but having some sort of episode that is preventing you from finishing your words? Where are we?" He raised his hand to his neck and felt the chain.

"Who am I, Thomas Wheridison?"

"What?"

She grimaced. "I think we're in a pigpen."

Trick grimaced and spat. "Do you ever wonder why no one laughs at your jokes?"

"Everyone laughs at my jokes all the time, only sometimes not out loud." Maybe the Thomas line wasn't her best work, but it rated a solid five out of ten. Seven, if graded to recognize the challenge of coming up with good lines in barns. "I mean, you know what I meant, right? Thomas Edison? The guy? I think he invented like, playing cards and windmills or something?" Why was she explaining herself to him?

Trick stared at her for several uncomfortable seconds. The restraints scratched at her neck, and it was an effort not to rub at it.

"Thomas Wheridison? Come on."

"What did you mean about every timeline being crappy?" she asked, ignoring his notes on her comedy. She didn't take notes. Some of the stuff he'd said before they were captured had been rattling around in her brain.

"I meant what I said." Trick maneuvered himself to a sitting position and yanked on his chain. They sat shoulder to shoulder. "Most of the timelines are terrible. It doesn't matter." He snapped his fingers. "The Padlock. Do you still have it?"

Vain checked her pockets. "Nope. My phone is gone, too. Looks like they took everything."

"Without it, we can't leave."

"That was the point," Vain said. "To keep the Padlock away from you and Arthur. And now you'll never get it back and you'll leave us alone."

Vain expected this to goad Trick into a fight, maybe drive him into a satisfying bout of anger, but he wasn't even looking at her. His eyes fixed on something behind her, then widened. She had never seen the blood drain from someone's face before and until now, thought it was an expression, but the colour literally poured from his cheeks, leaving behind a pale and terrified Trick. His mouth hung open.

"I so completely do not want to turn around right now," she said.

"Turn around," Trick said.

"You are not listening."

Feeling strongly like they were not on the same page, Vain reluctantly turned her head, bracing herself for what she would see.

A third captive was in the pigpen with them; Vain hadn't even noticed in her otherwise flawless SARCAC. He was unfortunately easy to overlook, what with his missing legs and missing arm that left him somewhat smaller than, for example, Trick.

"What the hell," Vain whispered.

"I think I know what this is," Trick said.

"What?"

The man also had a chain around his neck. Wet and bloody bandages covered his stumps, clearly recent. He drooled in a semi-conscious daze. A few empty syringes lay scattered about his body. Vain assumed it was something to help with the pain.

Before Trick could answer, the door to their prison crashed open and a silhouette filled the doorway. The sudden glare from the light outside forced her to shield her eyes.

The man who entered was dressed in ragged, threadbare clothes, kind of like he'd forgotten how actual clothes work and simply attached random strips of cloth to his body. His pants appeared to be an extra-large sweater that he'd crammed his legs through and held around his waist by extension cords. Instead of a jacket, several blankets were thrown over his white tank top. The bones in his beard rattled. Behind him, a woman huddled in his shadow, similarity attired. Vain couldn't tell if that was her real hair, or a wig made out of sheep's wool and straw.

"This cannot possibly be good for us," Vain said.

"Looks like our cows are awake." The man stepped into the barn and leaned over the gate.

"I am getting incredibly tired of these comments about my appearance," Vain said.

Trick made coughing noises and attempted to shush her.

"What do we call you?" Vain asked. "I assume your name is horrible."

"It's not. I still go by my name from the before times. You can call me… Smoove Dick."

Vain blinked. "I'm sorry, Smooth what?"

"Smoove," he corrected. "Not smooth. It's like 'groove',

but even smoother than that, so smoove." The sheep-haired woman rolled her eyes behind his back.

Vain attacked the linguistics of that sentence from several different angles but found it impenetrable. Unsure of how to respond, she nodded.

"I run this place," he said.

"Okay."

"Are you from the Green Reaches?"

"I don't know what that is," Vain said.

"Sure ya do. Your skin is unmarked, but everyone has burns from the Red Morning. So, you must be from the Green Reaches." He pulled out Vain's phone from somewhere inside his pant-sweater and waggled it at them. "You even got a phone. I haven't seen these in ages."

Before Vain could think of how to respond to that, he roared and kicked open the gate. In a flash, he had Trick's head pulled back and was growling in his face.

"Now you're gonna tell me a bunch of things," he said.

Trick's eyes were wide, and his nostrils flared.

"Things about how to get to the Green Reaches. And where you keep all your food that you have. And you're gonna tell me all these things fast and you're gonna tell me true."

Smoove Dick pushed Trick to the ground with a dismissive shove and gave him a kick to the thigh.

"Stop it,'" Vain said.

Trick glared, but kept his mouth shut.

Smoove Dick spat. "I'm not gonna ask you any questions now. It would be a waste. You'd lie, I bet. Something to stall for time, maybe. I know how the Reachers work. You're crafty."

"We are not from the Green Reaches," Trick said from between clenched teeth.

"See?" Smoove Dick shook his head like he was disappointed. "This is how it works with you. Liars to the core. What do you expect from the people who trashed this planet? I'm gonna give you a little encouragement." He snapped his fingers at the old crone who, up until now, had waited outside the pen in front of the Brazier. She bobbed her head and hobbled forward, holding a giant stump.

"I'm not from the Green Reaches," Trick said again.

He tried to back away, but Smoove Dick was faster and grabbed his chain. With a vicious yank, he hauled Trick towards the stump that the old woman had maneuvered to the centre of the pen. Vain could only blink, frozen by the immediate and unexpected violence.

He thumped Trick's hand down on the stump and put one knee on it, pushing down with the weight of his entire body. The woman pulled a rust-covered butcher knife from behind her back and slapped it into Smoove Dick's hand.

"No," Vain said. She lunged forward, but the crone was there first, putting herself between Vain and Trick.

Smoove Dick brought the butcher knife down with a loud thud that made Vain flinch. For a moment, the only sound was the man's harsh, ragged breathing before Trick's piercing cry filled the air.

"My fucking hand!" he screamed, and Vain covered her mouth in shock.

Trick held up his hand, which was now missing three digits, only the index finger and thumb surviving the massacre. Blood gushed out, soaking his wrist.

With pathological detachment, Smoove Dick picked up Trick's fingers from the filthy ground and popped one in his mouth, loudly crunching the bones. A mixture of blood and drool dripped from his lips as he chewed, the foamy pulp mixing with his beard. Vain choked back the acidic bubble of bile that crawled up her throat. He handed Trick's other finger to the crone, who chortled in insane glee and sucked the blood out like a popsicle.

"Now, we're gonna leave for a bit," Smoove Dick said around a mouthful of finger. He swallowed loudly. "When we come back, I'm gonna bring you the same stuff we give your buddy there." He gestured to the unconscious, one-limbed man. "If you tell us what we want to know, that is. You tell us about the Green Reaches, and I make your pain go away. Simple. On the other hand, you wanna still keep lying, well," Smoove Dick walked out of the pen and relatched the gate, "you still got six other fingers."

"Seven," Vain whispered.

"What?" Smoove Dick snapped at her.

She gaped and shook her head. "Nothing."

With a distrusting glare, he spat a bloody wad that splatted against her cheek. The warm moisture trickled down to her chin, but she couldn't make her arms move to wipe it away.

They left the barn without another word, slamming the door shut behind them, once again casting her and Trick into dim.

"Trick," she said. "Holy crap."

Trick's lower lip trembled and his eye twitched. He stared at his fingers, which continued to pump a staggering amount of blood.

"We have to stop the bleeding," she said. In the movies, the heroes would heroically rip their shirts or something, leaving only sexy, exposed midriff. But she was super cold because it was winter wherever they were and also, Trick already had a jacket.

"Did he eat my finger?" Trick said.

"Yep. I don't think we're getting that one back. Can you take off your jacket? We can use it to stop the bleeding, even though it's not that sexy."

"Vain," Trick said. He had not stopped staring at his fingers. "Without a word of a lie. On my honour. Swearing on everything I fundamentally hold dear in whatever is left of my miserable fucking life. If you spout one more non sequitur, I am going to punch you square in the temple. I won't even think twice."

Trick, Vain was learning, had a lot of unresolved animosity towards something, making it difficult to have a conversation with him. Not something she needed to deal with now. Blood pumped out of his hand like a fountain, and she eased him out of his jacket, ripped the sleeve off, and tore it into strips. Even in the poor lighting, Trick did not look well, and he leaned back to put his head on the wall.

Vain grabbed his hand and wrapped jacket-strips around it. He screamed in agony. Her hands shook, but she didn't stop wrapping him up until his fingers were totally covered. Blood, sticky and hot, covered her forearms, and her vision doubled.

"I completely do not have a problem with this much blood," she said before darkness washed over her.

She hit the floor with a thump.

Chapter 25: Emma discovers a new use for matches.

Arthur led Emma towards the Hotel at a brisk pace while she tried to catch a glimpse of Vain. Where would she have gone? Knowing her, she probably fooled Trick completely and had already doubled back to the Portal. All Emma needed to do was keep Arthur distracted for a while longer.

The Hotel's interior was not what she'd expected. Polished marble floors with white and black diamond patterns reflected the light from ostentatious ceiling lamps that dripped with crystal lace. Rectangular planters were placed at symmetrical intervals, each containing a single, perfectly pruned tree. Identical women in floral-patterned skirts and loose blouses scurried back and forth.

"What the hell," Emma said.

"Which part?" Arthur said.

"The identical women."

"Those are Janes. They're like housekeeping."

Emma had no idea how to react to any of it, so she kept her mouth shut. At the back of the room, a circular stone structure protruded from the floor, looking thematically out of place with the opulence of the lobby.

"Is that the Well?" She pointed at it.

"It is. I'll explain everything to you. Let's go to my room."

"Pass. Hard pass. Hard, unequivocal, emphatic pass."

"There's something I need to show you."

"I just bet there is."

Arthur glared at her and stroked his mustache. She crossed her arms. Finally, he reached out and grabbed a Jane.

"Get me the Camera from my room."

"Yes, Mr. Arthur."

The Jane scurried off and Emma took a seat. In addition to her general apprehension about being around Arthur, the Hotel made thinking a sticky, laborious chore. Even so, she knew enough not to walk into his bedroom. She didn't like going home with a guy after four dates, let alone after a superhero energy battle.

Arthur said, "Once you look through the Camera, we'll have a talk."

"Is it a Device?"

"Yes. It shows you the moment of the Hotel's creation."

Emma squinted at him. "You created a Device to show your backstory?"

"No." He sounded annoyed. "We wanted to review what happened. Maybe find a clue, something we could use."

The Jane returned, carrying a stubby old-fashioned film camera, the kind with the accordion-style front. Arthur handed it to her.

"Look through the lens."

Emma had no idea what to expect. She raised it up to her eye. With a rushing blur, her sense of self poured through the lens, and she tumbled through a tornado of memories. Her thoughts became jumbled, intertwined with someone else.

She was Emma.

She was someone else.

She was Emma.

She was—

*

"Arthur!"

Arthur blinked, brought out of his reverie by Trick's harsh whisper. He'd been thinking of home; of the dry, barren countryside of Arizona. A place he was unlikely to see again.

Rough bark scratched his back, but he knew from

experience that shifting around would bring no relief. The sun wasn't up, and he shivered against the cold ground, wondering if he'd die that night.

"What do you want, Trick?" His teeth chattered in the cold.

"I heard something." Trick had long ago lost the look of casual insouciance that he wore like a cloak. Two weeks on the run from German expeditionary forces had shredded his composure, leaving a haunted expression behind.

They'd survived the beach, the two of them. Most of their squad hadn't. They'd landed at Utah, not Omaha, thank Christ; he'd heard it was a woodchipper. Next came the slow, brutal grind to take back the surrounding French towns, a street-by-street fight where he didn't know who he was shooting at. In the last village, he and Trick became separated. Too much smoke and noise and confusion. They ran North when they should have run South, or they went West instead of East. Arthur had no idea. He only wanted to survive.

"Get some rest, Trick," Arthur said, even though he knew that was impossible. Although France in summer was hot during the day, the temperature would plummet at night, leaving them both shivering, trying to grab bits of sleep where they could.

Clouds blanketed the sky, reducing their vision to the meager space they occupied in the ditch off the dirt road. Behind them, through about two hundred feet of dense bush, was a ravine. The plan was to follow the road to the next town and see if they could locate allied forces.

"Strike a match."

Arthur sighed. Trick pressed him to light a match almost every hour. His nervousness made him relentless. There weren't that many left, certainly not enough to keep striking one as often as Trick wanted.

Creating the Matches had taken everything out of Arthur. After he told Trick about his weird abilities, the other man threw a couple hundred ideas at him. If there was one thing Trick didn't lack for, it was ideas. Arthur regretted telling him what he could do, but war brought people closer together. When every minute could be the one where you died, it made it easier to share personal stories.

When Arthur imbued an object with energy, he could influence it to do other things. Sort of. There were so many limitations, and Arthur barely understood how any of it worked. He only knew it was something he'd been able to do since he was a teenager, and creating things drained him, or at least made him sick. The bigger the thing, the worse it got.

"Leave it alone, Trick. I'm tired. We lit one before we bunked down. There's nobody around."

The Matches illuminated danger. A simple trick suggested, simply, by Trick. If they were in danger, red fire. No danger, normal fire. Arthur had found the simpler he made things, the better.

"Come on. One more and then I'll leave it alone." Trick rubbed his arms, peering intently at him with deep-sunken eyes. He looked like he'd lost ten pounds, easily. They both had. Arthur tried to remember the last time he'd eaten. Two days ago?

Trick nudged him again and Arthur sighed. He took out his matchbox. Only seven left. Trick made a protective cup with his hands, and Arthur scraped the precious match against the rough strip on the box. Once, twice, and finally, the match flared to life.

Bright, angry, red.

Trick cursed under his breath and knocked the match from Arthur's hands, stomping it out on the ground. They sat with their heads close together, breath intertwining to coalesce into a misty cloud before being sucked away into the night. Random noises ricocheted off the trees: the hoot of an owl, the chittering of a squirrel, the noise of a round being chambered in a Karabiner 98k.

Arthur flinched, banging his elbow against a rock. Before he could cry out, Trick covered his mouth and held up a finger. Straining to hear, he picked out the low murmur of voices coming through the bush, and the crackle of breaking branches. A beam of light poked at the tree line, sweeping back and forth, the final turn coming within feet of where they huddled.

They had long ago lost their guns. Arthur had no illusions about what the Germans would do. The war was basically over. They'd be tortured for information, then killed. Probably in rapid succession. Arthur had no interest in dying.

"The ravine," Arthur hissed. "Come on."

"We can't go that way." Trick craned his neck, trying to see over the tops of the bushes concealing their hiding spot. "It takes us further into the countryside."

A sharp voice cut through the night, and the flashlight trained even closer to them. "Americans," a voice called out in heavily accented German. "Come out. We won't hurt."

"I'm running," said Arthur. "Come or die. I don't care."

A crack of gunfire followed; a noise Arthur had come to know all too well. A patch of ground exploded beside his feet in a puff, and then Trick was off into the trees. Arthur swore and put his head down and pumped his arms, no longer caring about stealth or silence.

The bushes tore at his face with their barky fingers, and he couldn't tell if the moisture on his cheeks was blood or sweat. He ran in the direction he believed the ravine to be, not really caring where he was going, only knowing he had to get away from the Germans, away from death and torture. Several more shots rang out, one bullet whizzing close enough to his ear to cause a searing heat as it passed.

He ran faster.

Behind him, the Germans yelled and crashed through the brush. He had no idea where Trick was. The hot panting of his own breath filled his ears. His boots thudded against the uneven ground as he tore through the forest. His only warning of distress ahead was a startled yelp from Trick. Had the Germans somehow gotten in front of them?

He burst through the tree line and the ground disappeared beneath him. The next thing he knew, he was tumbling down the side of a steep hill. He had time to realize this was what Trick's startled yelp meant before the pain of impact made thought impossible.

Down, down, down the side of the ravine he fell, trying to tuck and prevent any substantial injury. He bounced off rock and trees, one hitting his head with enough force that his teeth clacked together and he saw stars. When he slid to a stop at the bottom of the ravine, he could hardly breathe.

Trick was there in seconds, tugging him to his feet.

"Are you okay?" he said.

Arthur wiped at his face and looked back the way they came. In fairness, the fall hadn't been as bad as it felt. Maybe forty feet, although the descent was mostly scrub and rock.

"We need to follow the gully."

"Did we lose them?" Trick wiped his nose.

To answer, a bullet whizzed past them and exploded against the cliff face on the other side. Four shapes on the crest of the hill pointed rifles.

"Run," Arthur said.

They ran through the downward-sloping path in the center of the valley. Freezing cold water trickled beneath their feet; not enough to call a stream, but large enough that Arthur's feet were soon soaked. They didn't look back or consider where they were going. In two weeks, this was as close as the Germans had come.

Without any moonlight to guide them, Arthur completely lost track of where they were. The stitch in his side reminded him that he didn't have much gas left. His knee clicked and complained. How had it come to this? All of his power, all of his abilities, and he'd been reduced to scurrying like a rat. Matches. Pah.

As they continued their breathless run, the gully narrowed. Already uneven, the terrain became littered with jagged rocks that they needed to climb over. Arthur couldn't imagine how they were going to get out of this. He suspected they were treading over parts that hadn't seen human feet in centuries. The walls narrowed to the point where they were pushing themselves through openings barely wide enough to fit.

Just as Arthur worried they'd hit a dead end and be trapped, the walls opened into a wide clearing lined on either side by tall pines that swayed in the darkness. Arthur looked back the way they came; the entrance was barely visible, nothing more than a slit in an otherwise unbroken strip of cliff. High above, the night sky twinkled with countless stars. A high escarpment at the opposite end fenced them in, blocking any exit.

In the center of the clearing was a giant, glowing purple doorway.

"That is unusual," Arthur said.

Trick spun in a circle, examining their surroundings. "What is this place? Where are we?"

"No idea."

"Do you think it's a German outpost?"

"Do I think a glowing purple doorway in the middle of a nearly inaccessible canyon is a German outpost? No, Trick. No, I don't think it's a German outpost."

They approached the door on exhausted legs, leaning on each other for support. Theoretically, they could turn around and go back the way they came, but what would be the point? The Germans couldn't follow them, not as deep into the gully as they were, and that door, strange as it was, had to lead somewhere.

Arthur brushed his fingertips against the purple nimbus, expecting a crackle of energy, but nothing happened.

"I'm going through," he said. "Better in than out." He didn't wait for Trick's response.

A low stone room with an otherworldly glow led them to another door. Passing through that, they emerged in a place that clearly wasn't Earth.

The endless and oppressive salmon sky gave him vertigo, and Arthur had to crouch to keep his balance. They stood on a faded patch of brown rock, surrounded by nothing.

"We've been here days." Trick wiped his mouth, like trying to work out a bad taste. "How are we not dead?"

"Hours, surely," Arthur said. Time didn't seem to work, but he couldn't make himself care. A narrow path stretched before him, lined with gray and white rocks that crunched when he stepped on them.

A flash of movement caught his eye, and he swung his head, trying to catch it. When he focused, there was nothing there. But still another flash bothered him. And another. Trick spun in a circle, whipping his head like a startled mule, trying to pin the ghostly images that flickered in and out of life all around them.

At the end of the path, only dozens of feet away, stood a building. A house. A structure.

A thing.

If a specifically insane child mashed together a version of a house based only on the remembered imaginings of fever dreams, that might have been the result. The windows sagged at awful angles that shouldn't have existed, angles that made his eyes water to look at. A dull black exterior made of wood and brick tilted inwards with eaves that squinted at him with monobrow disapproval. The building was close to ruin, held together by some horrible will that refused to let it collapse. A single-story misshapen lump of architecture, angry at its state.

Something pulled at him from inside the building. Not power. That wasn't quite it. Potential. Yes. Better. Potential pulled at him. Opportunity. The building needed something from him. And it was offering everything in exchange.

He took a step towards it, and those images flickered. Another step, and another flicker.. As he walked, the steps became easier, and the images clearer.

Them. The images were them.

Hundreds of Arthurs and Tricks. Some with guns, some with hats, some with bullet wounds, some with bandages. Infinite, endless versions of them stepped towards the shape from all directions, blinking in and out of existence.

"Are we us?" Trick breathed.

"Come on." Arthur didn't know how to answer that. He needed to get in the building. Thoughts assaulted him, alien thoughts. He wanted—

Power

Safety

Sanctuary

Strength

—This to be over, whatever this was, but somehow, the other Arthurs thoughts were blending with his, making coherent thought impossible. He remembered dancing at fifteen. No, wait, that was a different Arthur. He remembered falling down a hill. Not him.

"Get out of my head." Trick thumped his temples. "I never did that."

"The house." Arthur pointed. "In there. It will be better in there."

"It's not a house. I don't know what that is."

"We'll only stay the night." A jingle floated through his

head for a chain of hotels that had never existed in his world.

> Rest your feet, rest your bones,
> Now you'll never be alone.
> All the things you can be shown,
> Now the Hotel is your home.

"Did you say something?" Trick shook his head.

"I said we'll be safe in the Hotel."

Drunk with the baffling thoughts of an infinite number of Arthurs, Arthur lurched towards the Hotel. Around him, Arthurs blinked in and out of existence, all doing the same. All the Tricks looked worried.

"Use a match." Trick stopped Arthur with a hand on his shoulder. "Before we go further."

Arthur nodded. All the Arthurs nodded. With shaking hands, he took out the box of Matches, being careful not to drop any. It took him three tries before he got it to catch. Like a firework going off, the landscape exploded with the flame of thousands upon thousands of Matches, lit by an unbelievable number of Arthurs, filling the air with tiny pinpricks of light.

Bright red. Bright, terrifying, red.

"We're going to die here," Trick said and somehow Arthur heard millions of voices, joining together as one.

Arthur shrugged the other man away. The pull of the Hotel was too loud. He didn't care about the Matches. He wanted that potential. No longer bothered, he practically ran down the path and flew up the steps. Trick scrambled to keep up. Arthur reached the entrance, stopping before the rattletrap door with its tumorous knob, and paused on the threshold. Around him, an infinity of Arthurs did the same thing, all their hands coming together and collapsing into a single image like adjusting the blur on a camera.

The Arthurs turned the knob and entered the Hotel.

The air was moist and dry all at the same time, thick with the smell of decay and rot. Tiny sticks crunched under Arthur's feet as he stepped into the lobby, only they weren't sticks. They were bones. The skeletal remains of animals, birds, and rodents. People, perhaps.

Cobwebs hung from the ceiling, and as he walked through them, they settled on his head, a chiffon veil for this emerging union. No light came through the windows, but he could see perfectly. Broken tables and chairs lay scattered around the interior. In the center of all the debris, a stone well jutted from the ground, an improbable fixture in an already-improbable location. Arthur couldn't take his eyes off it.

The Well was the key to all of it.

"What is this?" Trick whispered. He wiped his finger on a table, leaving a straight line through the dust.

Arthur couldn't answer. He was too busy feeling the pull of that place, feeling the lure of the power. It called to him. And in that calling, he understood what it was. The potential it could hold.

The worlds it could unlock.

All the Arthurs approached the Well. All the Arthurs put their hands on the cold stone and breathed deeply, luxuriating in the heady currents of potential. Of need. Of want.

The Hotel, that place, it was like a lens. A focal point for everything, all of what was, all of what could be. A place outside time, outside everything, and because it stood outside, it wasn't constrained by cause and effect. He could be anything, there. An Arthur who was a king. An Arthur who was rich. Any Arthur in the world, really. It could all be his, all of it could be his, everything could be his.

All he needed to do was turn the Well on.

That's what the Hotel wanted. Activation. Purpose.

To live.

A single Arthur could create a match that sensed danger. All the Arthurs could create anything. And they took a breath, inhaling as one, pausing to appreciate this moment before they could seize their destiny. They knew exactly what they had to do. It was so simple, so obvious.

The Arthurs smiled.

"Don't," Trick said, but it was too late.

Arthurs activated the Well.

The power that shot out was unlike anything Arthurs had ever experienced. The Hotel screamed in pleasure, a soundless holler that echoed against time itself, scattering throughout everything. Tricks dropped to their knees and clapped their hands over their ears. Arthurs stared into the Well, feeling the power rush by, feeling the Hotel take all of it. They reached out, tried to take some of it, but it flowed through their fingers like water. Because the Well was the battery. The Well was the heart of the Hotel. The Well was at the bottom of everything. They gave it blood, and the Hotel wanted more. Arthurs tried to pull back, to stop what they'd done, but it was too late. Understanding came too late.

They'd been tricked.

There was no potential there, no sharing of power. The Hotel exhaled and pulled itself together, one brick at a time. The walls straightened and unbowed, coming to military attention. Stairs appeared, extending to a second floor that hadn't existed until that very moment. Light penetrated through the musky haze; a malignant light that promised nothing.

Arthurs fell back from the Well, clutching their hands to their chests, their palms burning. Oh, they'd turned the Well on alright. Had they ever.

Paintings straightened in their frames, carpets fizzled up from inside the floors, and at the back, a glowing golden elevator revealed itself from beneath peeling layers of rust, decay falling from the metal doors.

And still the Hotel devoured, the greed of the pull finally revealing a second betrayal. The Hotel would have its meal and the only course on the menu was Arthurs. Delicious Arthurs, brought there to fulfill that horrible act of creation, an act that would leave them spent and hollow. Desiccated husks.

"I can't turn it off," Arthurs said.

"What in the fuck is that!" Tricks screamed.

Arthurs looked where Tricks were pointing. Garish orange bulbs were coming to life one by one, but in one corner by the ceiling, there was a darkness. And inside that darkness, a thing. A presence.

The thing laughed, or attempted to mimic the noise of laughter. A low, broken-glass sound filled the empty space, a haunting clicking that scraped against Arthur's brain. Something dark and sinuous slithered down the walls of the re-forming Hotel to materialize in front of them.

To call it human would be like calling a scarecrow human. There were surface similarities, like a general human shape and things one ordinarily associated with people, like limbs and a head, but the thing that undulated down the stairs was not human.

It was evil.

All the Tricks screamed.

The creature's enormous eyes covered too much of its maggot-pale face, and it didn't blink. Its nicotine-stained whites were almost entirely consumed by black pupil. Its mouth was more of a slit that went nearly ear to ear, and instead of a nose, it had a single pencil-sized hole. When it stood, it towered at seven feet at least and the way its arms bent, Arthurs realized it had more joints than was ordinary. Darkness flowed around it like a cloak.

"Oh, my Jesus Christ protect me." Tricks moaned.

This was a creature of shadows, of eventide, and Arthurs mentally shifted to thinking of the monster by that name— Eventide. It must have woken up alongside the rest of the Hotel. Had it, too, been turned on like one of the many lamps appearing on the tables that were now dust-free?

"Stop," the thing hissed, a sound of scraping madness that caused Arthurs to gibber with insane terror, and the terror was enough for Arthur, this Arthur, to separate himself and come back into individuality.

Eventide blinked and appeared before him, the heavy smell of rot and decay assaulting his nose. The monster took him by the shoulder and pulled, somehow taking his energy, feeding off him. And it was worse than the Hotel, because where the Hotel acted on instinct, Arthur suffocated under the weight of anger that Eventide directed towards him.

"What have you done?" The monster glared at him with frantic eyes.

Arthur felt himself die by the thousands as the Hotel came to life, but in his entanglement with Eventide, he'd been thrown outside that circuit. Able to sense the power, but cut off from the Hotel's feast. He let Eventide drain him, and now, too late, much too late, he understood why bones littered the floor of this place.

Millions of Arthurs died to the Hotel, being sucked out of existence, their life force being directed to the Well.

With a ferocious roar, Trick lunged at the demon, somehow finding the strength to throw himself at the horrible creature from the beyond. The move took it by surprise, and it stumbled backwards, knocked off balance by Trick's attack. It teetered on the edge of the Well and hissed its hatred and fury, but Trick wasn't done. He kicked Eventide in the chest, and the monster screamed and toppled backwards into the Well, falling into the darkness. Trick dropped to his knees.

"Get up." Arthur pulled him to his feet. "We have to get out of here."

"We have to stop that thing." Trick said. "We can't let it get out. It's horrible. It's evil."

Almost as if to prove the point, the monster screamed from the depths of the inky blackness, a sound of madness and rage and hate.

"It was feeding on the Hotel," Arthur said. "Like a leech. I think I jarred it loose, somehow. It tried to feed on me, too."

"The Well," Trick said. "Turn it into a cell. A holding tank. I don't know. Something. Can you do that? Like you changed the Matches, can you change the Well? Turn it into a prison?"

Single Arthur couldn't do anything that profound. Single Arthur could create parlor tricks. But infinite Arthurs? Infinite Arthurs could do anything. The staggering energy of the Arthurs flowed through him, drawn out by the Hotel. And because he was now outside that circuit, knocked loose by Eventide, he could use it, but only until the last of the Arthurs were consumed. Soon it would be only him. What Trick suggested would be the biggest thing Arthur had ever created; far, far bigger than the Matches. But the Well already was something, wasn't it? It wasn't like he was creating it from scratch. He was only modifying it.

He placed his hands on its rim and focused. He didn't understand what he did, not really, but he took what was already available to him and changed it. Tiny nudges here and there. He turned the Well into a prison and packed energy on top of it like a cork in a wine bottle. The demon's enraged cries didn't stop, but they became muffled, and Arthur knew it was working. Somehow, it was working. The Hotel stopped growing, the energy now diverted to keep Eventide trapped, and dimly Arthur thought he could hear it howling in frustration. They'd stopped Eventide. For now.

Trick said. "How much is left? How much is possibly left?"

"Some," Arthur groaned with the pressure. "The Well is done. I don't think I have much time. I'll never be able to do this again. Not like this. Nothing this powerful." He stopped and tried to pay attention to what was happening. "Trick, that thing was eating me. Consuming my energy."

"So?"

"So the prison I created to hold it is made out of energy. It can eat its way out. The Hotel is going to take energy from the Well, too. It won't last."

Trick swore. "We need to figure out a way to put in more energy, then. Faster than it can consume it. You need to create more things," Trick said. "Weapons. Devices. Anything. Whatever we can think of that will help us keep that thing contained."

"But what?"

Trick looked around and spotted something on the rubble by his feet. He picked it up and threw it at Arthur.

It was a padlock.

"Start with that."

Chapter 26: Flute sees the sky.

Flute only had about ten minutes experience with the world outside the Hotel, but she was already quite the expert in dragging giant doors.

The lobby was bedlam, as Ernie had predicted. People rushed towards the entrance, not quite panicking, but certainly getting there. Several people gave them funny looks, and a few stopped to take pictures. One woman screamed.

"Whatever you're planning, time to do it, Sunrise," Hush said.

Sunrise nodded.

"Marvel movies!" he yelled. "Avengers prop! Out of the way. Movie stuff."

The guards pushed and hauled the tipped-over Portal through the lobby. Now that people believed it to be a giant prop, they no longer screamed and stared, they oohed and took pictures.

Sunrise was laboring to carry the semi-conscious Blunt, and Flute hurried to his side to help. She hated being at the back where she couldn't be more involved, but now that they were in the main lobby, the noise and the people and the everything had her overwhelmed.

"This way." Hush directed them to the front door, and they pulled the Portal behind them.

Abruptly there was a noise like yonk, then a single Wyatt tumbled out of the Portal onto the ground below. The group, apparently, had no specific way to respond to this, so they stopped dragging the Portal to stare. Ernie wiped his forehead with his sleeve. The Wyatt staggered to his feet and looked at his surroundings. Before anyone could do anything, he turned and punched a guy in a suit in the face and took his phone.

"Wyatts rule!" he yelled, and ran off through the crowd.

"We should probably try to stop future Wyatts from doing that," Charm said.

"Keep pulling," Hush said. "None of this matters."

While the group strained at the Portal, tugging it through the crowd and the bedlam, Hush shouted a few more commands into his phone. Charm yelled something about Guardians of the Galaxy.

Flute missed the quiet routine of the Hotel.

She felt a tickle in the back of her throat and a tight clenching of her chest. Even though she was positive she was breathing, there didn't seem to be enough oxygen, and her mouth got all heavy and turned downwards no matter how hard she tried to make it stop.

"Hey," Sunrise said from across Blunt's sagging head. "I got you." He maneuvered to rub her forearm, the best he could manage with a semi-conscious human between them.

Sweat poured down his cheeks, and his baggy sweatshirt was soaked through at the neck and armpits. Blunt was probably six inches taller than him, and Sunrise had been carrying his weight that whole time. He was also surrounded by a world of weird collapsing buildings and blaring alarms and huge crowds. And despite that, he reached out to tell her, 'I got you'. She wasn't alone.

"I know you do. Thank you." She smiled at him and immediately felt better. It helped that she needed to be brave for him. Go back to the Hotel? They'd have to drag her back, kicking and screaming.

They made it to the front doors, which were thankfully large enough to haul the Portal through. Outside, chaos ruled, and Flute resigned herself to the reality that she'd never have a moment of silence again. The building opened onto a street packed with madness. Cars and trucks honked, and people milled about, blocking traffic. Huge, towering skyscrapers leered at them from high, high above.

But the sky was blue.

It was the kind of blue that made Flute think if this were the only color she ever saw again in her life, she'd be okay with that. A blue with weight. With depth. It went on forever, and she swam in the color.

"No lightning," Sunrise said, eyes wet with emotion.

"No lightning," she agreed. Whatever this place was, they were home.

"Pull harder, you idiots," Hush said.

Ernie and Mickey and Ron all blinked stupidly at one another. Flute assumed Hush's powers were wearing off. It didn't look like Blunt was in any shape to lend him any more energy. Ernie slapped himself on the face, and Mickey yelped in surprise.

"What the hell just happened?" Ernie said.

"Thanks for your help guys." Hush reached into his pockets and handed wads of cash to each of them. "After being under this long, you might be screwy. Don't go near a TV for an hour, and if you can manage it, don't listen to any R.E.M."

"I am going to get drunk," Ron said before running inside. With a final, confused glance, Mickey and Ernie followed.

There were on their own.

"Come on," Flute said.

She let Sunrise take the full burden of Blunt and ran to the front of the tipped-over Portal. It was heavy, but not as heavy as she'd expect an inter-dimensional gate to be. Sort of fridge heavy. With her hands under the frame, she hoisted it a foot off the ground and started to drag it. Charm was there beside her in an instant, helping, and then, surprise of surprises, Hush joined in from the other side and pushed.

They pulled and strained and sweat trickled down her back. It had been at least twenty minutes since she'd been free from the Hotel, twenty individual minutes she could remember completely and clearly and distinctly, each thought coming in logical sequence with no weird cramming together. She grinned like a sap, realizing she could spend the rest of her life watching minutes tick by and be content.

"Around the corner," Hush said. "They got us a truck. We should be able to fit the Portal in the back. Nearly there."

They pushed past a row of firetrucks and policemen who screamed at them to get behind the gates, which was exactly what Flute was trying to do, so she didn't quite understand how the screaming helped. Her hands were sore and blistered from the exertion, but she didn't stop.

When they made it around the corner, they maneuvered Portal further down the street where a flatbed truck was waiting. Hush stopped pushing and yelled at the men who lounged against the side, playing on their phones. They lugged the Portal into the back and Flute followed the group into another vehicle.

Inside, Hush was practically limp with relief, and Charm hugged herself. Flute wasn't sure what would happen next.

"When we get to the restaurant, you need to heal Roman, okay?" Charm reached forward to place her hand on Flute's knee. "Then we figure out how to save our friends."

Flute nodded. So that was what would happen next.

Chapter 27: Trick oversells his own prowess.

Trick tried to come up with a reasonable estimate for how many worlds he and Arthur had visited since trapping Eventide in the Well. He'd seen a few thousand, easy. Arthur had gone to twice that many. How many worlds had killed them? Probably a third. And still, no answers, after all that time and all the worlds they'd seen. Not a single whisper of a solution to the unknowable monster barely kept under cover by constantly flooding more energy into his prison than it could absorb. It grated on him. But there had to be an answer somewhere. On some version of Earth. There had to be.

His missing fingers throbbed and blood soaked through the makeshift bandages. Sadly, that had not been his first time losing digits, but unlike juggling or vase-making, forced limb-removal was not something one could really become an expert at.

Vain snored softly at his feet, curled up into a ball, sleeping after her faint. He'd placed his single-armed jacket over her shoulders because she seemed cold. When she slept, the anger lines normally present when she looked at him melted from her face. He lightly brushed a single hair back from her cheek, and she groaned and swatted his hand.

"Only ham deliveries," she muttered.

Trick sighed. At some point he'd need to check the chains

around their necks and see if he could find a way to open them, but he was too dizzy from blood loss. Too irritated from being held in captivity. Too everything.

Vain yawned and stretched, the contour of her body clearly visible while she arched her back. It made him feel creepy to stare at her, so he looked away. She sat up, smacking her lips. His jacket slid off her shoulders like it'd never been there.

"Trick," she breathed. "Your hand."

"My hand," he agreed.

They admired their respective limb-naming abilities for a few moments.

"I told you we should have run," he said.

"They would have caught us, anyway."

"That's incredibly annoying, do you know that?"

"What is?"

"Your complete inability to take responsibility for your actions. We are here because of you. My fingers are missing because of you. If you had listened to me—"

"Then we'd have run and then you'd talk with your hot face and you'd confuse me. This is better."

"You think I'm hot?"

"What the hell is this place? Why are they like this?"

"Seriously? Are you completely immune to subtext? The Green Reaches? The Red Morning? Eating my raw severed finger? There's obviously been a series of incidents that resulted in global catastrophe, leading to a world where agriculture and livestock no longer exist, and people turned towards cannibalism for basic sustenance. Did the bones in his beard not clue you in? How are you not getting this? Do you need it spelled out in a formal report with bullet-points and an executive summary?"

"Huh," Vain said. "So that's what that feels like."

Trick grunted, confused by the several abrupt pivots the conversation had already taken. He tried to inspect the keyhole on the metal bar around his neck. Vain busied herself by taking several deep breaths. When she was done, some of her swagger had returned. Maybe they'd get out of there, after all.

"You don't happen to have two pieces of metal on you, do you?" he asked without any real expectation of success.

"My bra has metal wiring in it." She squinted at him. "Is this a line to get me to take my bra off because I said you were good looking?"

"Can you think of a single other reason I would want a thin strip of metal while I'm trapped by a collar with a lock? A lock that is probably susceptible to picking? Take your time. I'm not in any rush." He hummed the theme to Jeopardy.

"Oh," she said. Then, "I don't want to escape. If you escape, then you'll get the Padlock, and all of this will be for nothing."

"If we don't get the Padlock, you'll die here, too."

"I'm okay with that. At least you won't bother us anymore."

"Vain." He tucked his bloody hand to his chest. "What do you think we do this for? All of it. The Hotel. The pairs. The energy in the Well. I'm curious."

"Because you're evil," she said. "You probably have a plan to take over the universe or something, you and Arthur and all the Wyatts. I bet when you're sitting up there with him you laugh and drink brandy and talk about all the hot evil you're going to do."

He didn't respond, because in his experience, when people said profoundly stupid things, it was best to let silence argue with them first. This tactic, however, only worked on people blessed with a modicum of self-reflection. Vain took his silence as agreement.

"I knew it," she said. "You suck so much."

His hand hurt too much to argue, so he ignored her and concentrated on how he could get out of there. It would be impossible to fight Smoove Dick while chained to the wall, and there was probably no chance he could make up a lie realistic enough to convince them he knew anything about the Green Reaches. Vain probably wouldn't make it, either. Why would he even care about that? It would be better if she didn't make it. One less thing to worry about. He didn't care if she died at all. And the image of her huge, pretty eyes closed forever wasn't why he felt like someone had kicked him in the stomach. It was probably the blood loss.

"What did you mean when you said Arthur can't create

another Padlock?" she asked.

"I meant literally that sentence. We only have the one."

"But he's all-powerful."

"He is exceptionally limited. He can only create little things. Trifles. The compass that helps us find pairs. Timepieces that make life in the Hotel more tolerable. All the big stuff was created at the beginning, and we've never been able to replicate that."

"What do you mean, the beginning?"

"Does any of this matter, Vain? Are you going to believe me even if I tell you?" His finger stumps were in agony, and he hoped she'd say yes. Talking was better than sitting there, waiting to die. "And before I tell you, why did you even come back? Why did you open the Portal in the first place?"

She bit her bottom lip, an affectation she always did when she was thinking. It was kind of endearing. His fingers throbbed.

"Roman was shot," she said. "We needed to heal him."

"Oh. I'm sorry to hear that." He recalled Vain had some small measure of attachment to Roman.

"Whatever. By now Flute has escaped and Roman is better. We don't even need to worry about that anymore."

"You kidnapped Flute?" He was so startled, he brought himself to his knees, the chain rattling behind him. "She was our best producer. God, you really are trying to kill all of us, aren't you?"

"Yuh."

"Why?" he asked. "What did we ever do that was so awful?"

Vain's mouth dropped open. "You fucking tortured me."

He shrugged, a pointless gesture given her fairly valid argument, and said, "Arthur did that. I suggested other approaches."

"It doesn't matter who gave the order, you were always there."

"Do you think I like any of this? Trust me, I don't love Arthur's methods either."

"When we kidnapped that Wyatt, he said you were going to kill us. Torture Roman."

"Yes, that's what I told the Wyatts. I wasn't actually going to do that. But Wyatts work better with simple and violent instructions."

"What about taking our memories? Stealing our lives? Making us prisoners?"

Trick waved his good hand, shooing away the accusation. "I did what I had to do. Same as you would have done if you were up against an impossible choice. If you had followed instructions, like everyone else in that forsaken place, we'd have left you alone. I didn't like it when it happened, but we needed your energy. If you had just done your job—"

"My job?" She poked him in the chest. "I never asked for any of this! What's so important about the stupid Well? Tell me Trick. I'm ready to hear the whole thing. What's so important that you created this nightmare?"

So, he told her.

All of it. The run from the Germans, Eventide, the impossible moment of creation, how things seemed to be degrading in the Hotel since the Portal broke. She listened through the whole thing, miraculously not interrupting even once. It took about fifteen minutes and when he was done, he blew at the tips of his throbbing fingers through the bandages, strangely exhausted.

Vain didn't respond. Her giant eyes consumed him, considering. Why did butterflies dance in his stomach when he looked at her? More importantly, what in all hell was wrong with his stomach? Unable to stand her silence any longer, he spoke.

"Well?"

"Yes, you mentioned the Well. I am processing that."

"No, that's not what I meant." Why was he asking her anything? He didn't care what she thought. "What do you think?"

"It is the stupidest origin story I have ever heard, and I am aware of the Teenage Mutant Ninja Turtles."

Trick couldn't help but grin, and he waited, drowning in her eyes while she thought. Again, she bit her bottom lip. What would it be like to bite her—

"Where is the energy going?"

Trick shook his head to clear it. "Eventide is consuming it, presumably becoming stronger and more dangerous in the process."

He continued to blow on his throbbing fingers, a blinking traffic light of searing pain; on, off, on, off. The pain was made worse by slow pace at which Vain trundled towards the conclusion he needed her to get to. But if he said anything, it would break the spell. She needed to get there on her own. People were frustrating. Anyway, he liked watching her think, watching her brain in action.

Vain picked up some hay and broke it into pieces while she talked. "Why do you even need the Padlock? You have the Portal."

"Because the worlds are dangerous. Look at us. We've been here less than twenty-four hours, and already we've been captured by cannibals, and I've lost three fingers. At least with the Padlock we have a sure-fire way to get back."

"How many times have you both died?"

"Dozens. Hundreds. I don't know. We stopped counting."

"What will Eventide do if it gets out?"

"Who knows? I think if it escaped and had access to all the worlds, it would be the end of everything."

"But if it's been feeding off the energy in the Well, its appetite must be—"

"Unquenchable," Trick agreed. "It will probably devour its way through the entire multi-verse, likely starting with our world through the Portal."

"And kill Roman," she said.

"All of your friends. Yes."

Vain stared at him for several beats, and he could almost see the wheels spinning. Inwardly, he allowed himself a moment of relief. She got there.

She pulled her hands inside her shirt and began unclothing.

"What are you doing?" he asked. It wouldn't have been the first time that had happened to him. What weird timing, though. Apparently, she was turned on by energy demons and heroic origins. And, despite the circumstances, he found himself interested. But the chains would be a problem. Maybe once they got out.

"Vain, I find you incredibly attractive. And sure, in another circumstance I would certainly do this and, if I'm being honest, show you a spectacular time, even one-handed. Like mind-blowing. I'm talking multiples on multiples. That said, I don't think now is a great time."

"I'm giving you my bra." Her arm popped out of her sleeve, holding a black bra. "You said we could escape with this."

"Right. Escape." He took a deep breath. "Wow. I need to shift gears. Okay. Escaping. Good. Pull the wire out." He shook his head to clear out the other thoughts that danced through.

With ripping and mutual swearing, they managed to pull the underwire out, giving them two long strips of metal to work with.

"This isn't very much." He frowned.

"Fuck you, Trick," Vain snapped, her face flushed. "Excuse me if I'm not Tits McGee or whatever gets you going. God, I am so sick of all these comments about my appearance."

"Down. Easy. I am not commenting on the size of your—I think you have quite wonderful—I simply meant it's not as much wire to work with as I had hoped. Can you see if you snap off a piece? Try to get a more sharp or jagged end when you do it.

Vain eyed him sideways but did as he asked, flexing the wire until it snapped, and she had two fairly solid strips of metal, each no bigger than the length of a match, but with enough tensile strength that he thought he'd be able to manage the lock.

Although missing fingers was going to make that tough.

There wasn't a ton of light coming in through the rickety slats in the building, but it was enough to make out the keyhole and see what he was dealing with. On a good day, he could pick a lock like this in seconds. Funny how many skills one was able to acquire when living multiple lifetimes trying to stop a demon from consuming the universe.

"Hold your lock steady," he said. Vain secured it and he got to work. One handed, it was challenging, but not impossible.

He thrust the piece of metal into the lock and began working the tumblers. Tension on one. Click out of two, that's binding. Nothing on three, click out of four. Back to one, good click there. One more push, and he had it.

Her collar clicked open and fell to the ground. Black and blue bruises covered her neck to her chin.

"Oh, Vain."

"Trick, holy shit!" Vain clapped. "You have to show me how you did that."

"Apparently our sadistic cannibal friends aren't great locksmiths," he said. "Come here, lean closer to me. Same as last time, hold my lock."

She leaned close, which he found somewhat distracting. After another minute of picking, his collar fell to the floor.

"Now what?" she asked. "What's the plan?"

Trick noticed she was shivering, and he handed his jacket to her. She was so silly for not keeping it on. Stubborn. Like him. He didn't care if she wore a jacket. Some people would say she was being foolish, but not him. He'd punch anyone who called her silly.

He was only wearing a shirt, but he'd picked up a few mental tricks that let him ignore the cold, a little. Besides, the heat from his fingers was keeping him plenty warm. Fever-warm, actually. Vain pulled his jacket back around her shoulders.

"What's to plan?" he asked. "We escape, kill a bunch of cannibals, get the Padlock, then," he mimicked a gun to his head, "get out of here."

"Consider this, though. There's two basic types of cannibals."

Several seconds passed where Vain stared at him, unblinking.

"And?" He finally said, unable to wait any longer.

"And what?"

"You said there's two types of cannibals."

"That's right." She nodded. "We should try to find a weapon."

"What are the two types of— you know what? Forget it." Trick rubbed his eyes with the palm of his hand. "I don't know how I'm supposed to play team up with you."

"Because I'm adorable, remember?" Vain gave him a massive, and he had to admit, adorable smile. "Okay, I agree we're playing team up now, but this doesn't mean we're friends. This is temporary. As soon as we get back to the Hotel and I save the universe because you're so bad at it, we go back to being enemies. Deal?"

She stuck out her hand for a shake and he took it.

"Do you see why I did those things?" He didn't let go. Something like a fist crushed his chest, taking his breath away. He needed her to understand.

"I see someone who did horrible things because they were too scared to do the right thing." She snatched her hand back.

"Really. And what was the right thing? What would you have done in that exact same scenario?"

"Fought, somehow. Done something. Not hold people captive and take their memories."

"Not even to save Roman?"

She didn't answer.

"If Flute had been unwilling to come with you, what would you have done?"

Still no answer.

"I used to have Romans. People I cared about very much."

"And you don't, anymore?"

"There's one person I seem to find myself caring about." He didn't blink.

A flush rose in her cheeks and she pushed herself off the dirty straw. Finally able to stand upright after so long, she stretched and cracked her back.

"Okay," she said. "Let go punch some cannibals."

<u>Chapter 28: Emma demonstrates casual misandry.</u>

Emma drew an enormous lungful of air, surfacing back to the present. With a sputter, she threw the camera across the lobby, leaning back in the tall-backed wooden chair. He smiled wryly at her.

"It's something, alright."

Emma couldn't find her words. The sensation of being Arthur still drenched her body, and her own authentic self struggled to swim through the oil slick of memories.

"You," she gasped. That seemed like a good start. "That thing. Well." She was really bringing it home.

"True," Arthur agreed. "I've watched it a dozen times now, and it never gets better. The dizziness will pass."

Emma groaned and put her head in her hands, trying to make sense of what she had witnessed. The Hotel was a prison. And although the trip through Arthur's past answered a few questions, it left her with about a thousand new ones.

"What the hell was that?"

Arthur shrugged. "I'm not sure what the Hotel is, exactly. Maybe a pocket dimension or something."

"I was asking about the thing in the Well."

"It's a monster that feeds off energy. How was that not clear?"

"I saw the Elevator."

"Yes, it sprang to life with the Hotel."

"How many worlds have you visited?" she asked.

"A few thousand. I don't know. You sort of lose count after a while."

"Why?"

"Two reasons. Trick thinks Eventide had to come from somewhere. If we can find where it came from, we might be able to figure out a way to beat it."

"It's pointless. The chances of a random world having a solution to Eventide is microscopic."

Arthur waved his hand. "Eventide is Trick's problem, although he's been screwing that up lately."

"You said two reasons."

"Infinite worlds, Emma. Infinite. Do you get what that means? I've already set myself up as a billionaire in three universes. I met Mozart. I was there when Rome burned. Time is infinite here in the Hotel. There must be a universe where they've cured aging. And I'll see all of it. All the futures, all the pasts. It's like being God."

"What's the alcohol content of that power you're drinking?"

"Come again?

"Because you're drunk on it."

Arthur brushed back his hair and straightened his glasses. "I went too fast for you. I forget how simple you are. I'll start again. Let's pretend you have an apple and then I show you a second apple, only this one is made out of money and wishes."

"I understand what you're doing," Emma interrupted. "Many worlds. Power. I'm still sort of stuck on the problem with the energy demon you and Trick trapped in the bottom of the Well. You've had forever to figure this out. Why can't you kill it? Trick was able to push it into the Well easily enough. Let it out and destroy it."

"Let it out?" Arthur blew out a breath through his mustache. "You keep saying you're not a moron, but then you say moronic things. The thing that eats power has access to infinite power. Who knows how strong it is now? The only reason Trick managed to kick it into the Well was because it was such a dumb and improbable move, it caught everyone by surprise, including Trick."

"If you let it out of the Well though, it won't have access to that power anymore. It would deflate. Eventually."

"Thanks. Trick and I have never once thought of that in the countless millennia we've been working in this timeless nightmare prison. Let me call Trick and tell him to shut it all down. Thank God you've come to Emmasplain the situation to me."

Emma flushed in irritation. "Why not, though?"

"Because, think of the damage he could do before he runs out of energy. That's assuming it's finite."

Emma rose from the chair.

"I did what you said. I listened to your story. Can I leave now?"

"You're serious? After everything you've heard, you still want to leave?"

"Yes, please."

"You're not seeing the possibility. Imagine if we didn't have to deal with Eventide. We'd have all of existence to explore. Forever."

"You just said we can't let him out."

"We can't. But we can build a better prison."

"How are you going to do that?"

"Not me, Emma. You."

He took off his glasses and polished them on his shirt and glared at her with his shark's eyes. Emma looked around the room, trying to find something comforting in the strange surroundings. Something that would take her mind off the horrible situation she was in. More than anything, she wanted to hug her mother. One year ago, her biggest worry had been whether she could finish schoolwork in time to watch Grey's Anatomy.

Emma hiccupped and choked back a sob. She turned from stupid Arthur and pushed away from the table. The lobby was empty, something she was thankful for. She rested her head against the cold plaster of the wall.

For a single moment, Emma allowed herself to hate Vain. Truly, honestly and deeply hate the woman that had, effectively, ruined her life. Vain gave her those powers, Vain pulled her into that stupid world of magic and demons, Vain destroyed any chance she had at a safe and reasonable future.

Emma had not given herself any space to grieve about Vain's destruction of her life. Many horrible things had happened to her over the past six months. Everything she knew entirely changed. She was absolutely allowed to feel unhappy and depressed about that. Instead, she'd fought against the emotion, tried to pretend like everything was okay.

Everything was not okay. Vain destroyed her because she had to rob an ATM and get pushed off a roof. But still, a smaller part of her brain yelled that she was being unfair; that she would have done the exact same thing in Vain's place.

Emma turned back from the wall to face Arthur. "What exactly do you think I'm going to be able to do about this?"

"Imagine a bottle filled with water. Now imagine there was a creature on the bottom that drank the water. Okay, now this is going to get challenging for you, but imagine someone is always filling that bottle."

"Enough, Arthur. I understand the Well. You want me to dump on more power? I knew it. You're going to pair me, aren't you? You're going to take my memory and give me a weird name like Perspicacity, or Sagacious, or something."

Arthur squinted at her. "Maybe you're the one we should have called Vain. But no, I'm not planning to pair you. You can't pair people like us, anyway. It creates brutal feedback. It would be catastrophic. You say you get it, but then you keep saying dumb things. I'm honestly not sure how to react here."

Hot shame rushed to Emma's cheeks. "What, then?"

"I want to you to plug the Well."

"How?"

"I'm going to teach you how to make a Device. You don't appear to have the same limitations I do. You can create a Device to seal the Well. Forever. No more putting in power. No more pairs. All of this, done. I understand you want to go home, back to your normal life, where you can go to school and get married and become an environmental lawyer or something. Simple dreams. If you could create Devices, you could have that. You can create a

Device to help you manage this. Maybe turn an EpiPen into a power sucking pen or something. I don't know, I feel like I've done a lot of lifting on this plan and you're not meeting me halfway. You clog the Well and fix everything, and in return you get the ability to be normal."

Emma turned away again so he wouldn't see the tears spring back to her eyes. To be normal again. She could hardly imagine. But she'd seen the power of Devices firsthand. They could seemingly do anything. Could Arthur really teach her? Already, she thought of several Devices she could make. One to help manage the power. One to let her eat again.

One to stop Emma of Death from taking over.

It wasn't like it was that much of a commitment. If he wanted to kill her, he already could have. All she was doing was getting more information.

She wiped her cheek and squared her shoulders.

"Okay. Let's look at the Well."

Chapter 29: Roman forgets his manners.

The last thing Roman remembered was seeing Vain on the couch surrounded by Wyatts with a terrible welt on her face. Before he was aware of moving, his feet had carried him past Emma's shield and into the line of fire. Searing pain, a blinding flash of red light, then nothing.

And knock-knock jokes. For some reason, he remembered knock-knock jokes.

He groaned and opened his eyes, rubbing the disorientation away. He seemed to be in a hospital bed, but from the surrounding décor, he suspected he was in the twins' apartments. A blurry group of figures stood watch, and he blinked a few times until they came into focus.

Charm was crying and laughing at the same time, holding his hand. Blunt wore an enormous grin, and Hush looked sort of happy, or as much as happy would fit onto that pinched and distrustful face.

Even Flute seemed relieved to see him, and she clapped her hands in delight.

Wait, Flute?

Flute was in the Hotel.

Flute was standing beside his bed. Jesus Christ, was he back in the Hotel? His stomach plummeted. But no, this was clearly the restaurant, because time still worked. He remembered a sharp pain in his forehead. Gunfire. Vain wasn't there. Flute was.

Bile rushed up his throat, and he nearly gagged on its bitterness. The top of his head became magma-hot. What had she done? What had she convinced them to do?

"Welcome back, sweetie." Charm leaned over to give him a huge hug. "I know you must be confused at what's happening."

"I was shot. Vain somehow convinced you to re-open the Portal to the Hotel, kidnap Flute and get her out here to heal me. The fact that Emma and Vain aren't here means they are dead or captured."

"Um, yes," Charm said. "That's exactly right."

"God fucking damn it to fuck. Fuck."

Roman pushed the covers back, unconcerned that he only wore a flimsy dressing gown. Let them all look at whatever they wanted to. Wires and tubes covered his arms and chest and he pulled them off, not caring how much they ripped and tore at his skin. Charm tried to get him to stop.

"You should have let me die," he said. "You should have killed me or done something else. Convinced her to stop. Anything. I can't believe you opened the Portal. After everything it took to shut it down, you drag us back into this nightmare. What's wrong with you? What's wrong with all of you?" His voice grew to a yell by the end, although he was still weak enough that his head spun.

Hush snorted. "That's a funny way of saying thank you."

"He didn't say thank you," Blunt said.

"I know, boss."

"What happened?" Roman pulled on the sweater than Charm handed him. "Tell me everything."

The glances they exchanged told him how badly they'd messed up before they started speaking, but Charm nonetheless gave him the details of the past week, complete with guilty looks and lots of excuses. He wasn't surprised Vain had come up with something like that, but he was surprised Emma went along with it. Of course, she'd be the one to re-power the Portal. Who else could? And knowing her, she was wrestling with the power and losing herself. Assuming she was still alive.

Roman swung his legs out of bed alongside protests from Charm that he should not swing his legs out of bed, that he needed more rest, and that he was too weak to move.

"Enough, Charm." He moved her out of the way. "You know how Hotel healing works. There's no need for recovery. I'm probably healthier than I've ever been in my life. Where's Mark?"

"Downstairs, guarding the Portal," Hush said. "Flute healed him first. He wanted to run in there and storm the Hotel by himself. We convinced him to wait for you so we could decide our next step together."

"What's to decide?" Roman said. "We have to go in and get them. Somehow."

"It's the somehow that's the problem," Hush said. "This entire thing was screwed right from the beginning. And you know how time works over there. From the way Charm explained it, it seems like she was in there for maybe a half hour, but it was only minutes for us. Maybe it's been years for them at this point."

"Then we go in and find out," Roman said. He turned to Charm. "Someone get my pants."

That line had sounded more heroic in his head.

They left him alone to shower and clean up. As he let the hot water run down his body, he thought about how he'd charged, forehead-first, into a group of Wyatts pointing guns at him, without any thought at all for his own safety. The sight of Vain on that couch with marks on her face had driven him past rational thought.

Was the entire thing his fault? If he had kept his head and stayed behind Emma, she'd have fought the Wyatts off and none of it would have happened.

While steam from the hot shower filled the bathroom, a memory came to him of a time he and Vain spent together a few months before. They'd agreed to meet for a coffee because they hadn't seen each other much, and they sipped at their over-priced lattes that he'd ordered and made forced small talk. He hated it. Vain had been restless and jittery through the whole thing, and it was her idea to do something different.

"This sucks," she'd said. "Wanna get a motel room and a box of pizza and hide out for a couple days? Like we used to?"

Roman thought that sounded wonderful because anything would be better than that weird, stilted conversation where neither of them had anything to say. They found a motel by the highway, checked in, and binged on movies and pizza without a care. It was wonderful. Just like the old days.

Now, two versions of that experience presented themselves to Roman with stark, terrifying clarity.

In version one, he spent a few days catching up with a friend, watching movies, eating pizza, and laughing about nothing. He enjoyed being around Vain; all of her energy pointed at him, that energy and drive that always made his day more vivid, somehow. They turned off their phones, swapped stupid jokes, and napped when they were tired.

In the second version, two adults in committed relationships with other people rented a motel room without telling their partners, slept in the same bed, and recreated the "good old days" when they were being hunted by duplicate thugs because it was the only life they felt comfortable in, and they had nothing to talk about otherwise.

The revelation took the wind out of him, and he dropped to his knees in the shower. What was even wrong with him? What was wrong with both of them? And he'd charged face-first into a hail of bullets for her.

Even now, he wasn't mad at her. Intellectually, he understood that she caused the whole mess to happen. According to Charm, she'd followed the Wyatts and got herself captured. This was unequivocally Vain's fault. But he couldn't make himself blame her. His defences kicked in with jarring efficiency. "You don't understand. Vain had to do it. She had a plan. There's a reason. Leave her alone."

He turned the shower off and leaned against the cold linoleum, heartsick and exhausted. All the moments with Emma came back to him when he'd talked about Vain, or checked in on Vain, or been completely unavailable emotionally because he was thinking about Vain. It was horrible. He was horrible. He thought he'd been separating from Vain, giving her space; but he hadn't really separated from anything. All he'd done was create physical distance, something that he couldn't deal with, apparently. His chest constricted, and he struggled for breath.

Emma was trapped too, and the only way he'd thought about her since waking up was in regard to her relational proximity to Vain. When this was over, assuming they survived, it was time for therapy. Tons and tons of therapy.

As he ran a toothbrush through his mouth, he tried to think of a single thing he could do to fix anything, both in the short and long term. Hush and Blunt could theoretically handle a couple Wyatts. Mark could get another few. Hell, maybe even he and Charm could take one or two down. But what then? There were hundreds of Wyatts. And there was Arthur, who could kill them all without blinking. The only one who had a chance to save them was Emma. But Emma was captured or hurt. He needed her to save her.

Joseph Heller could eat all the shit.

By the time he got to the basement of the restaurant, he had almost worked himself into a full-blown panic attack and could not settle his feelings on who he was supposed to worry about.

The scene in the common area did not bring him any calm.

A single Wyatt sat against the wall, head hanging between his knees. One eye had swollen shut, and Mark towered over him, rubbing his hands together, looking as angry as Roman had ever seen him.

The Portal leaned against the wall, and it was a good thing Hush was obsessed with opulence and had a den area with twenty-foot-high ceilings that could accommodate magic Portals to also-magic Hotels. The pool table and leather couches had been pushed to the side to make room.

"What's with the Wyatt?" he asked.

"They keep popping out of the Portal," Charm said. "Mark punched this one, and we tied him up."

"I just wanna escape, man," the Wyatt said. "I don't want to tangle with you guys anymore. Everything has gone to hell. I only want out."

"Where's V—Emma?" Roman hauled the Wyatt to his feet. He felt sick for saying Emma's name. He felt sick for nearly saying Vain's name. He felt sick.

"Who is Vemma?" the Wyatt said. "Do you mean Vixen? The pair to Meagre? I haven't seen them in ages. I'm not sure they're still alive."

"Emma," Roman said. He threw the Wyatt against the wall. No one stopped him. "Vain. Where are they?"

"I don't know where Vain is," said the Wyatt. "She attacked me and tried to break my neck. The redhead went crazy and nearly killed me, even though I didn't even do anything and was minding my own business. I don't know what happened after that."

"Enough waiting," Mark said. "I'm going in. You said once Roman was here, we'd go."

"I said we'd talk," Charm said. "We need to figure out what to do next. Together."

"There's nothing to talk about," Hush said. "They either come out or they don't. We keep punching Wyatts. If we go in, we die."

"I think we should have a glass of chocolate milk," Blunt said. "We'll all feel better."

In moments, they were all arguing, talking over each other, throwing out dumb ideas. The last time that had happened, they had the same stupid and pointless series of arguments about how to escape the building. Emma had pulled energy from them and calmed them all down. They'd gone out the window, escaping via a magical energy bridge. He'd panicked, and she held his hand and told him stupid jokes about superheroes because he was scared, and she was lovely. That was the moment Roman understood he could love her.

God, he wanted her back. And he didn't want to think about how Vain fit into that. It was too big and too confusing. He wanted his Emma, and the unambiguous simplicity of that thought brought him some measure of calm.

"I have an idea," Flute said. Roman had barely remembered she was there. In the Hotel, she'd been one of the perfect pairs that Vain hated. No one but Roman noticed she'd spoken. She hopped up on to the couch and cupped her hands around her mouth to be heard.

"I have an idea," she shouted. The group quieted down

and looked at her.

"No one cares, princess," Hush said. "This isn't the Hotel. In the real world, we do things on merit, not who kisses the most ass."

Flute put her hands on her hips. "Okay, what's your idea?"

Hush opened and closed his mouth a few times. Mark cracked his knuckles. The Wyatt whispered to Roman, "This is awkward."

The silence in the room grew to pregnant proportions and was close to requiring a c-section when Hush finally said, "If I had a leaf blower—"

"Enough," Charm said. "Why is it always a leaf blower with you? What do you think a leaf blower actually is?"

"What's your idea, Flute?" Roman asked. He didn't want to hear her idea. He wanted to follow Mark into the Portal. Time ticked by. How long on the other side? A second? A year? What were they doing to Emma?

"They might not know I escaped yet," Flute said. "I can take a look. If there's Wyatt's guarding the Portal, I can tell them you kidnapped me or something. But assuming it's clear, then you can all follow me."

"And what do we do once we're inside?" Hush said. "Assuming there aren't any Wyatts?"

"We rush the place." Mark pulled a gun out from under his jacket. Everyone recoiled and flinched, except Roman. "We get our girls back. And we shoot anyone who tries to stop us."

"I can get you an Umbrella," the Wyatt said.

Now the group turned their attention to the monster on the floor. Flute said, "I don't think rain is an issue in the Hotel. There's no weather."

"It blocks energy." Roman rubbed his chin and gave the Wyatt a considering look. "How?"

"We're in Minneapolis, right? I know where Trick has some supplies stashed. He had a locker at the train station. Umbrellas, maybe more. He's always got a gadget or two."

"A few of those could give us a shot," Mark said.

"We're in your restaurant, right?" the Wyatt asked. "I think it's like a half-hour round trip. I'll get you the gear, then you let me go. You can storm the Hotel or whatever the hell you're planning. We never see each other again. Deal?"

"We're not letting you loose on the world," Charm said.

Roman ignored her. He and Mark stared at each other.

"Less than an hour," Mark said. "And we go in protected."

"We could lose them."

"We could."

Roman rubbed his chin. The group stared at him. He realized it was somehow his decision to make. Even though they were all in it, they were waiting for him to decide.

"How can you be sure the stash of stuff is still there?" he asked the Wyatt.

"I can't."

Roman looked around the room. They were waiting for an answer. Vain and Emma were both waiting for an answer. Time kept moving forward, step by step.

"We get the Umbrellas, and whatever else might be in there." he said. "Then we get our girls."

Chapter 30: Vain puts a crack in the glass ceiling.

Vain kicked the gate open and Trick grabbed her by the arm.

"Wait," he said.

"Why?"

"What about him?" Trick gestured to the one-limbed man on the ground.

"Oh." She bit her lip. "Shit."

"What should we do? Should we take him with us?"

"I don't know. Maybe. If we had a sling or something. Can you make a sling?" Vain tried to imagine how it was going to work, but couldn't. Did she even need to get involved? Why had Trick pointed it out?

"He's going to slow us down," Trick said. "Do you think we can risk it?"

"I guess we have to," Vain said. "We can't leave him here."

"If we screw this up, Roman's going to die." Trick put a regretful expression on his face. "Your friends are going to die. All of this will have been for nothing."

Vain continued to gnaw at her bottom lip and Trick pressed on, leaning closer towards her, dropping his voice. "How are we going to fight them, carrying him between us? How would that work? We'd have no chance."

"You don't know that," Vain said. But she didn't move towards the man. Trick was playing with her and she knew it. That didn't make it any easier.

"What would we even save him for?" Trick asked. "He's going to be dead in a week, anyway. We'd almost be doing him a favor, leaving him here. They have him drugged, he's not in pain. And we can still save Roman."

"I know what you're doing, Trick," she said. She already knew what her decision was going to be. Her stomach clenched.

"I'm simply talking to you about options."

"You're making a point. Sometimes you have to do terrible things because the alternative is even worse. But you don't understand, not really. Having a reason to do the terrible thing doesn't make the terrible thing any less terrible. It just makes you a shitty person for doing it. So, I get it. I'm a shitty person. Fine. But I'm not going to pretend like good reasons make the bad decisions any less shitty." She turned to him and tilted her head upward so she could look him in the eyes. "I know who I am, Trick. Do you?"

He opened his mouth, blinked, and closed his mouth again. She spun towards the barn door.

"No more screwing around. We have to get out of here." Horrible thoughts pinged through her mind. It was never like that when she had adventures with Roman. He didn't confuse her with ham-fisted metaphorical lessons and violently amputated fingers.

Before she could call them back, an avalanche of words fell from her mouth.

"I mean, they don't have agriculture or livestock or phones, but they somehow figured out a way to eat humans one limb at a time using stashes of medical-grade heroin and also keep them restrained with neck collar chains? Where would they even get those, do they have sacks of them lying around? Hey Pete, shame about this famine apocalypse we're suffering through, too bad about your family and everyone you love dying, but hey, what's your favorite part of the human to eat because I really like leg thigh, it's super tender, and speaking of stuff I like, your skeleton beret is so cunning, that's a clever use of every part of the body and do you by chance have an enormous fucking sack of neck collar chains in your garage? I need to restrain human cows."

The last word snapped off, and her chest heaved with exertion. Trick stared at her for several moments.

"I can see you're upset," he said.

"Fuck you," she snapped. She gave her head a shake and took a few more breaths. Focus on escape. Soon it would all be over, and she'd be back in the safety of the horrible Hotel, fighting hell demons and holy hell, she did not think that day could get any worse.

Vain opened the door to the barn a whisper-crack; a tiny sliver that allowed her to peek out with a single eye and check if any cannibals were waiting to attack them.

There were not. Score.

But there did seem to be a single farmhouse with lights pouring out the windows showing her the path through the dark. It would be easy enough to sneak over there; it was pitch black.

"Let me see." Trick moved her aside. After a moment, he pulled back and said, "It's dark out, so we should have no trouble sneaking over there."

"Save it," Vain said. "I'm already past that part of the plan. You know Trick, a good plan is a lot like wrestling."

"I get it."

"It's not a list of… wait, you do?"

"Yeah, it's a series of big spots, followed by a finish. Lock up, table spot, suplex, done. The best plans are loose and fluid."

"Totally." Her stomach fluttered and she wondered how she'd beaten Trick so easily all those other times since he seemed to have some fraction of intelligence.

"Once we get to the farmhouse, we find an open door and pick them off one at a time. How many do you think you can handle?"

"Eighteen," she said without hesitation. She assumed the iron-deficiency inherent to cannibals would make them easy to punch.

Trick sighed for some reason. "Let's say two. You can take two, and I can maybe do two with my good hand. If there's more than four in any building, we think of something else. Agreed?"

"Agreed. Although, I don't think they have any spinach or pomegranate."

"Stop." Trick exhaled deeply while looking at the ceiling. He held up a finger for her to wait. "I can do this." Thirty seconds passed before he spoke. "Okay. I think I've worked this out. At first, I thought you were making a Popeye reference because of the spinach, but the pomegranate threw me. But it's iron, right? You think cannibals are iron deficient and therefore easier to beat up."

"Yes. That's exactly it." Vain was surprised at how not stupid Trick was. He smiled, and why did her hands tremble? Trick pushed open the barn door and they stepped outside.

The snow between the barn and the house was packed down and made for easy sneaking. Vain was glad she didn't need to navigate the heavy snow drifts from before. Even with Trick's jacket, she couldn't stop herself from shivering, and her shoes weren't exactly designed for that kind of weather.

Mark had taught her to crouch and be stealthy, so she snuck her way over to the house. Trick didn't crouch at all.

"Get down, you idiot," she hissed.

"Why? There's no one outside. It's pitch black. Come on, let's go around the side."

Feeling foolish even though her crouching was top notch, she followed him to the far end of the building. Light poured from two evenly spaced windows. They huddled beneath the closest one with their backs against the cold metal, and she experienced a moment of déjà vu. It was the Wyatt den all over again. That mistake had cost Roman his life, and she resolved to be careful. Enough people had died because of her stubborn impulsiveness.

"Look inside," she whispered. Her lips brushed against his earlobe, and a tiny tingle ran through her body. He nodded and stretched upward to peek inside. After a moment, he dropped back beside her.

"There's two of them. Small guys. We go in the door and rush them. I'll go left, you go right."

"Are either of them Smoove Dick?"

"Don't you think if one were Smoove Dick, I would have said 'It's Smoove Dick and another guy'? Why would I generically refer to the person who cut off my fingers? I have enormous amounts of personal stake in this."

He smiled while he spoke, teasing. She swatted his arm and looked at his earlobes.

"We need code names," she said.

"D'uh. I'm Hot Granite."

"Ha. And they call me Vain. Fine, Hot Granite, then what's my name?"

"Gorgeous eyes."

Vain felt heat rise to her face and tried to ignore it. "Dick-punch Nine, it is."

"Why nine?"

"Because I already punched eight dicks."

Trick snorted, and she weirdly found herself wondering if Roman or Mark would have laughed at that joke. To be fair, it was an awesome joke, but they didn't always get her humor. But having code names brightened her mood immensely and playing secret agent made the terrifying, terrifying thing they were doing ever so slightly less horrifying. She couldn't stop clenching and unclenching her hands. Some of this must have showed, because Trick took her by the shoulder with his good hand and pulled her close.

"Hey. They're only murderous, violent cannibals. They can only kill us once."

"And I can bite off my own tongue if they capture me."

"Exactly. See? You're all good." Trick stood up and dusted off his pants. "We should talk into our wrists from now on."

"Like we have wrist-communicators!"

"Exactly. Dick-punch Nine, do you read me?"

"Loud and clear Hot Granite. Over."

"I'll kick the door open. Remember. You go right. Got it? Over?"

"Roger. That's a code ten." She saluted.

"A code ten is a bomb threat. Do you, by chance, have a bomb on you?"

"I don't. How do you know what a code ten is? I thought I made it up."

"Vain, I've been around for a while. I kind of know everything."

She couldn't decide whether she found that weirdly attractive or grotesquely condescending, and she landed somewhere in the middle, which ended up feeling like… hunger? Only with shame, somehow?

"We can do this, Vain," Trick said. "We take these two out, fast. As fast as possible. They're in a kitchen, so there must be something in there we can use as a weapon. We might have to kill them."

"Please stop talking." If Trick laid down one more inspirational speech, she was going to throw up on his pants. "Is your hand okay?"

He nodded. "As good as it's going to get. I can punch ambidextrously."

That time, she experienced zero ambiguity. She found that hot. Huh, maybe she did have impulse issues.

Trick took a position on the other side of the door and held up three fingers. She wiped her hands on her jeans. He mouthed, "Three, two, one," then he was up and kicking the door open and Vain was seriously not ready, but she followed him and screamed for some reason.

All of Vain's training evaporated. Her vision narrowed to a young and scared-looking red-haired boy holding a knife. Vain surprised herself by leaping into the air and kicking him in the face. He flew backwards and landed against the kitchen counter hard enough that his back bent at a horribly unnatural angle. Vain fell awkwardly on her side, her own elbow driving into her ribs and forcing the air from her body. Beside her, Trick disarmed his cannibal much more smoothly, doing some weird takedown maneuver that ended with a single blow to the temple. Even one-handed, he was better at fighting than she was.

"Next time, make more noise," he hissed.

Vain clambered to her feet while he ran to the boy cannibal and knocked him out with a punch to the jaw.

"Check their pockets for the Padlock. Hurry."

Vain bent to the cannibal closest to her who was wearing a bunch of potato sacks stitched together with shoelaces.

"They have fucking electricity," she bit back a sob, "but pants are apparently a bridge too far." Unfortunately, calling attention to the inconsistency did not solve for his potato-sack pants lacking any pockets.

"Nothing here." Trick stood up from his investigation of the unconscious boy. He cast a look around the filthy kitchen and found a knife on the counter. "You should grab one too," he said.

"Pass." Vain was okay with stabbing Wyatts, but that was where she drew the line.

Trick peered out the door that led into the rest of the house, keeping his back to the wall.

"What in hell is that racket!" someone yelled. Above them, what sounded like several people's worth of boots clomped towards the stairs.

"Shit." Trick backed away from the door. He cast her a worried glance. "Vain. Please. Take something to protect yourself."

Something. Not a knife. She scanned the kitchen. Can opener, no. Cutting board, maybe? If she used it like a plank? Cheese grater? Wait. There. A cast iron pan. She gave it a few experimental swings, holding it like a baseball bat.

Trick nodded and got his knife ready. The footsteps stomped closer, and Vain wiped her sweaty palms on her pants before readjusting her grip on the pan.

A bearded cannibal burst through the door.

Trick lashed out, quick as a viper, stabbing the cannibal in the knee. Cannibeard screamed in agony and fell to the ground, ripping the knife from Trick's hand. Another cannibal, this one with a shaved head, rushed through and tripped over them both. He stumbled towards Vain, arms pinwheeling for balance.

Vain swung from the hip and connected solidly with his unprotected skull. It sounded exactly like a cast iron pan connecting solidly with an unprotected skull. He fell on the boy cannibal, unconscious. She gagged and dropped the pan with a loud crash. Trick finished with Cannibeard, and now they had four unconscious or dead cannibals in the kitchen, and the place was getting pretty crowded with bodies.

Smoove Dick appeared in the doorway.

"What in fuck?" was as far as he got before Trick pounced, knocking him to the ground. A flurry of one-armed punches followed and Smoove Dick brought his forearms up to block. The witch woman stepped through the doorway, glanced at Trick and Smoove Dick wrestling on the ground, then took a look at Vain. She smiled and cracked her knuckles.

Vain held up her hands. "I want you to know that the only reason I'm fighting you is because Smoove Dick came through first. If it had been the other way around, Trick would be fighting you and I'd be fighting Smoove Dick. I'm only saying that in case you think the reason we're fighting is because we're women. I reject that trope."

The witch woman tilted her head and Vain congratulated herself for landing another huge blow for equality, because Charm said you break that ceiling one chip at a time.

The snarling woman hurled herself at Vain, and they both tumbled to the ground with Vain on the bottom. Rancid, fetid breath puffed into Vain's face, and she gagged and turned her head. The witch woman clawed, and it was all Vain could do to keep those fingernails away from her eyes. One got through and raked a hot line of searing pain across her cheek. The woman cackled and bent forward to bite Vain's shoulder.

"What even the fuck!" Vain screamed as the woman's teeth tore through her shirt and pierced her skin. She released the woman's wrists and started pounding on her head. Hot moisture covered her shoulder where the Witch Woman gnawed at her flesh. Vain delivered a solid blow to her temple. Before she could capitalize any further, the witch woman brought an elbow down on Vain's head. Stars exploded behind her eyes, and the room swam.

The witch woman bit her other shoulder.

Vain screamed and began throwing blind punches. Head, stomach, temple, neck; she hardly even knew what she was doing, only that she was going to die, she'd never see Roman again, and the cannibal witch was going to eat her alive.

She landed a savage blow and was rewarded with a grunt of pain from the witch. The witch grabbed her sides and rolled off Vain. Vain scrambled to her knees, her shoulders screaming at her in agony, and threw a looping hook that connected with the hag's jaw, knocking her down. Before she could recover, Vain grabbed her by the hair.

She slammed her head down into the floor.

Some part of Vain recognized that the wet and meaty sound would stay with her forever, but that didn't stop her from pulling the witch woman's head up a second time and driving it back into tile.

That time, when she raised the woman's head, a thick stream of blood poured from her nose and mouth. Vain choked back a sob.

She slammed her head again.

"I'm sorry."

And again.

The hag's face was hamburger, her nose completely driven into her skull, and her tooth poked through her upper lip.

Vain couldn't stop. Again.

Vain couldn't stop crying. Again.

Again.

She stopped and let go, holding her blood-sticky hands up. The witch woman wasn't moving.

Vain screamed.

She kicked herself away, scrambling as far back as she could get. Her elbow hit the counter, but she still pushed with her legs, unable to take her eyes off the woman she'd just murdered. A pool of blood grew underneath her body, expanding, the red wave covering the kitchen tiles as it creeped forward, getting closer to Vain, to her feet, and oh my God, it was going to touch her, the blood was going to touch her.

"Vain!"

Trick pulled her to her feet and took her by the arms. A nasty welt under his eye was the only evidence he'd been in a fight. He pulled her into a tight hug, and she let him do it, although she didn't hug him back.

"It's okay. Shh. It's okay. It's finished. It's done."

He repeated it, saying it was finished, telling her to shh, telling her it was okay, but it wasn't okay, nothing was okay, and her adventures with Roman were never like that, not for one second, and she missed Roman so much, so fucking much that it almost felt like she was dying. With a broken sob, she pushed her head into Trick's chest and hugged him tight and hated herself a bit more.

"Shh. Okay. It's okay."

Over and over.

She didn't believe a word of it.

<u>Chapter 31: Emma figures stuff out.</u>

Emma rested her hands against the cool, rough stone of the Well, surprised at how satisfying it felt. Waves of power emanated from the dark hole in the center.

As far as wells went, it was disappointingly plain, if a bit wider than usual. She'd expected something more magicky. A lightning bolt on the side or something. The circumference was easily twenty feet across, and no amount of light could penetrate that blackness at the center. She waved her hand over the top and a crackle of blue static caused her to pull back with a hiss, sticking her burned fingers in her mouth.

"Careful," Arthur said. "The amount of energy we packed in there would flash fry a mastodon."

"Are you speaking from experience?" Emma waved her hand over the Well once more, letting it slice through the hot currents.

"Actually, yes," Arthur said. "We found a world with dinosaurs, and you know Trick, he thought they'd be good to eat, so we went hunting. They are not. You think authentic dinosaur steak is going to be something exciting, then it tastes like rancid meat. There's a lesson there."

"A lesson about Wells and demons?"

"If that helps you flounder towards understanding."

She ignored him, and reached out with her mind, casting it downwards through the depths, trying to reach the bottom. The enormous amounts of energy acted as a barrier to her mental probing, and she strained with the effort. There, near the bottom, her mind brushed against a presence.

Hatred.

Pure, undiluted hatred.

With a cry, she stumbled back from the Well, her brain recoiling from what it touched.

"I felt it. Eventide. For a second, I rubbed up against it."

"And?"

"It's angry. I've never experienced anything like it."

"All the more reason to work with me to contain it."

She wiped her mouth. "What would I even make? I don't know how."

"I can show you. There's a world I visit when I'm practicing. It's empty and safe."

"And then I get to leave?"

"Yes. You help me close the Well and then you can go."

"You'll stop chasing us? You'll call off Trick? No more Wyatt attacks?"

"As long as you give me the Padlock back, yes. I'll let the pairs go, too. I don't need them if I can keep Eventide secure."

Emma imagined a life where this was all over, a life built with Roman. They'd buy a tiny house in the country and would they have a tree with a tire swing? Sure, why not. The fantasy was absurd, but every moment she kept Arthur from the Portal gave Vain more chances.

"Okay. Show me the empty world."

Arthur gestured and led her to a door near the back of the Lobby. He opened it but didn't step through right away.

"You never know where this thing is going to open. Sometimes, there's stairs. Looks like a hallway this time. Follow me."

He led her down a narrow pathway lit by blue candles. The Elevator waited at the end of the tunnel, and Emma was marginally disappointed by how little fanfare there was.

"This is it?" she asked.

"Yes. You push these buttons and then it goes."

"Nothing in this place looks that magical. Why is that?"

"Oh, hold on a second. Let me grab my feedback box, a thing that doesn't exist because I don't care what you or anyone else thinks, and then I'll get you some paper and a pen and you can rate your Hotel vacation. Miracle traveling Elevator to everywhere wasn't sufficiently wondrous. One star."

Emma frowned and wondered why she even bothered to talk to him. She was getting mighty fed up with being put down, but swallowed her anger, and kept working on the problem. She poked her head in the contraption and brushed her fingertips against a row of buttons. "How do you know what to press?"

"It's random. Trial and error. We've never been able to find any connection between the worlds, and their button sequences, but logically there must be one."

"I am going to step into this with you and you are going to take me to another world."

"Yes."

"This is a lot to take in."

"Even more so given your modest intellect."

Emma was getting to be an expert in ignoring Arthur's jabs. She stepped into the Elevator.

"Show me."

Arthur followed behind her. "The world we are about to visit seems to have stopped around the mid-eighties, but it's a decent place to experiment in. There's little danger. The button sequence is peacock, peacock, peacock, five."

"What's peacock, peacock, peacock, one through four?"

"Do not visit those worlds. All four killed me."

"Are any of them filled with peacocks?"

"No. Okay, ready?"

Emma was enormously confused by the opaque rules of that system, but was also tired of Arthur insulting her intelligence, so she nodded. He pressed the buttons.

The doors closed, and the Elevator hummed to life.

To say the sensation of traveling to another universe was unnerving would be the same as saying Vain's jokes were "sort of" inaccessible. It was like nothing Emma had ever experienced, the strangeness invading her very molecules. While it wasn't painful, it was disorienting, and when the Elevator dinged to a stop, she felt like she was coming out of a long sleep.

"Welcome to a new universe." Arthur opened the doors and bowed with a flourish to the outside.

The new universe looked exactly like the world she'd come from, only abandoned. Wherever they were, it was an empty city with green shrubs breaking through the pavement and rusted, dirty cars littering the streets. A gasp escaped her lips as time slammed back into place.

"It will pass," Arthur said. "Breathe through it."

"What is this?" She spun in a circle to try to take it all in.

"Empty." Arthur followed her out and wedged a few traffic cones between the Elevator doors. At her raised eyebrow, he said, "If the door closes, we're trapped here. There's no way to open an Elevator door from this side. Only from the Hotel."

"Traffic cones? That's all that stands between us and being stranded?"

"Do you have a more elegant solution?"

"Several dozen, yes."

Arthur glared at her and muttered something about uppity youth, and Emma experienced a moment of satisfaction having pushed back on him a bit. Arthur finished piling objects in front of the door and dusted off his hands. "There isn't any weird end of days scenarios here, or anything like that. I don't know why it's empty, but it is and that's good enough for me."

"What city is this?"

"Toronto. Canada. Follow me."

Emma thought an alternate universe would be somehow more alien. Different colored skies, or two suns, or something to let her know she wasn't home anymore. Aside from the emptiness, that place seemed exactly like her planet.

Arthur led her a few stores down, past a store called Sam the Record Man, and stopped in front of a Pawn Shop. She sneezed when he opened the door. Dust and cobwebs covered everything in the store, although footprints through the dirt revealed the times Arthur had been there.

"I used to come here to practice. There are enough

random things in here to experiment with. This is where I came up with the Handcuffs. The best way to start making Devices is with small things. Here."

He picked something off the counter and flicked it at her. It sparkled as it tumbled through the air, and she caught it one-handed. She was sort of proud of that. It was silver and covered in little dimples. A thimble.

"What am I supposed to do?"

"You pour your energy into the object and think about what you want it to become. It helps when the thing you're trying to create is related to the object."

"What would I make out of a thimble?"

"It's up to you."

The innocent item rolled around in her palm. Around her, energy pulsed. It was hers for the taking. What could she make with a thimble? What did a thimble do? It protected your finger from needles. Made your finger harder, in essence. Sort of made your finger indestructible.

"What's the holdup? Start." Arthur crossed his arms.

Emma licked her lips. "I'm afraid of the power." It was hard to admit that to him.

"Why?"

"I lose myself when I draw too much power. My emotions. They change."

"And you're afraid of that?"

"Yes."

"Emotions are brittle things. Let me ask you a question. Have you ever had a relationship end? One where your partner broke it off with you?"

"Sure." She thought of Scott Stilton, a boy she'd dated briefly in her first year of college.

"And at the time, how did you feel about the breakup?"

"I was sad, obviously."

"And are you sad now? When you think about it? Right at this moment, does the thought of that breakup make you sad?"

"No. It was long ago."

"Nothing about the event has changed. The only difference is your feeling towards it. And so it goes with emotions.

They are temporary. Storms that are unpredictable and to be endured. But not something to be afraid of. You're only afraid of this now because you've made that decision."

She shook her head. "You don't understand. I do things when I'm using the power."

"If I understand this correctly, when you are attacked, you get angry. And this, to you, reads as losing control of your emotions, somehow."

"It's not like that. You're twisting my words."

"I'm straightening them out. You're the one making this complicated."

"The power makes me do things."

"Is it the power? Regardless, I'm not your therapist and I don't care about any of this. We're not friends. I want you to make a Device to stop a demon and then I don't care if I ever see you again. If you're not going to help me, then you're telling me you are without any use." He leaned forward and dropped his voice. "Is that what you're telling me, Emma? That you have no use to me?"

"I'm not saying that." She swallowed and hoped he didn't notice.

"Then stop talking and get to work."

The thimble sat on her palm, and she started to pull the power. Same as she did with the Portal, she imaged the energy as something outside of herself, going through a funnel. She connected the end to the thimble and thought about protection while she attempted to push energy into it.

At first, nothing happened. The energy flowed around the thimble, like a stream going around a rock. She concentrated harder, and tiny flickers of energy started to be absorbed by it. Slowly, at first, but with gaining momentum, the power made its way into the thimble. It grew warmer in her hand.

"It's working," she said.

"You have to keep going," Arthur said. "Don't stop."

Now that she had a connection, the thimble started to drink energy. As with the Portal and the Padlock, she directed the currents into the Device while trying to keep as much away from her as possible. The strain was immense, but she clenched her hands and continued to push, ignoring Arthur, ignoring the store, ignoring everything. The only thing that existed was her and the thimble.

It changed as energy surged into it. The tarnished silver began to gleam, and the dimples vanished, leaving behind a smooth surface. With an almost-audible pop, the Thimble jumped in her hand. She broke off the connection and dropped to her knees.

Breathing hard, she held up the Thimble to investigate it more closely. As with the Padlock, it seemed heavier and thrummed with power. She'd done it. She'd created a Device.

"I did it." She blew a strand of hair from her eyes and got to her feet.

"You did." Arthur eyed the Device and snapped at her. "Give it to me."

His tone alerted her something was off. He stared greedily at the thing she'd created. With deliberate motions, she put in on her finger and put her hand behind her back. Right away, she felt the Devices power on her skin. It was like the energy shields she created, but now available to anyone wearing the Thimble.

"I don't think so, Arthur," she said. "Take me back to the Hotel. Let's create your cork and be done with each other."

He looked like he was going to argue, but instead gave her a single sharp nod and took her out of the store.

They didn't say anything on the way back to the Elevator, but she realized she was in more danger now than ever. She could do something that Arthur wanted. And that look he gave her. Hungry. And as much as he said he only wanted her to help, she was beginning to realize that wasn't true.

He wasn't going to let her leave.

Chapter 32: Roman eats pizza but Mark kind of ruins it.

It didn't take long to get the Umbrellas. Mark, obviously distracted, didn't move to stop the Wyatt when he pushed Roman to the ground and ran off in the opposite direction, yelling that Wyatts ruled. Roman wasn't sure if he cared. He had bigger problems than a stray Wyatt.

Back at the restaurant, the mood was grim. Hush was making all the Conduits eat. It made sense. Filling them up with energy would make them slightly harder to hurt, slightly stronger, and if Vain was around, give her something to draw on. Roman sat at a table groaning with food and started to eat, trying not to think about anything.

Mark tapped his gun against his pants. His mouth worked like he was trying to swallow a tough piece of meat. The Portal hummed in the corner. Nobody had come out. There wasn't really any more planning to do. They were willingly going to run into that godforsaken place again and get their girls or die trying.

"You ready?" Mark asked. The question was for Roman alone.

Roman nodded and took a huge bite of pizza.

"She loves you." Mark held his gun up and did some move where he made the bullet holder come out of the bottom. He gave it a once-over before slamming it back into the grip with a loud clack. "She pretends she doesn't, but she does. I tried to be enough for her."

"Don't, man." The pizza stuck in Roman's throat, and he washed it down with water to avoid choking.

"It's true. She didn't visit me in the hospital, you know that? She didn't leave your side. Charm had to physically pull her out."

The hot and sickening knot of guilt that had been busy eating at Roman's stomach took another few chomps. "Please. Stop. I can't do this."

"If we survive, you need to cut it off, or be with her. You can't have it both ways. Not anymore. You need to decide."

"Stop, Mark."

The bigger man finally looked at him with wild and bloodshot eyes. "You need to make a choice, my man. She'll keep burning the world to the ground until she figures out what she's missing is you. And she's never going to figure that out."

"We're only friends."

Mark barked out a laugh and tucked his gun into his holster. "Sure. Totally normal friends, both of whom go literally insane if they don't spend enough time together. When we're inside, if something happens, who are you going to save? Emma or Vain?"

Roman turned back to his meal and concentrated on shoveling food in his mouth. There wasn't anything to decide. Once Emma was safe, he'd set some reasonable boundaries with Vain, that was all. No more waking each other up with texts, maybe. His hands shook when he tried to take a sip of water. He tilted his head back and let the cool liquid stream down his throat, not caring that it poured down his cheeks and into his sweater.

When he was finished, he deliberately set the glass down on the table, wiped his face, and stood up.

"It's time."

The room quieted and everyone looked at him.

"We go in together. Flute pops her head through to see if there are any Wyatts. If there are, we handle them. Maybe we can take them by surprise. Hush, you need to keep your commands focused. Charm, stay at the back. Flute, you heal anyone who gets hurt, got it?"

Everyone stared with pale faces and trembling lips, and Roman tried not to think about love. It was strange, but the thought of attacking a magical death-hotel with an umbrella held less menace.

"If there's no one there, we run straight to the Hotel and find them."

"What if we run into Arthur?" Charm said.

"Mark and I will have the Umbrellas open. I don't know. Maybe he can get a clean shot."

Charm bared her teeth and nodded. The Portal loomed before them. Calling to him. Vain was there. Emma, too.

He stepped through.

*

They gathered at the opposite end of the stone room, ready to go through the door. None of them looked brave or heroic. Blunt burped, probably on the edge of being physically sick. Charm looked like she might faint.

"Okay." Flute swallowed and brushed her long black hair from her face. Sunrise hovered by her shoulder. "I'll poke my head through. If there's no one there, I'll come get you."

"And if there is someone there?" Hush said.

"Wait five minutes."

"Five normal minutes or five Hotel minutes?"

Flute stared at him and Roman realized how insanely, desperately unprepared for this they were.

"This is nuts," he said. "Screw the plan. All of it. We go in together. If there are any Wyatts, we attack and we attack hard."

"You're changing my plan?" Flute looked irritated.

"The concept of a plan for what we're attempting is insane in the first place."

"He's right," Mark nodded. "This was a waste of time. I'm done waiting."

Mark dove through the door. Roman followed. Someone behind him screamed.

The immediate absence of time reminded him how badly his body enjoyed the concept of ticking seconds, the way they divided moments from then and now and here and there. At least a dozen Wyatts blinked at him in ponderous surprise as he stumbled through the doorway.

In the distance, the Hotel leered at him, grinning maniacally with its lopsided windows and seesaw gutters. Welcome home, Roman, it said. I've been keeping your seat warm. I knew you'd be back.

Roman ignored the nauseating icicles lancing through his stomach and charged directly at the closest Wyatt. The smell of whiskey made his eyes water and oddly, his mouth water, but Roman threw sloppy haymaker fists, hoping to solve the fight as quickly as possible. He had no idea whether anyone had followed him. He only knew that they were there, it was happening, and he needed to knock that Wyatt out.

His fists found their target, slamming into the side of the Wyatt's head. Roman kept punching. He didn't know how many punches it took to knock a Wyatt unconscious, but he knew if he stopped, he'd die, so he kept punching. At any moment, another Wyatt would attack him.

"All Wyatts drop dead!" Hush's voice ripped through the air, grinding against Roman's brain and nearly causing him to fall. His body wanted to obey the command, but he wasn't a Wyatt. He rolled off the Wyatt and got to his feet.

Several Wyatts were on the ground, dead. Some were only staggered, Hush's power not sufficient to stop them all. One vomited a bright red geyser of blood before collapsing. There were about six Wyatts left.

There was one Mark.

Roman knew Mark could fight—you didn't open your own security service if you didn't have some familiarity with contact—but the sheer methodical ferocity of Mark's attack took him by surprise. It also took the Wyatts by surprise.

Mark tore through them with arms and fists and elbows, knocking them down with brutal shots that sounded like someone hitting a piece of meat with a sledgehammer. Seeing him fight, Roman realized the Wyatts never stood a chance. Not really. Not against that.

The group watched open-mouthed as Mark dispatched the last of the Wyatts with a vicious shot to the temple. He spun around, looking for more enemies to fight, but between Hush's command and the surprise of the attack, there wasn't anyone left. Mark breathed heavily, arms at his sides.

"That it?"

Flute rushed over to inspect him, and Charm helped Roman off the ground. Wyatts lay in heaps around them.

"I hate this place," Charm said.

"Me too." Roman peered through the garden but couldn't see any further Wyatts. "Is everyone okay?"

"I think so. We're going to have to carry Blunt."

"Get Sunrise and Hush to do it. We need Mark unoccupied in case we run in to more Wyatts."

"Here," Charm said. "The Umbrellas."

Right. The Umbrellas. Roman had forgotten. He was so bad at this. For about a million reasons, he wished Vain were there. "Here." He handed the second one to Mark, who took it without looking at him.

"How long have we been here?"

"Don't think about it. Thinking about it makes it worse."

"I think it's been a week. How is that possible? It doesn't take a week to beat up six people."

"Don't think about it," Roman repeated, although he knew how pointless that advice was.

"She lived here? She tolerated this?"

"I wouldn't say she tolerated it, no."

Mark turned towards him and Roman had to crane his neck upward to meet his eyes. Mark tapped him on the chest.

"When this is over, I don't ever want her back here. You understand?"

"That was always the plan. But you have a hand in that too."

"She's not my problem anymore."

Before Roman could process the meaning of that sentence, Mark yelled at the group.

"Let's go."

Roman popped open his Umbrella and Mark did the same. Blunt regained consciousness, supported by Hush and Sunrise. Flute and Charm brought up the rear. His little army. The Hotel glowered at them, an object of solitary dread, starkly lit against the disturbing red sky.

"We head into the Hotel," Roman said to the group. "We find them, we get them, and we stay together. All of us. No more splitting up. Clear?"

Everyone nodded.

"Let's end this."

Chapter 33: Trick does some light cleaning.

Trick held Vain close to his body, waiting for the shaking to stop, rubbing her back and making soft noises. That scratch on her cheek. His heart was going light speed, and he wanted to kill someone. Her poor shoulders. It was all he could do to keep his muscles from clenching. He stroked her hair and told her it was okay and tried to will some of his strength into her weary frame.

After a few minutes, her tremors subsided, so he spun her around and walked her out of the abattoir they'd created in the kitchen. She didn't seem to mind Trick's arm around her waist, so he kept it there. He walked her to the dirty, tattered couch in the middle of the living room, bending over to brush off a stack of old newspapers. Unsurprisingly, a group of ravenous cannibals did not keep a clean living room and, garbage clung to every available surface. The TV had a boot through it.

Vain didn't seem to notice the mess, and hugged herself, rocking back and forth with haunted, faraway eyes. He had to get her out of there. And keep her occupied. A distraction.

"You look around for the Padlock, okay?" Giving her something to do would help her come back. Vain, he suspected, would not respond well to softer measures. "Can you do that?"

She gave him hangdog eyes from beneath her choppy bangs, but nodded and stood. He gave her a nod back and turned back to the kitchen. He knew the Padlock's exact location. It was on a chain around Smoove Dick's neck. Or more accurately, a chain around his corpse's neck.

Walking gently over the bodies and trying to keep his feet from stepping in any of the blood, he bent over Smoove Dick and pulled the Padlock off the chain with a sharp jerk. Trick wanted to yell for joy, but settled for pumping his fist. The Padlock. He had it back. Finally, after all that time. It was like being reunited with an old friend. The warm, soft buzzing from the burnished gold base. The way the word 'safe' tickled against the side of his palm. He squeezed it with both hands and breathed a huge sigh of relief.

Now that he had it back, what was he going to do about Vain?

His stomach clenched. Did he eat some bad tofu before this adventure started? Thinking about how to deal with Vain made him tremble, so he pushed those thoughts away. There were some things that needed to be taken care of before they could go. He'd have to move fast.

He shouldered the back door open and ran into the night air. On the way to the house, he'd spotted a garage off to the side; a small, single-car building. He hadn't thought anything of it at the time, but now he realized it could hold something useful. Cold, biting snow nipped at his bare arms, but he ignored the chill and sprinted towards the garage. The door was unlocked. Inside, he flipped on the light.

An assortment of equipment hung on the walls; a rusty shovel, a set of bolt cutters, a garden rake, a rifle and, there it was. A handgun. An old Colt Diamondback with a long, angry barrel and a cherry-wood grip. With a practiced flick, he checked the cylinder. Full. Okay. He tucked it into his waistband and ran back out into the night.

Next stop; the barn.

The coals in the brazier still burned, letting him see where he was going without too much trouble. He made his way back to the pig pen and pulled the gun from his pants.

"Sorry man," he said, and pulled the trigger.

Everything was taken care of. He had a gun, he had a way out, he had the Padlock, he could leave clean. He could leave right now. The heat from the Padlock warmed his thigh. Put his hand around it, put the gun to his head, boom, express trip back to the Hotel. No more Vain to worry about, she'd be trapped there forever. He'd have no way of finding her again, even if he wanted to. Vain, all alone, hurt, wounded, by herself, forever wondering if he abandoned her, thinking he was awful for leaving her.

His knees went weak, and it became hard to breathe. Probably the hay. Weird that his stomach was flopping around again, it certainly couldn't have anything to do with her. He ran back into the snow. One bullet, right through his head. Leave her behind. His breath thrummed in his ears. It was the smart play, getting her out of his hair. He'd never have to see her again. He picked up his pace, running towards the house. Vain's smile, extinguished. All he had to do was stop; stop moving and do it. The back door rose before him, the bright light from the kitchen causing him to squint. Time to do it. Leave Vain behind. He should. He could.

He stepped into the kitchen and yelled, "Vain, are you okay?"

"I'm okay," she yelled from the other room, and suddenly it was easier to breathe again, and somehow the lights in the kitchen seemed brighter. Christ, his head was hot. He stared at the gun in his hand before tucking it behind his belt. He hopped over the bodies, avoiding the blood so Vain wouldn't have to see any more of it, and jumped into the living room.

She stood by a battered credenza and was rooting through the drawers, pushing aside broken dishes.

"I can't find it." Some color had returned to her cheeks and she looked more present.

"I found it." He swallowed against a lump. He held up the Padlock. "And I came right back here without any internal debate because I would never leave you here by yourself."

She cocked an eyebrow at him. "Was that ever on the table?"

"There isn't even a table." He rushed to her side and grabbed her arm. "Are you okay?"

"Yeah man, I'm fine. Quit it." She shrugged his hand off. "I just need some time to process it. Let's get out of here."

"Okay." He pulled the gun from his waistband and held it up. Vain flinched.

"What the hell?"

"It's our way out. How else did you think we'd leave? You know how the Padlock works. We have to die."

"You're going to shoot us? At the same time? How?"

"Put our heads together, squeeze them tight. Cheek to cheek. This is a Colt Diamondback. At that range, it will explode both of our heads like water balloons."

Vain paled and swayed on her feet. "Hooray," she said weakly.

"Sit down. I won't leave you. I promise."

He pulled her down on the couch. She fiddled with her hands.

"You keep saying you won't leave me."

"I won't."

"Everyone says that to me. Roman, Mark, Charm, they all say it. But they all leave, because the amount of them I want, the amount I need back from them, it's too much. It's too much for anyone. I don't know how to split my focus, Trick. So if you get me, you get all of me. It's awful and there's something wrong with the way I am."

"I'm sorry." Stupid words. He couldn't work any moisture in to his mouth. "You're wrong though."

"What, you're going to tell me it's not awful?"

"There's nothing wrong with the way you are."

She stopped playing with her fingers and locked her huge, endless eyes onto his.

"Why are you being so nice to me?"

"We're playing team-up, remember? And teammates stay with each other, they don't leave. Even if one teammate did something that he wishes he never had to do, wishes he had come up with some other way to handle business and knows that no amount of sorry will make a difference, they still stay together."

"Are teammates sorry?"

"Yeah. They are. They know no amount of apologies will make a difference. But it's all they have."

"Do teammates do anything else for each other?"

He thought his mouth was dry before; now it was dust. "Yes. Sometimes, teammates are there for each other in a bunch of different ways."

The merest whisper of a smile appeared on her lips, and his heart started beating again.

"Take me home, Trick."

She squeezed in so their hips were touching and he wrapped his bad arm around her and pulled her close. Their cheeks were flush, their lips barely inches apart. Her warm breath blew onto his mouth. He removed his arm and put the Padlock in his ruined hand. Vain covered it with hers and squeezed.

"Too hard?"

"It's okay."

"Give me warning?" Her breath came in gasps, and he could feel her shaking.

"I will." Trick put the gun to his temple. "We'll do a countdown together. You won't feel a thing. I've done this thousands of times."

"Okay. Okay. Okay."

"Three," Trick said, and pulled the trigger.

<u>Chapter 34: Vain tells a joke.</u>

Vain screamed.

Awareness returned in gasps, her heartbeat dividing the moments, and she concentrated on each thump.

Thump.

Trick had pulled the trigger. On three, the prick.

Thump.

She was warm. The freezing cold that had become a permanent fixture in her bones had departed.

Thump.

Her shoulders didn't hurt. Her neck didn't hurt. Nothing hurt.

Thump.

The Well. Her back was against the Well. The gritty stone scratched at her back. She was leaning against it. She was back in the empty Hotel lobby.

Thump.

The now-open Padlock rested in her hand.

"Vain." Trick sat beside her. He took her face in his hands, gently, so gently, and inspected her, looking for injuries. He had all his fingers back. "Are you okay?"

"Yeah." Her mouth contained a sour, soapy taste and she spat on the ground, missing Trick by inches. She tried to brush his soft hands away, but now one stroked her hair and the other rubbed her arm. His expression was only of concern, and she pushed him away, confused. "Why are you doing this?"

"Doing what?" He kneeled in front of her, not moving his body out of her space, filling up her vision.

"Whatever you're doing."

"I—" Trick started to speak, then snapped his mouth shut. He tried a few more times, searching for the right words. "I'm going to get you out of here. For real, this time. For permanent. No more chasing you. No more hunting. You're free."

"Why?" She leaned closer to him, their faces inches apart. She had to know. "What's so special about me?"

Trick barked out a short laugh and took her hands. "You always ask the wrong questions."

"What's the right question?" She couldn't catch her breath. Her heart was loud in her chest.

"What isn't special about you?"

They stared at each other across inches that were somehow cavernous, and she wondered whether she wanted to shrink them.

"Why do I attract men that pick the weirdest fucking times to have moments?" she whispered.

This time Trick's laugh was genuine, and he shook his head and helped her to her feet. She kept a close grip on the Padlock, while she turned and looked into the Well.

"He's in there," she said.

"He is."

"Getting stronger every minute."

"Yes."

"You have absolutely no plan to stop this."

"We're working on it."

"You've had forever."

Trick grinned, a perfectly gorgeous look on a perfectly gorgeous face, and no one could blame her if her heart skipped a couple of beats. "Give me another couple days."

"What happens now? With us?"

"I thought we were a team."

"I want this over, Trick. Not for a day, not for a month. Forever. All of it. I want this to stop." She swung her arm to encompass the entirety of the Hotel.

"This isn't your problem. I'm sorry about everything we did. And I told you the truth; I'll let you go."

"I want everyone freed," she said, thinking back to what Blunt had wished for. "The pairs."

"I can't do that."

"That's the difference between you and me, Trick. You spend a lot of time worrying about shit you can't do. And we have something now that you never had before."

"What's that, exactly?"

"An Emma."

"Arthur and I—"

Before Trick could finish, the door leading to the Elevator slammed open and Emma and Arthur came out. Vain's mouth dropped open.

Arthur crossed the distance in a half-dozen steps, and Trick positioned himself in front of Vain.

"Easy, Arthur."

"Give me my Padlock." Arthur reached around Trick's shoulder. "Now. Trick, what have you been doing this whole time?"

"We had some business to take care of. Vain, it's okay. Give Arthur the Padlock."

"He'll kill me," Vain said. This seemed obvious to her. Without the Padlock, she was useless.

"No, he won't." Emma stepped forward. "We have an agreement. Right Arthur?"

"Our agreement was for me to get my Padlock back."

"After our business is concluded. Yes."

Arthur glared pure venomous murder at Emma, but Emma didn't back down. With a grunt of disgust, he turned away. Vain had no idea what was going on.

"Hey Emma," she said. "Where have you been?"

"With Arthur."

"Should we hug?"

"I'm good."

"Yeah, me too. Do you know if Charm got out?"

"I assumed you circled around and got out with her. Why

are you even here?"

"Trick and I were fighting cannibals on an alternate earth. Why are you here?"

"Arthur and I went to Toronto."

Throughout the conversation, none of which was providing Vain with any sort of understanding towards what had passed between Emma and Arthur, she sensed something else. A knot in her head. Growing. The knot she took for granted, the one that gave her strength, that made her feel special. The presence of the person she'd spent every waking moment with for eternity. Getting closer. Could it be? How was it possible? But there was no denying what she felt. Roman. Roman was back in her head.

A crash from the opposite end of the lobby caused them all to jump, and Vain spun, frantically searching. A group of people burst through the front doors of the Hotel, brandishing open umbrellas in front of them. Charm peeked from behind one. And Flute. Christ, she'd done it. And if they were here, that meant—

Roman stepped forward, and Vain gasped.

Her Roman. Alive.

All hell erupted.

Mark yelled to get down, get down, get down, while Hush yelled something that sounded like "hurricane Thursday" but that couldn't have been right. Charm screamed and pointed, and out of nowhere, Sunrise bellowed and ran straight at Arthur, knocking Trick out of the way.

Arthur pushed Sunrise aside with a wave of energy, and then Mark was there, taking a swing at Trick, who swatted his hand away. Mark threw a series of elbows and fists, punching faster than Vain could track, and somehow Trick blocked or dodged them all. Vain was about to attack, although she truthfully had no idea who to punch and debated knocking their heads together, when Emma yelled and clapped her hands.

"Enough!"

A lethargy passed through Vain, and she sagged against the Well. Emma was putting them to sleep, making them relaxed.

"Stop fighting," Emma said. "Everyone stop, or I'll make you stop."

"You're both okay," Roman said softly.

He lowered the Umbrella, a look of wonder on his face, his eyes ping-ponging back and forth between her and Emma. Vain swallowed through the lump in her throat; through the terrible, burning heat that rose to consume her head. If her heart was loud before, it was nuclear now. Roman's face, his perfect face, broke into a smile and he took a step forward, and without any conscious thought, so did Vain. It worked. Her Roman was back. Her Roman. Her Roman. She reached out towards him.

"Emma," he gasped.

He went to Emma first.

He went to Emma first without a glace sideways, and Vain's heart—her brittle, weary heart that had seen her through so much, that had so many exhausting fucking miles on it—shattered. It didn't break with fanfare or complaint, but it broke nonetheless, and the pieces fell into her stomach.

He went to Emma first, and Vain collapsed second.

They hugged in the middle of the room. Her hug. The hug she deserved, the hug she wanted. Emma took it from her and Vain watched and wondered how it was possible to hurt that much without dying.

Then the hug was over, and Roman finally had eyes for her. He caught her with them, and a lock of his silly brown hair flipped in front of his face. He grabbed her in a rough embrace and said, "Vain. I'm so glad you're okay. I'm so glad. I was so worried about you."

Vain did not hug him back. Too many emotions assaulted her at once, and she couldn't think. But that wasn't the time to deal with any of it. She had to lock it all down and keep going. So, she squirmed out of his embrace and did the hardest thing she'd ever done.

She smiled.

"I'm glad you're okay too, Roman." Her voice didn't even tremble. She needed a joke. "You sure can't take a bullet to the head." A bad one. The moment she'd wanted, given to Emma. But ha-ha, Vain was always good for a laugh, good old Vain. Good old reliable Vain, always joking. Turning that frown upside down and keeping her upper lip stiff and doing all the mouth things that meant 'I will bury my pain'.

Why wasn't she dead? How can she live without a heart?

"What are you all doing here? I remember some of you." Arthur stood with Trick behind Emma. His eyes locked on one person in particular.

"Hello, Charm."

Charm paled but stood her ground. "Hello, Arthur."

A group of Wyatts burst into the room, followed by some Janes. They stopped to stare at everyone.

"We all good here, boss? We heard fighting." A Wyatt asked.

"Yes," Emma said. "No one is fighting. Arthur, call off your Wyatts."

"I don't answer to you."

"Please."

The amount of time Arthur waited seemed specifically designed to demonstrate his feelings about Emma asking him to do something, but he gave her a curt nod.

"Stand down, Wyatts. Trick will explain."

"We're all buddies now?" Hush said. "Great. Then we're leaving."

"I'm not leaving," Vain said.

"Me neither," Emma said.

Hush sighed theatrically, a noise also designed to demonstrate his feelings towards everything, and Vain reflected that men were somewhat passive aggressive in their responses.

Emma gestured to the tables. "Everyone, take a seat, please. There's a lot to talk about."

"You want us to sit down with Trick and Arthur and a bunch of Wyatts?" Roman frowned. "We came in here to rescue you. How long have you been in here for? It's been about half a day outside. Are you okay?" He cut himself off, and said to Vain, "I want you to tell all your friends about me."

"I'm Batman," Vain said. "It's fine, Roman. We haven't been turned by Arthur."

"Wait," Trick said. "Was that your safe phrase?"

"Yeah," she nodded. "We worked it out when we were outside. If I was ever coerced, I was supposed to say I'm Superman, which would tip Roman off, because that's not the line from the movie."

"Do you get that those phrases are supposed to be subtle? Actually, never mind, I know the answer. You're about sixty percent of way there every time. It's fascinating."

"We're all okay, Roman," Emma said. She stroked his cheek and Vain's stomach plummeted. "Now sit. All of you. There are things you need to hear about what happens next. There's a way to stop all of this. Forever."

With mutters and curses, the group did what she asked, each eying the other with suspicion. The Hotel's current configuration included long, metal tables and dim, hostile lighting. Vain suspected the screwy nature of the place was dulling everyone's ability to think clearly, because even Hush didn't complain.

As Emma gathered everyone around the table, Vain watched Roman pull up a seat beside her and take her hand.

She concentrated on listening and not crying.

<u>Chapter 35: Trick knows eavesdropping is rude.</u>

Trick yawned as Emma explained everything to the group. He knew the story too well to be invested in the telling. He couldn't keep his eyes from Vain, who sat at the table playing with her hands, blinking and taking deep breaths. She was devastated. How could people miss it? Roman killed her, sure as if he'd stabbed her.

The Janes ran back and forth, getting drinks and appetizers, while the Wyatts lounged at the periphery, swapping jokes and laughing. Emma had been going on for ages. Trick noticed that once Emma got going, she really got going. Maybe it was a school thing, but she certainly did enjoy the sound of her own voice. The only thing that interrupted her was the constant stream of questions from her idiot friends. What did she mean, there was a monster? What did she mean, the destruction of everything? Baa baa. Catch up, people.

She got to the part of her plan for creating a Device to trap Eventide forever, the only interesting component in the whole tale. Not a bad idea, Trick had to admit, and he was impressed with Arthur for coming up with it. Her friends didn't see it that way. Hush called her a twice-dappled, redheaded nut job, which made Trick chuckle a bit, although Emma didn't appear to appreciate the zinger.

"Can you create something like that?" Roman asked.

"I think I can. I made this." She held out the Thimble she'd created on Arthur's practice world.

"How is this any different from burying Eventide under energy?" Charm asked. "All a Device does is refocus concentrated energy into a singular task."

"Ha," Arthur snorted. "Let's all listen to the Conduit. Please, explain to us all how this works. What else should we do, Charm?" He rested his head on his hands in an exaggerated pose of attention.

Charm blushed, and Vain shot to her feet.

"How about I take my foot and shove—"

"Because there's nothing to leech," Trick interrupted before Vain could get herself into trouble. "We're pumping raw energy into the Well, that's why he's able to absorb it. He can't feed off a Device. Eventually, he'll grow weaker and die. Or at least get to the point where he's not a threat."

"How big a Device are we talking?" Roman asked.

"Big," Trick said. "Portal big, maybe. It would have to be, to keep him down there."

Roman shook his head. "I don't like this. It's too dangerous for Emma."

"I can do this, Roman." Emma rested her hand on his, and Trick watched as Vain studiously avoided looking at them.

"But you lose yourself," Roman said. "Something this big, it would be insane to come back from."

"I'll have you here to bring me back."

Trick didn't visibly gag, and he was sort of proud of that. He caught Vain's wet eyes, made a face at her, and rolled his eyes at Emma. Vain gave him a weak smile before wiping her cheeks. It was something.

"Besides," Emma continued. "I'm stronger now, I think. After the Portal and creating the Thimble, the amount I can handle has increased. Look, I'll show you. Who has the Padlock now?"

"I do," Vain said.

She took the open Padlock out and placed it on the table, giving Arthur the side-eye as she did. Emma placed her hand over the Device and closed her eyes.

The air took on weight and the table groaned. The hair on

the back of Trick's neck stood up, and his ears popped. Normally it took Arthur ages to recharge the Padlock, something he could only do in small bursts before succumbing to exhaustion, but Emma was doing it all at once. The pressure built, becoming claustrophobic in its weight, as the Device was creating its own gravity. Even the air seemed thinner.

"Emma?" Roman reached out with a tentative hand.

With a pop, the pressure vanished. Emma opened her eyes and her hand. The Padlock was locked and glowing again, returned to pristine condition.

Everyone gasped, seemingly surprised by Emma's growing power, reinforcing Trick's belief that Vain's friends were all complete morons, and she could do better. He would have to talk to her about that.

"I'll take that." Arthur reached out to snatch the Device, but Emma pulled her hand away.

"When this is over," she said. "Consider it insurance."

Arthur looked mad enough to chew rocks but didn't argue. Trick knew his partner well enough to know that Emma was probably in more danger now than she'd been five minutes before. Arthur was going to kill her the second her usefulness came to an end. He didn't tolerate disobedience. Trick wondered how he would keep Vain safe.

"Are you okay?" Roman asked.

"Yeah." Emma's face had lost some color, but she seemed otherwise unaffected by her display. "I told you. I can do this."

"What were you thinking of using to cover the Well?" Hush asked.

"Good question," Emma said. "Maybe a blanket? That covers things."

"A manhole cover?" Blunt asked.

"Too small, I think," Emma said.

"A pool cover?" Flute said. "It would be big enough."

Emma nodded. "That could work. That's a great idea."

Flute preened under the attention.

While they continued to hash out finer details, Vain excused herself and wandered down a hallway that led to the living quarters. Without a word, Mark followed. No one noticed when

Trick got up and followed behind Mark.

The hallway twisted around in a way that would be problematic if this were an actual Hotel with paying customers. There was no way guests would appreciate a hallway that curved this much, and those spots where the space narrowed were disorienting. He followed Mark and Vain at a distance until Vain came to a stop in front of a long wooden bench with no back or sides that sat in the middle of the open hallway. She plopped herself down and Mark sat beside her. Trick parked himself around the corner to listen.

They didn't say anything, and Trick wasn't sure who would break the silence first. Finally, Vain spoke.

"I'm sorry I didn't visit you. I should have. My head wasn't working right. I'm sorry."

"Okay."

"I'm glad you're okay. I used your training when I fought cannibals. I did a pretty good SARCAC and I crouched across snow."

"Okay."

"Is that all you're going to say to me? I said I was sorry."

"I'm not sure I can forgive you."

"Why? Roman was hurt."

"So was I."

"I can't be in two places at once. What was I supposed to do? Leave him?"

Mark sighed and Trick could imagine him pinching the bridge of his nose. "Of all the damage Roman did, never saying no to you was probably the worst."

"What does that mean?"

"Don't worry about it."

"I don't know why you're bringing Roman up. He doesn't even like me anymore."

A tremor crept into Vain's voice. Trick doubted Mark noticed.

"Why on Earth would you say that?"

"He hugged Emma first."

"Jeeeee-sus Christ. Do you hear yourself?"

"Can you not hear me? Is that a Hotel thing? I know time

is funny, but do sound waves not work now?" She raised her voice. "Is this better?"

"I want to ask you something," Mark said.

"Okay."

"Do you like me?"

"Yuh."

"Are we in a relationship?"

"We kissed, so I guess so? You're back on the label thing?" Vain didn't sound delighted. She sounded miserable.

"If Roman and I were standing side by side and both of us were attacked, who would you save?"

"That's such a dumb and unfair question. It's like you're trying to lay a trap for me or like you're trying to prove something. I acted badly and I apologized. Roman and I have been each other's entire world for as long as I can remember. I'm trying to fit you into that, but you're not helping. Say what you mean, Mark."

"Okay, I will. We're done, Vain. I'll stick around to see this through, because I promised I would, but once this is over, you and I are finished. I don't want to see you anymore."

"You're leaving me, too?" Vain was in agony, and Trick's heart snapped. "Why? I told you I'm sorry. I don't know what else to do. Is it because I didn't date properly? I tried my hardest."

"It doesn't matter. There is no us."

"What about hanging out and learning to fight and stuff? I still want to do that. I like you, Mark. I tried to like you the way you like me. I don't think it worked, but that doesn't have to mean the end of all of it."

"It sort of does, Vain. There's an inequality here that makes this a problem. If you don't have those feelings for me, that's fine. It sounds like you never had them. But it doesn't change how I feel about you and the amount you're willing to offer isn't enough."

"But that doesn't make any sense. If you want more of me, how is none of me better than some of me?"

"Tell you what. When you figure out why only some of Roman is such a problem, give me a call."

"Why is everyone leaving me?" Vain asked in a small voice. Mark sighed and Trick heard the sound of him getting up from the bench.

"I think you're confused about who left who, Vain. Take care of yourself."

Before Trick had time to hide, Mark came around the corner and glared at him from his insanely tall height.

"Hello," Trick said. "I was eavesdropping."

Trick did not care enough about Mark to expend energy in a lie. He wanted to get to Vain. Mark shouldered past, knocking Trick back up against the wall. Trick rubbed his arm and rushed around the corner.

Vain rocked herself, unblinking, tears running down her cheeks. When she saw him, she wiped her face and sat up straighter.

"I think the Janes are cooking French onion soup," she said.

Trick sat close enough that their shoulders were touching. She didn't move away. He didn't say anything. After a moment, she rested her head on his shoulder and he put his arm around her. They sat in silence like that for a few minutes.

"Do you care about anyone, Trick?" she said.

"Until recently, no. Not really. It's too hard. Emotions are tricky."

"They are." She sniffled loudly. "I don't think Roman loves me anymore."

The easiest thing in the world would be to agree. Tell her Roman doesn't love her, then swoop in. He could break them apart in a second. She'd be his.

"He still loves you, Vain. But he loves Emma, too. I don't think he meant to hurt you. He was confused and scared. I think he loves Emma differently, and he doesn't know how to deal with that."

"He hurt me. A lot."

"I know."

"How does he love Emma differently?"

"Their relationship has additional elements."

"Oh. I see. Sex is very confusing."

"It is," Trick agreed. "It can complicate a lot of feelings."

"Mark broke up with me. I told him the truth, and he left

me. How are you supposed to have a relationship without truth?"

"I don't know."

"My heart hurts, Trick."

"I know it does. I'm here to listen."

"Until you get bored and leave."

"I won't leave."

"Promise?"

"Promise."

She sniffled and rubbed her nose on his sleeve before snuggling in closer. After some maneuvering, she was in his lap with both his hands around her waist.

"I'm glad your fingers are back."

"Me too. Are all your hurts gone?"

"Yuh."

"Are you okay?"

"Not really, no. I'm losing my best friend, my sort-of boyfriend dumped me, and I'm cuddling with my arch-nemesis. I don't think I'm okay at all. Not going to lie Trick, this is not how I saw this day turning out."

"Sometimes you can't help what your heart does."

"My heart didn't help me with Mark. I tried to be attracted to him. I tried so hard. I thought if I could make myself, I could be normal."

A thought occurred to Trick. "Vain, do you find people attractive? At all? Is that something you feel?"

She lifted her head up and put her face close to his. "I find one person very attractive, yes." Her cheeks were beet red.

Trick's knees melted. He brushed her hair back and let his breath mingle with hers.

"There's one person I find very attractive, too."

"What do normal people do in this situation?"

"Many of them would probably try kissing."

"I'm not weird," she whispered. Their lips were inches apart. "I know how to kiss."

"Show me," Trick said.

She did.

<u>Chapter 36: Roman totally nails it.</u>

Roman noticed Vain leave the table and moved to follow, but Mark beat him to it. And Trick, strangely. Giving her some space with Mark seemed like the right thing to do, but at some point, he'd have to figure out what she'd been through. He didn't like Trick getting that close.

Speaking of things he didn't like to be close to, he scootched his chair a little further away from Arthur. Of all the scenarios he'd envisioned, having a casual chat with the person who enslaved him wasn't one that occurred to him. Plus, he was surrounded by Wyatts. And Janes. The entire thing was nuts.

"I can run and get a pool cover," Hush said. "Only problem is, I don't know how long I'll be outside compared to in here. If it takes me a couple hours, how long is that?"

Arthur grunted. "That's not how time works here. There is no time. It's like asking how tall Saturday is."

"I don't understand."

"I know. Get your pool cover." Arthur waved Hush away and stood up. "Janes, make our guests comfortable. We have work to do."

"Arthur?" Charm played with her hands, her voice small. "Can we visit with the other pairs? Please?"

Arthur hesitated a moment and then snapped at a Jane.

"Fine. Jane, let the pairs out so the puppies can play. Call me when the small angry one gets back with the pool cover."

Arthur spun away from the table, leaving a somewhat dazed and bewildered group. With plans made and animosity ignored, the Hotel burst to life. Dozens of Janes emerged from doors that Roman didn't remember seeing. Pairs wandered out of their rooms with bemused glances, some pausing to talk, others going to get dinner or walk the paths of the garden. And in the middle of all of it, the Wyatts bounced around, shouldering their way past people, barking orders at anyone that didn't move fast enough and making a general pain of themselves.

Charm and Blunt got up from the table, happy to reunite with old friends. A few nodded warily at Roman, but none of them came over to talk.

"Do you have anyone you want to visit?" Emma said.

"Not really. The pairs never talked to us much. Vain kind of kept them away."

"I understand. Can you follow me to that secluded corner, please?"

"Why?"

"I'm barely keeping it together, Roman. I thought you were dead. I love you beyond description and I would like some time to demonstrate to you, in extensive detail, the depth of my affection." She pushed herself away from the table and hauled him to his feet. "Secluded corner. Now."

Emma was thorough and demonstrative, and for several minutes, they didn't talk at all. It left Roman with a full heart, weak knees, and a dizzy head.

"I missed you so much." She rested against his chest. "I thought I'd lost you forever."

"I'm sorry. I acted dumb."

"When this is over, we need to talk about your relationship with Vain. Not now. But it's something we need to deal with."

"I know. We can talk now."

"It's okay. You saying you understand is enough. It doesn't need to be anything more than that right now." She hugged him tighter.

"I don't like any of this plan, Emma."

"I know you don't, but I can do this. And once it's done, we're free forever. From all of it. The Hotel, the Wyatts, the insane near-death adventures; we can live our lives. Really live."

"You can't trust Arthur."

"I don't. But I felt that thing down there. Arthur sucks, but he's practical. As long as I can show him he's getting the better deal by working with us, he'll leave us alone."

"And then what? We leave him to gallop around the multiverse?"

"I don't care what he does when this is over. I only care about us."

Vain emerged at the other side of the room, and Roman glanced over. Emma sighed and gave him a small push.

"Go say hi to your friend. She'll be happy to see you. I'm going to get myself ready." She pressed the Thimble into his hands. "Take this, okay? Promise me you'll wear it. I can't deal with losing you again."

"You said this makes you invulnerable?"

"It should, yeah. It's not like we had time to test it. Put it on."

Roman slipped the Thimble on his pinky finger. A slight weight settled on his body, and the air shimmered.

"What does it feel like?" Emma asked.

Roman inspected himself. "Like a weight. Not that heavy, but almost a thickness."

"Don't take it off. Promise?"

"I promise."

"Stay safe." She kissed him on the cheek.

Vain was looking at him with sad and heavy eyes, and as he approached, he was surprised to find his heart in his throat. She gave him a fake smile.

"Hi."

"Hi." She folded her arms around herself, like she did when she was dealing with too much emotion. She couldn't look at him.

"I'm glad we get some time to talk."

"I'm sure you can barely tolerate it." Her voice was chilly. "Shouldn't you be holding hands with Emma or whatever?"

"I wanted to see you."

"You're only doing this because you have to, Roman."

To hell with subtly. He grabbed her and pulled her close. She kept her arms folded around her own body and didn't hug him back.

"Hey," he said. "I missed you. I'm sorry I scared you. I know what you did for me. You did all of this. Thank you. You saved my life."

"I did." She pushed herself away from him and wiped her cheeks, flushed with embarrassment.

"Do you find it weird that there's so much pollen in the Hotel air?" he asked. "My allergies are going nuts."

Vain gave a brief laugh and sniffled. "Mine too."

"Now is not a great time, but when this is over, you and I are going to have a long talk. Is that okay?"

"Why? Are you going to leave me too?" The agony in her voice almost broke his heart.

"Never. Why would you say that?"

"Because you love Emma now. And Mark dumped me."

"Mark did what? That piece of shit." Roman rubbed his cheeks. "Don't worry about Emma, okay?"

"How can I not?"

"Vain, whatever happens, we're still us."

"We don't feel like us. Not anymore."

He took a deep breath. "I'm going to tell you something that I should have told you ages ago. I've been struggling with this, too. It's not the same now, is it? When we were running, everything was so simple. You. Me. Us. But now there's more people to deal with and it's weird, right? Especially when you consider the different types of love. I'm sure at some point I had parents that I loved. That's family love, you know? Then I have friends like Charm and Blunt, and hell, I guess even Hush, too. Friend love. And yeah, I love Emma, as my partner. Relationship love. They're all different, but they're all the same. Sometimes they overlap, sometimes they don't, but one isn't better than the other, one doesn't mean more than the other. People are going to come in and out of my life."

She bit her lip and sniffled again. "Which am I?"

"You're not any of those."

"I knew it."

"You're Vain love."

Her huge eyes widened. And even though they were surrounded by the bustle of the Hotel, they were the only people in each other's world in that moment.

He continued, "You are the only person who gets to be Vain love. Eventually, I might have other friends, and maybe Emma and I don't work out, and I might have other relationships. I will only have one Vain. You're a category to yourself and no one else ever gets to be that. There is no overlap. I love you like I love Vain. Forever. And whatever happens with Emma, you and I will figure it out together. Like we always do, like we should have done from the start. And whatever we come up with, it will be something we both agree on. Because you're my Vain. My only Vain. And I'll never let you go."

Tears poured down Vain's cheeks, and she turned away with shaking shoulders. He gave her a few moments to collect herself, and when she turned back, her eyes were bright and clear.

"I Roman love you too, Roman. Can we hug again? I think my elbows were locked last time or something, the Hotel maybe gave me lupus."

"As many as you want, for as long as you want."

This hug felt way better, and she squeezed him hard enough to make his ribs ache. He didn't mind, and he didn't tell her to stop. When she pushed away, her face was dry.

"You're so silly, Roman, getting all mushy like that. Have you been stressed about us this whole time? Of course we're okay. You shouldn't have worried."

He smiled. "I know."

She bounced on her feet. "Roman, I can't wait to tell you all what happened. Do you know I fought cannibals? That part was awful, but I went to a different world. That was kind of neat. There was snow and like they had electricity but no pants. Oh, and we maybe collapsed a building opening the Portal. Our adventures certainly do include a lot of destruction of infrastructure. Wait, are we criminals? Also, Trick taught me how to pick a lock."

Vain was fully animated now, back to gesturing at him

while she talked, and although he'd been smiling through the whole thing, he stopped her at the last comment.

"What is going on with you and Trick, anyway? I saw him follow you."

"Okay. You are not going to like this part of the story, but hear me out. Trick and I totally kissed."

"What?" Roman's mouth dropped open, and he goggled at her. "What the hell did you do that for?"

"Don't worry Roman, he's a good kisser."

"One hundred percent not what I was worried about."

"I'll explain when all this is over, but we're maybe dating now. I'm not sure. He gets all my jokes."

Roman still couldn't close his mouth. "This is an insane amount of information to take in."

"I know, right? No one gets my jokes even though they're awesome."

"Again. Not the part that I'm struggling with."

"Hey, why did you come talk to me, anyway? Emma's preparing to do big, magic, Emma things. Shouldn't you be helping her?" Vain gave him a small push. "Go be a good boyfriend, you ninny. She needs you. I'm basically an expert on dating and you were right to come to me for advice. My advice is this: stay with Emma until this is over and then we'll talk and go out, but not for coffee. I don't think I get coffee shops."

Still reeling from the Trick information, Roman could only shake his head in wonderment.

"Are you okay, Vain? Honestly? The Trick thing has me a bit shook."

"I'm okay. I promise we'll go through it all when Emma fixes everything. Once I explain it, you'll see it's not that bad."

"But the things they did to you."

Vain reached out and put her hand on his cheek, a show of intimacy that was well beyond anything she'd ever demonstrated. "Trust me on this one. Okay?"

A commotion by the front doors grabbed his attention.

"Sorry I'm late." Hush was there, struggling with a rolled up, light-blue pool cover. "That took longer than I expected."

Vain and Roman made their way to the front.

"How long did this take you to get?"

"About half a day. Has it been centuries here?"

"Or two minutes," Vain said. She turned and waved to a couple of Janes. "Can you help us drag this?"

They hauled the pool cover over and unrolled it in front of the Well. Roman's head vibrated with all the new information. Trick and Vain. Together. That was harder to accept than working with Arthur and he couldn't help but feel partially responsible. If he had paid more attention to Vain, maybe been less up his own ass with Emma, none of this would have happened. But believing that would require him to believe Vain had no agency, that somehow, her behavior reflected his actions. And he couldn't quite get himself to that point. Vain made weird decisions, sure, but she was always authentic to herself.

For sure though, he would not be best man at the wedding, if it came to that. The image of a reception filled with Wyatts flashed through his mind. At the same time, Trick shot Roman with gun fingers and stood beside Vain. Roman's stomach clenched. Vain and Trick.

He was almost relieved when Emma said she was going to get started.

Trick and Vain. Too weird.

Chapter 37: Vain can't be blamed for missing that throw.

Vain had no idea if this would work, but the moment felt like the culmination of everything she'd fought for. They'd plug up the stupid, demon infested Well, and then be done with that dumb place forever. Except Trick. She didn't want to be done with Trick.

The talk with Roman had lifted a couple tons of weight off her chest. Why had she ever thought he'd leave her? He was Roman. She was Vain. They were practically a tautology.

Ha. Not even Emma could come up with something that clever. She leaned over and whispered it to Trick so he could be impressed. He gave her that sideways smile that made her stomach go all stupid.

"Feeling better, then? You two had a talk?"

"Yep."

"That's good. It's bad to let stuff like that fester."

"Did you like my tautology line?"

"It's really slick. I bet not even Emma could come up with something like that."

"Right?"

Emma coughed, and Vain realized everyone was staring at them.

"Are you two idiots finished?" Arthur asked.

Emma rubbed her hands together. "I'm ready to get started."

Everyone was focused on Emma and her preparations with the pool cover, so no one was paying attention to Arthur. No one except Vain. She'd spent too many countless eternities in that place to ever relax with him around. Even Trick wasn't paying any attention. So no one except her noticed when Arthur leaned over and whispered something to a Wyatt. The Wyatt's face hardly changed, but he raised his eyebrow and nodded. A chill ran down Vain's spine.

To someone unfamiliar with Wyatts, that raised eyebrow meant nothing. To someone who had been on the receiving end of a couple dozen Wyatt beatings, that raised eyebrow meant everything. The Wyatt walked over to another one and whispered. Another raised eyebrow. Another nod. Both of them went to go talk to two more. And then two more.

The room was suddenly very crowded with Wyatts, most of whom had quite strategically placed themselves in front of doors. And hallways. And exits. Arthur had taken a step away from Emma and was looking like the cat that ate the canary.

"Trick," she murmured.

"What."

"The Wyatts."

Trick looked around the room, and his face darkened. He was a smart guy.

"Okay."

"Arthur's going to betray us, the second this is over."

He licked his lips. "Yes."

"Are you on my side, or his?"

For once, Trick seemed at a loss for words. "I'm on the side that doesn't want you to get hurt."

"That doesn't answer the question I asked."

Before Trick could explain further, Emma closed her eyes and started to pull power.

It washed over Vain, smothering her, making further conversation impossible. Emma's hands hovered above the pool cover, and even though nothing had changed, a rushing noise filled Vain's ears. A weight settled on her shoulders. She opened her mouth but couldn't make words come out.

Vain stepped away from Trick and moved closer to Roman, trying to figure out some way to warn him. The keening noise and the pressure dropped her to one knee. She'd never experienced anything like that before. It wasn't like that when she recharged the Portal or the Padlock. And still, Emma directed that horrible pressure at the pool cover.

The Hotel itself shuddered and trembled. Flakes of stone fell from the lip of the Well. Two lights popped far above them. On the second floor, pairs screamed. Whatever Emma was doing, it was causing the Hotel to collapse. It was too much. It was the building in Minneapolis all over again.

"Stop!" Arthur yelled. "You're pulling from the Well!"

But Emma didn't stop. Her entire body trembled and her lips pulled back from her teeth. Only the whites of her eyes showed.

"Roman. Bring her back! This is crazy!" Vain had to scream to be heard, even though there was no noise. Every single word seemed to take a minute. Roman nodded in slow motion, and Charm also moved closer to help. High above them the chandelier exploded in a flash of light and breaking glass.

Emma screamed.

The pool cover started to glow; a sickly greenish hue that reminded Vain of algae, and cracks appeared on the surface. Crackles of blue electricity bounced and danced on the cover, not settling into the object as Vain would have suspected. A bolt lanced out and struck the side of the Hotel, and Blunt yelped in surprise. Arthur looked furious, although Vain was learning that might have been his resting face.

At the other side of the lobby, the door to the Elevator slammed open, causing Vain to jump. It filled the wall it had materialized into, somehow malevolently demanding they stop their assault on the Hotel, even though it was only gold gating and a rectangular box. Whatever Emma was doing had pulled it from its lair, and it wasn't happy.

"Enough!" Arthur yelled over the cacophony. "Stop her, or I'm ending this!"

Roman and Charm had placed themselves on either side of

Emma, stroking her cheek, whispering into her ears, rubbing her shoulders, everything they could think of to bring her back, to prevent her from her from bringing the whole place down around them. Vain was quite certain she would not be welcome in those efforts, but it drove her nuts to only watch. Surely there was something she could do.

The Wyatts had them surrounded, and Vain searched frantically for anything she could use; any exit, any plan. The moment they got Emma under control, the Wyatts were going to pounce on them. Why had she trusted Arthur? Why had she trusted Trick? It was the same. It would never stop. No matter what she did, it would never—

It stopped.

It was like the silence after a brutal thunderstorm. Emma collapsed to her knees and cried against Roman's shoulder.

"It needed too much," she sobbed. "Too much. I had no idea. I had no idea how hard it would be. It almost killed me."

Roman stroked her hair, and everyone looked on, dumfounded, not sure what to do next. The pool cover had returned to its original color. Whatever Emma had tried to birth, it was back to being an ordinary piece of plastic at the foot of the Well.

"Well, that was a complete waste of time," Arthur said. "I knew it wouldn't work." He clapped. "Wyatts. Take them."

Everything happened at once.

The Wyatt's rushed the group, but Hush was faster.

"Wyatts die!" he yelled.

At least half the Wyatts dropped to the ground, puppets with their strings cut. Several others staggered, wobbling on their feet like bowling pins that refused to fall. The distraction gave Mark all the opening he needed and he set to his favorite activity, namely punching Wyatts. Half-dead or not, there were still a lot of them and they were still dangerous.

"Emma!" Vain yelled. "Throw me the Padlock!"

If she got the Padlock, maybe she could attack Arthur somehow. At least she'd have a chance. Trick hadn't moved to stop her, but he didn't move to help, either.

Emma looked up, dazed, but did what Vain asked and

lobbed the Padlock at her.

"No!" Arthur yelled.

He jumped between Vain and Emma with his hands outstretched. His fingertips brushed the Padlock, and he jarred it off course, sending it tumbling through the air, where it bounced on the lip of the Well.

One bounce. Two bounces.

Vain felt sick.

The Padlock fell into the Well with a sickening clink.

"No!" Arthur screamed again, loudly enough that the remaining Wyatts stopped their attack to see what had happened. No one moved. Vain could hear her own heartbeat.

"Does Eventide know what the Padlock does?" Vain whispered.

No one answered.

The ground rumbled beneath her feet.

"Arthur," she said again. "Does Eventide know what the Padlock does?"

With shaking hands, Arthur took off his glasses and polished them on his shirt. He didn't look at any of them. The ground rumbled again, and he put them back on.

"I believe he does."

Vain looked around at her friends.

"Get everyone out of the Hotel right now."

Chapter 38: Emma did not see that coming.

Emma could hardly summon the energy to raise her head. Roman sat with his arms around her shoulders. Vain waved her hands in the air.

"Everyone, get out of here!"

She'd failed. Profoundly and deeply. How had she been so arrogant to think she could do it? And now, the Padlock was in the Well, she was exhausted, and she'd handed a one-way-ticket out of anywhere to a creature that had spent the past eternity pissed off.

Roman hauled her to her feet and supported her around her waist. For a moment, she let herself be comforted by his touch and leaned against his shoulder.

"Oh, Roman," she whispered.

"I know." He kissed her on the head.

During those moments when she'd tried to transform the pool cover, she'd almost completely lost herself, her imagination filling with visions of head crushing. She'd flinched away from the power, too afraid that drawing more would lead her down the path of no return. Even with both Roman and Charm to keep her grounded, it had been a close thing.

"You idiot!" Arthur yelled at her. "You've ruined everything."

Emma could only stare at him, beaten and exhausted. It

seemed like she should retort, but she couldn't make herself speak. And besides, wasn't he right? Hadn't she ruined everything?

"Get the pairs out of the Hotel," Vain said. "All of them."

"Enough of this," Arthur said. "Wyatts, take them."

"Wyatts, stop." Trick stepped forward. Arthur glared at him, his jaw dropping in surprise. The few remaining Wyatts looked at each other, seemingly not sure whether to attack or to stand down.

Arthur spoke in a deadly quiet voice. So deadly. "Are we doing this, Trick?"

"We can fight when this is over." Trick ran his hand through his hair. Emma noticed he'd placed himself between Arthur and Vain.

The Hotel lurched and let out a wailing noise like it was crying out in pain. Vain jumped forward and wagged her finger in Arthur's face. She had to scream to make herself heard over the sound of the collapsing Hotel. "Put your Wyatts to work. They need to help get everyone to safety. If we stay, there won't be anything left."

Arthur slapped her hand away, his face red and flushed. He'd lost his glasses in the commotion.

"We're going to need the pairs to help, boss. If Eventide is coming out, we'll need everyone."

"He might not be coming out," Arthur said. "The Hotel might be collapsing for completely unrelated reasons that coincidentally line up with the moment the immortality Padlock that transports people to the outside of the Well fell into the hell demon's hands and, gaaaaah fine." Arthur raised his voice and started issuing commands. "Wyatts, get everyone outside. Janes, you help. Deactivate the Handcuffs when you're getting the pairs."

"I can help, too," Flute said. "If anyone's hurt, they'll need me."

"It's too dangerous," Roman said. "Just get yourselves outside."

Flute shook her head. "I'm not leaving anyone behind. Not again. We're getting out together."

Sunrise stepped up beside Flute and said, "We'll be okay."

Roman gave them a considering look before nodding. Flute gestured at Sunrise and they ran up the trembling stairs, taking them two at a time.

Another huge rumble made its way up through the floor, and a chunk of ceiling hit the ground with a booming crash. The Hotel sagged inwards. People screamed in the distance, but Emma could hardly make herself care.

"I need help with Blunt." Hush struggled to get his unconscious brother upright. "Please." He was almost in tears.

A massive detonation sent all of them to the ground, and the air was knocked from Emma's lungs. A Wyatt hoisted Blunt on his shoulders while Roman dragged Emma towards the doors. She was almost dizzy with exhaustion, but each step she took helped her to regain her strength. To speed the process along, she soaked up the ambient energy. By the time they hit the front doors, she was able to stand unassisted and stepped away from Roman.

Pairs and Janes and Wyatts pushed outside. It was impossible to tell how much time had passed. Somehow, in the commotion, she'd lost track of half of her friends. Roman was with her, obviously, but she couldn't locate Mark or Charm or Vain. Hush managed to make it out with Blunt.

The Hotel convulsed in its death throes. Huge chunks of the building plummeted towards the ground and the windows shattered. What seemed like minutes passed as Emma looked at the destruction of the Hotel in slack-jawed amazement. How long had Flute been in there for? It was impossible to tell. Pairs poured from the doors, bumping into each other and screaming, marshaled by angry-looking Wyatts and worried Janes.

"Create a barrier around the Hotel!" Vain appeared at her side, flushed and out of breath. "Hey, you stupid, cow-eyed pairs! Listen to me, Vain, your leader! If you can make a barrier, make a barrier. It's all coming down."

Unsurprisingly, Vain's speech did not motivate anyone to action. A bunch of pairs ran off towards the garden, while more stumbled their way out of the Hotel. Emma had no idea how many there were, but close to a hundred people had gathered. Vain had made a good point. If the Hotel was going to explode, they should put up a shield around it. She began to shape an energy barrier, but there was no way she could cover the entire structure by herself. Maybe with enough time, she could—

The Hotel exploded.

The detonation blew it apart, debris and rubble hurtling through the air. Everyone was sent flying, screams of terror mixing with the booming sounds of the explosion. Emma and Roman crouched behind her hastily assembled barrier, hugging each other. Roman's mouth was moving, but she couldn't make out the words. Chunks of the Hotel fell all around, one huge piece missing her by a mere foot.

As debris rained from the sky, the ground shook and trembled, this rumble so severe she thought the rock that held them might split in half. They were sitting on a floating island hurtling through the nether outside of time, how much structural integrity did it even have? Emma coughed and rubbed her eyes, while Roman fanned the air in front of his face. What was that? Was something moving? She squinted into the dust cloud.

"There's so much energy," Roman said. "I've never felt anything like it."

"Roman!" Vain yelled and ran towards them, with Trick by her side and Mark following close behind. They were all covered in dust and grime. Smoke filled the air, making it hard to see. "Are you okay?"

"Yeah. Where's everyone else?"

"I'm here." Charm made her way over, a nasty cut on her forehead. Arthur followed, his face red with outrage. Charm said, "Has anyone seen Hush or Blunt?"

Mark pointed. "I think they were by the garden."

"You've killed us all." Arthur ran his hand through his hair.

Emma shook her head in disbelief. "This was all your idea. Everything."

"My idea was for you to not screw this up."

"What the hell is that?" Vain pointed through the dust.

Wavering at first, but growing more distinct, a shape floated its way through the rubble.

Eventide emerged.

This was Emma's first look at pure, hot evil, and she did not care for it. It took most of her control to stop herself from falling to her knees in terror. The too-big eyes. The broken limbs. Eventide was a creature of madness. Until that moment, the mental image she had held of that thing was David Blaine, the weird street magician. 'Too much eyeshadow' scary, not 'doubt reality' scary.

It didn't walk, not exactly. Its legs jerked, and one weird skip later, it would simply be closer. Almost as if it blinked through space while its limbs struggled to catch up.

Mark pulled his gun and shot at it, the noise deafening at that close range. Eventide didn't even flinch, it just kept walking, coming closer. There wasn't any ricochet or deflection, the bullets simply… weren't. It continued its halting, jerky march through the rubble.

"Behind me," Emma growled.

Eventide gave another stuttering leap and suddenly appeared ten feet away. Vain gasped and stumbled backwards. Emma didn't move.

It held up its hand, and something glittered in its palm. No, not something. The Padlock. It held the Padlock. With a too-wide grin that almost extended beyond the boundaries of its face, it closed its fist on the Device. A blinding flash of light spilled out, and cold, poisonous air washed over Emma. Her head rang from a high-pitched whine that came from everywhere, and she screamed and covered her ears.

When Eventide opened its hand, gold dust drifted from its palm to settle on the rubble at its feet.

The Padlock was no more.

"Free," it rasped.

Arthur screamed and threw his power at it. Eventide raised its hand and deflected, but the distraction bought them a moment.

"We need everyone," Vain said. "Someone has to round up the pairs and get them over here to help. We can't take it by ourselves."

"I'll go," Mark said. "I'm useless here, anyway."

"Me too," Trick said. Mark eyed him sideways.

"Vain, pull as much from me as you need," Roman said. "There's so much in the air, I don't think I can run out. I have Emma's Thimble, so I'll be fine."

A blast of energy from Eventide struck Roman in the chest and he went flying off, landing several dozen feet away.

"Roman!" Vain screamed.

Emma threw a shield up in front of the group as Eventide attacked with a wave. And another. And another. The air crackled with sparks as the power slammed into her barrier, but she managed to keep it up. The amount it summoned was staggering, each volley carrying enough force to shatter entire buildings. But she endured. To the side, Arthur threw more shots at the monster, distracting it.

"Go," she gasped to Vain. "I'll keep him busy."

Vain gave her a short nod and smacked her on the ass. "You got this." She ran off in the direction Roman had sailed.

Eventide slammed her with another blast that pushed her back several feet. While keeping her barrier up, she lashed out with her own volley, but the creature deflected it easily. In moments, they were trading blows, neither able to get the upper hand.

Her friends were scattered, and Arthur couldn't summon enough power to make a difference.

She was on her own.

Chapter 39: Flute kicks ass.

As the Hotel trembled and lurched, Flute ran from room to room, pounding on the doors, yelling at her friends. "Everyone out. You have to get out. Now!"

Sunrise went down one hallway, and she went down the other. For once, it seemed like the Hotel's daffy architecture was helping them. There were times when even finding someone's room took an eternity walking down endless winding hallways, but now, the Hotel arranged them all side by side.

It was hard, being back here, after so recently escaping. Had it only been that morning she was trying to learn to play the clarinet? Surely, it had been days ago? But she hadn't slept and so she must have been experiencing the single longest day of her life. When this was all over, she was going to sleep for a week. Not a Hotel-week where time made no sense and sleeping left her feeling more disoriented than when she went to bed, but a real sleep where minutes were actual things with tangible heft.

A staggering rumble sent her to the ground and Sunrise was there in an instant, helping her back to her feet. By now they'd gotten close to two dozen pairs out, and they all looked at her with wild, horrified eyes. She didn't want this responsibility. But then again, no one forced her to run up the stairs. No one forced her back to the Hotel. It made no sense to be mad at other people for choices she made, so she squashed her terror into the dark corners of her mind and, for good measure, hopped up and down on it a couple times.

"Everyone, follow me."

It didn't seem so bad after she said that.

She led the group back towards the main lobby and away from the collapsing building. A whole section of the floor above, including a truck-sized chandelier, crashed through the landing, inches in front of them, blocking off their exit.

"What now?" That was from Ever, a Utility she'd known for ages. His Conduit, Noble, held his hand. "Why is this happening, Flute?"

"This is an adventure, and it's all part of how adventures work. Trust me, I'm an expert now. They're always yelling and things collapsing. Everything will work out. I promise. I'll get us out."

Picking a door at random, she kicked it open and pushed her way into one of the rooms. It was painted a garish shade of orange, and it made her eyes water.

"This way." She led the group to the window and threw it open.

"We're four stories up," Ever said.

Another Utility, Diamond, shook her head. "No, my room is on the ninth floor."

"Look." Flute pointed outside. "We're on the ground. Everyone, stop talking and get out the window. Move."

She clapped her hands together once, sharply, and with Sunrise's help, pushed and prodded the pairs out. There was another deafening explosion, and the walls collapsed inwards, plunging them into darkness. The red-tinged sky was visible through the window, and they stumbled towards it. Dust and smoke clogged the air, and she coughed. The Hotel groaned in agony, and Flute silently begged it to hold together. They didn't need much more time.

The pairs jumped out the window, not caring about the broken glass. When the final pair made it out, she pointed to Sunrise. "You first."

"No chance." There was no shrug that time, and no time

to argue. She dove out, hitting the ground rolling. Sunrise followed behind, tripping on the windowsill and stumbling out.

They were beside the Hotel, fifty feet away from where the rocky ground dropped off into space. Even looking at it gave Flute vertigo. This wasn't the manicured perfection of the garden. This section of earth was damaged and uneven, with huge rocks jutting from the ground like jagged teeth. Small tufts of faded brown grass poked from between zig-zagging cracks. They weren't safe there.

She yelled, "Everyone into the garden!" and led the group to the front of the building.

"So much energy." Sunrise came to a stop, flexing his hands in the air as if he were kneading invisible bread.

Before Flute had time to ask him what he meant, the Hotel exploded.

The detonation tossed her back through the air and for the second time in minutes, she hit the earth with a hard thud. She was getting extremely tired of being thrown to the ground. Honestly.

Flaming tables and a chunk of bathtub fell from the air, and she screamed and covered her head with her arms. Pulling at Sunrise, she shuffled towards one of the rock outcroppings, thinking they could hide underneath it. Sunrise panted in terror as they both crawled across the uneven earth, neither caring about the sharp rocks that jabbed their hands and knees.

They made it to safety just as a huge steel girder slammed down on the ground in front of them. It had missed them by seconds. She hugged Sunrise close and tried to push her way further back into the safety of the rock.

Through the bedlam, she spotted Ever and Noble only twenty feet away, clinging to each other in terror.

"This way!" She raised her arms and got their attention. "Come on, you can do it."

They stood up on shaky legs and made their way over to the rock, but they were going too slow and Flute yelled at them to hurry. An enormous section of plaster wall slammed to the ground beside them. They were almost there. Ten feet to go.

Noble's eyes caught hers and he grinned with a relived look on his face. Ever looked up at the sky and pushed Noble out of the way, just as freezer fell between them. Noble stumbled into the outcropping, but Ever had nowhere to go and the freezer landed on his legs. He screamed in agony. He had a lovely singing voice, and even his screams had the flavor of melody to them. Flute almost threw up.

Not moments ago she'd promised to get them all out, and now one of them was hurt. Adventures were nightmares, for real. That terror she'd so effectively squashed poked its head out to say hi. Flute figured she had two options. Be scared and sad and do nothing, or try her hardest to fix things. She smacked her terror in the face and pulled Sunrise close.

"We have to help."

Sunrise tried to lift it, but it was too heavy. Noble got on his knees beside Ever, trying to find purchase beneath the heavy equipment, but the wreckage must have weighed hundreds of pounds. Ever's screams were reaching crescendo pitch.

"Flute!"

Then Blunt and Hush were there, helping to lift, and she'd never been so glad to see her friends. Blunt looked exhausted, but his face was set in grim determination.

"You do what you need to, Hush," he said. "I can take it. There's energy in the air."

Hush nodded and put his hand on Sunrise's shoulder. "This is going to feel weird, big man," he said, and then commanded, "Be strong enough to lift this."

Sunrise bent over to lift the huge appliance off Ever's legs, tossing it aside with relative ease. He stared at his hands in wonder.

"Superman," he said to Flute, and smiled.

"You are wonderful," Flute agreed.

Ever's legs were a splintered mess of bone and pulpy flesh. Sunrise gagged and turned away, but Flute rolled up her sleeves and got down on her knees.

"Sunrise, I'm going to work. Are you ready?"

Sunrise nodded and waved at her to start. She opened herself up to him and let the energy flow into her. As always, she felt… more. Sweat dripped down her cheeks, and she smacked her lips around her dry mouth. Ever had passed out, poor thing. She placed her hands on his legs.

Healing was easy; compared to putting energy into the

Well, it was a snap. The bones knitted together under her skillful hands, and color returned to his face as she willed his broken body back to health. In moments, the deed was done, and she dusted her palms on her pants.

"You okay?" She asked Sunrise.

He gave her a thumbs up.

"Can you see what's happening?" Hush said.

She stood on her toes. "Not sure."

A huge eruption of power knocked them backwards. Flute wiped dust out of her eyes.

"Eventide must be out." She grabbed Hush by the arm. "We have to get the pairs over there to help." She cupped her hands to her mouth and yelled, "Everyone to the front. We need to help Emma."

It seemed so natural to her. There was a problem they could help fix, and so they should be trying to fix it. What else was there? Life did not get any more simple than that. It's not like she was a hero, she had absolutely no desire to fight a demon, but staying out of it simply wasn't an option.

The pairs were not having any of it, and ran around in every direction. To be fair, some merely cowered in terror. Also, she realized that not a single one of them would have any idea who Emma was, and so that probably wasn't the best way to encourage them. Being in charge was kind of hard, and she reflected she maybe gave Hush too hard a time during the Portal escape. They weren't listening to her, but if they just stood here like docile sheep, Eventide would pick them off one at a time.

"Hush, do something. Yell at them. Tell them they need to fight."

Hush glanced at Blunt, who gave him a weary nod and sat down on the ground. Hush said, "Cover your ears. You too, Sunrise."

Flute stuck her fingers in her ears and hummed a Joy Division song. Hush yelled something and all the pairs stopped moving. Blunt slumped over against a piece of concrete.

The pairs started attacking each other.

Ever shot fire out of his hands, hitting another pair square in the chest. Two went down in a heap, throwing punches at one another. It was bedlam.

Flute screamed as Hush dove to the ground, avoiding another blast of fire.

"What did you do?" she yelled.

"I said 'everyone, fight' and now they're—oh shit, yeah, I see what happened."

"How? How are you so bad at this? I was going to apologize to you."

"Down!" Sunrise tackled her out of the way as Ever launched a volley of fire at them. The skin on Flute's back burned. Another set of pairs fought beside them, trading massive blows of energy, filling the air with thunderous concussions. All of them had a wild, faraway look in their eyes that lacked any semblance of consciousness.

"I have an idea," Hush said, and then a Conduit named Prattle hit him on the head with a rock.

Flute dove to the side as Prattle snarled and lunged at her. Sunrise was there in an instant, knocking him over.

The scene was pure chaos. Everywhere she looked, pairs were fighting, throwing enormous blasts of energy and fire at each other. Already, some groaned on the ground, casualties of the violent battle, while others cowered and waited for death to come. She looked at her hands, still covered in Ever's blood, and wiped them on her pants. This adventure wasn't fun anymore. Her friends were dying. Everyone was dying. But she couldn't stand there and do nothing. She was a healer. The best one the Hotel had.

It was time to prove it.

"We have to help," she said and turned to Blunt. "We have to get Hush somewhere safe. How much longer will this last?"

"Five minutes maybe. Ten, tops." Blunt wiped his forehead. For all he'd been through, she was surprised he was still upright.

"Okay. Sunrise, how much can we do? No shrugs, now. Full sentences. I need to be sure."

Sunrise took a deep breath. "There's energy everywhere, Flute. It's coming into me through the air, I think it's because of the Well. Way more than we've ever had. I've got a lot."

She surveyed the rocky landscape, trying to figure out where she could be of the greatest help. Most of the pairs seemed to have made it into the garden. That way, then. That's where she'd go.

"Time to go to work."

<u>Chapter 40: Trick makes a deal.</u>

Trick and Mark weaved between chunks of Hotel and stray energy blasts. While he didn't like leaving Vain alone, part of him was glad he wouldn't have to face Eventide again. It had been sheer luck to get it in the Well the last time, and the thing that emerged this time seemed far removed from that long-ago monster that slithered down the stairs. This was an Eventide at maximum power, filled with rage and hatred.

Whatever else happened, his operation with Arthur was finished. There was no coming back from this. Strangely, the thought filled him with relief. No more pairs. No more living in day-to-day terror of Eventide. No matter what the after-effects of that fight would be, he was free. Finally, forever free. The worst thing he could have imagined was happening, and now all he had to do was face it.

The Hotel itself would be fine; Trick wasn't concerned about that. In the early days, he and Arthur blew it up dozens of times. It would always pull itself back together. The Hotel always was, and always would be.

They ran through the maze of the garden, down the gravel-paved path, between thick green hedges. Trick was leading them to the clearing in the center. If the pairs were anywhere, they'd be there. None of them would go near the Portal section.

Oddly, thick black smoke poured from the direction of the clearing, but why would that be? The wreckage from the Hotel hadn't made it that far. Were the Wyatts setting fire to the pairs? It made no sense.

"So, you and Vain, huh?" Mark interrupted his thoughts with absurd, ill-timed blather.

"We're doing this now?" Trick jumped over a smoldering bunk bed. "This feels like the right time to have this conversation? Would you like me to run back to the Hotel and see if I can get a Jane to make us some tea?"

"You hurt her, and I'll find you," Mark said.

"How tedious. Here's an idea you might want to try, Mark. I'll give this one to you for free. What would it be like to treat her like a human?"

"What the fuck are you talking about?" Mark asked.

"In brief," he said, "you're suggesting that if I am unhappy in the relationship, I should bury my feelings and remain so to avoid causing her distress. Further, you're suggesting that she, by herself, has no agency to make the relationship last and that it's up to you to ensure she suffers no distress. Lastly, you're suggesting that she is somehow unable to manage negative emotions. Have you ever met her? This entire thing is insulting to Vain. That's what the fuck I'm talking about."

Mark flushed crimson and sputtered something about equality that Trick studiously ignored. None of these idiots deserved Vain. Not like he did. He understood that now.

They continued forward and the hedges opened up into the clearing.

Chaos ruled. Pairs fought with pairs while Wyatts tried to stop them. Everywhere he turned, the garden was burning. Trees blazed like birthday candles. The gazebo where the pairs sometimes put on plays for each other was engulfed, and a single Jane lay at the foot of the structure, unmoving. Half the hedges that ran down the side had been reduced to ash. Even parts of the ground smoldered, all courtesy of the fire-wielding pairs that shot out huge gouts of flame indiscriminately into the air and each other.

"What the hell is this?" Mark said.

"I have no idea."

A Wyatt spotted them and ran over, his shirt ripped and torn, burns covering his arm.

"The pairs have gone nuts, boss," he said. "They're killing everything."

Before Trick could respond, the Wyatts head exploded.

He slumped to the ground, and behind him, a Utility named Spindle stood with a single arm outstretched. Spindle was an energy user, like Vain. His eyes were completely vacant, and a thin line of drool dripped from his lips.

Both he and Mark yelled to move at the same time, and they both pushed each other out of the way as a tree exploded behind them. Spindle was shooting energy at them.

While Trick didn't agree with Mark's opinion on how to gracefully move on from a relationship, he also didn't think Vain would appreciate it if he let her recent ex-boyfriend be murdered. That said, he had no idea how to fight pairs. They had all the powers and he had none.

Mark pulled out his gun and pointed it at Spindle.

"Stop!" Trick yelled.

His cry got Spindle's attention, and he fired off an energy blast that would have killed Trick had he not rolled out of the way. Mark's shot clipped Spindle in the shoulder, and he fell to the ground.

Another pair spotted them and ran at them with raised hands. Territory. A fire Utility. A fire Utility running straight at them. Mark stood up and pointed his gun. Territory's sleeves were smoldering, and he wore the same vacant expression Spindle had. Years of working with the pairs had taught Trick to have a healthy respect for what they could do. Mark, unfortunately, did not have the same experience, and he stood in Territory's path, a look of confusion on his face. Trick had about a single second to act, but he already knew it wasn't going to be enough.

"Mark, get down!"

It was too late. Spindle spewed a massive gout of fire in Mark's face. Mark screamed and put his hands up. At that distance, and at that temperature, it wasn't even fair to say he burned to death. It was more like he melted to death. His hands were first, burning down to the bone in seconds. His head and skull followed next. Trick choked on bile that rose from his stomach. Mark dropped to the ground, a smoldering ruin, and Territory turned in a circle, looking for his next victim. Trick shoved his hand in his mouth to stop from screaming and scrambled through the hedges, trying to find a spot to hide, hoping Territory wouldn't follow.

He could hardly fathom the abruptness of what had happened. There wasn't any point in going back to check on Mark, he was clearly gone. Trick emerged from the hedges on a path that ran parallel to the clearing. It seemed to be empty, and he followed it while crouching, trying to look everywhere at once. At the end of the path, he spotted Flute and Sunrise kneeling over a body, and headed towards them. Blunt was with them, carrying an unconscious Hush.

Flute finished her work on a bloody, broken, Conduit. She gasped and sagged against Sunrise, who seemed equally exhausted. Blood covered her forearms.

"What the hell happened here?" Trick said as he approached.

"The pairs turned on each other. Hush yelled at them. I've saved as many as I could. I'm exhausted." Flute brushed sweat-soaked hair from her eyes, and Sunrise nodded.

"I'm done."

Blunt sat Hush up and rubbed his back. Hush blinked, slowly coming back to consciousness. A group of pairs came around the corner and saw them, and Trick flinched. But these pairs didn't attack. They seemed dizzy, confused, and relieved to see them.

"It must be wearing off," Blunt said. "Finally."

"There's more in the clearing," Trick said. "I don't know how many will be left alive. It was insane. We need everyone with Emma. All the pairs need to help fight Eventide."

"I'm taking my brother and getting out of here," Hush spat on the ground. "Enough is enough.

"You might need to push the pairs again." Trick said.

"Why would I care about that?"

Trick sighed. They were making it hard. None of this was his fault. "Because if you don't, I'll find you and I'll kill you, Hush. Straight up murder you. That's why. I'm not going to die, I never die. I have more back doors than you could imagine. But you know who will die? Charm. Vain. Roman. Everyone. And in the sheer seconds we have between Eventide escaping and devouring every world in his path, I will find you and kill you using a guitar pick, a tablespoon of salt, and a staple gun."

While Hush worked out the logistics of his pretty cool threat, Trick turned to Flute.

"Can you help me?"

Flute slapped him. Not the reaction he expected.

"You made me a slave." Her nostrils flared.

"I did."

"Why?"

He gestured. "To avoid this. If we survive, I'll let you slap me some more if it makes you feel better. Agreed? But for now, we have to save Vain."

"I thought you said Emma?" Blunt said.

"I did say Emma." Trick shook his head. "Can we stop arguing semantics? They need our help. I don't care how you do it, get the pairs over there. I'm not sure how much longer Emma and Arthur can hold out against that thing."

They looked at him with weary, distrustful eyes, and he wanted to scream in frustration. Vain could be getting attacked at that very moment and he was wasting time trying to play nice with people who had been, up until quite recently, his employees.

All his life, he'd gotten by with tricks. It was kind of his thing. His looks certainly helped, but he'd mostly played fast and loose with people, viewing them as no more than game pieces he could move around. Only he was out of moves and the dice seemed loaded against him. But he remembered his conversation with Vain. Teammates. That's what he'd said they were. So, okay. He'd try it that way.

"Please," he said. "Help me. I'm terrified for Vain. This isn't a prank."

Flute sighed and exchanged a glance with Sunrise, who nodded. Hush scowled and jabbed his finger at Trick.

"Slaps won't do it. If we survive, we each get to kick you in the balls. One solid kick, each of us."

"Deal," Trick said. Crushed balls would probably help him go at a pace Vain was more comfortable with, anyway. Ha. Even when getting his balls ruined, he could still find a way to come out on top. He ruled.

He let none of this show on his face.

"Thank you, everyone. Now let's go help our friends."

Chapter 41: Emma would make a good therapist.

Eventide attacked, and it was all Emma could do to stay alive.

She'd never seen something human-shaped that was so clearly not human, and the wrongness offended her. Only offended wasn't the right word—offended was getting cut off in traffic, or when someone said, "you're the smartest female grad I know" instead of "you're the smartest grad I know." No, what she experienced looking at that grotesque, multi-limbed creature was so much stronger than offence. It was abhorrence.

To her surprise, she felt no fear, despite being locked in a literal life or death struggle with an unstoppable super demon. The angry part of her that existed anytime she used the power had seized control, and she fought against that as hard as she fought against Eventide, unwilling to surrender to what she'd become if she gave into that rage.

Arthur attacked from one side, making throwing motions with his arms as he lobbed energy balls at Eventide. His salvos were powerful, but only a fraction of what she was handling. He'd still be able to take probably ten pairs in a fight, but it wasn't enough. But her attacks weren't faring much better. She used as much as she was able to summon; more than she'd used all those months ago in the fight against Trick, more than she'd used to re-energize the Portal. Ten times that amount. A hundred. And she poured all of it at Eventide. The power couldn't hurt her anymore, not like it used to. She'd learned how to control the power outside herself and not funnel it all through her body like she did in the early days. There was no fingernail popping or skin splitting. She'd moved well beyond that.

Eventide took everything she had and hardly flinched.

It shimmered in and out of reality, like an image on a grainy VHS tape. And its mouth stayed twisted into that parody of a grin, almost like it was enjoying the fight.

Almost like it was enjoying the energy.

Because of course it was. It fed off it.

Emma realized, with sinking horror, and much too late, that she was pouring energy at a demon who survived on the very thing she was dumping on it. Of course, she wasn't hurting it. It was like trying to put out a fire by throwing fire at it.

"Stop!" she yelled at Arthur. "Stop attacking." Arthur ignored her and kept hurling power. But after the feast Emma had given it, his offerings were like individual raisins.

She dropped her hands and stopped fighting. There had to be some other way to defeat it. Instead of attacking, she directed all of her forces into protection; into a barrier.

And just in time. Eventide retaliated.

A tremendous burst of energy exploded against her barrier, and she was thrown back. She hit the ground and bit her tongue, her mouth flooding with hot, coppery blood. Some shred of instinctual self-preservation had her create an energy barrier around her body, even as she shook her head to try to get rid of the ringing. Eventide charged, lashing out with blows that she could feel slam up against her barrier. It was just enough to keep them from killing her, but each one staggered her back. There was no way to measure the amount of energy it was using to attack her, but each blow seemed to carry Padlock-levels of power. Megatons.

A blow hit her on the face and her head whipped back. Another followed, striking her in the chest, causing her to hiccup as her heart skipped a beat. Then, one hit her arms that sent a sharp pain up her elbow. Eventide grinned and pushed at her with both hands, crashing against her defenses and sending her flying through the air.

She landed just in time to see Eventide lash out against Arthur and send him flying in the opposite direction. Had he been able to put up a shield in time? She had no way to tell. Regardless, he was out of the fight. Eventide closed in on her and lashed out with a pale fist that caught her on the cheek and sent her spinning. She spat blood into the earth and barely managed to get her arm up in time to block a follow-up shot punch. It was attacking with both energy and body now, battering her. Somehow, she'd lost her sleeve. Roman had bought her that sweater. It kicked her in the ribs and she sailed half a dozen feet through the air, only her protective barrier preventing her bones from being pulverized. It followed that up with a crushing energy blow on her back that drove the air from her lungs.

It was literally beating her to death.

It was going to kill her. There was no way for her to win that fight. She was going to die. There. Alone in a strange place, far away from home, far away from her mom and Doreen and her old life. Eventide was going to kill her. It barely paid any attention to Arthur, recognizing her as the bigger threat.

Where was Vain? Where was Roman? Why wasn't anyone helping her?

She staggered to her feet. Eventide charged her and hit her with both his fists and the power, and there was a concussive detonation that, again, knocked her back half a dozen feet. Her arm twisted at an unnatural angle. Even though she was pouring every ounce of energy she could muster into defending her body, his blows were still getting through. Eventide picked her up and threw her deep into the Hotel rubble. On instinct, she put up a shield that buffeted her, even as she tumbled across the ruin of metal and plaster. Coming to a stop, she groaned and raised her head. Something glittered behind her. The Elevator. The Elevator was still standing, somehow. And Eventide was moving towards it.

Through it all, Emma of Death tormented her, begging to be let out, begging to be fully unleashed. Was that her only option? Let Eventide kill her, or give in to that madness? Maybe become as dark and twisted as Eventide in the process?

It slammed another burst of energy against her, and she felt something snap inside her chest. She coughed, and a torrent of thick, goopy blood poured from her mouth. There was no way she could take any more of that. Anything she had left was going into survival, in keeping some measure of protection up around her poor body, but it wasn't enough. The next blow would kill her. She had nothing left.

Emma of Death screamed at her.

And so, without any other options, she surrendered.

She let her herself feel all the anger, all the rage, all the hatred she'd kept bottled up inside. She let it flow through her, let it fill her up. And with all that rattling through her brain, tired, beaten and hopeless, a new thought started to form.

She was allowed to be mad. She'd been kidnapped. Attacked. Used. Not only her, but Roman. They'd killed her boyfriend. And she should be mad at that. Furious. There wasn't anything wrong with her; feelings were completely natural. They told your body when something was wrong. They needed to be listened to. Respected.

Eventide struck at her, but she was able to take the blow. Arthur, still hovering in the distance, threw a few more of his pathetic shots at Eventide, and they managed to distract the monster long enough for her to roll out of the way.

Her body ached with dozens of cuts and bruises, but now they seemed like someone else's problem. Still there, floating off in the distance, but unable to affect her directly. Eventide glared at her with malevolence, but before he could attack again, she yelled and lashed out with an explosive eruption of power. More than she'd ever done. More, she suspected, than anyone had ever done.

The monster staggered back.

Somehow, she'd staggered it.

People were coming towards her, barely visible through the smoke. Friends or new enemies, she hardly knew which, and she hardly cared. Emma let all the anger and rage flow into her. It was unrealistic to expect to be able to draw from this power and not change; change would be inevitable. But she didn't need to be that wild, uncontrollable force that put her hands around Vain's neck and squeezed, squeezed, squeezed. She could still be Emma, albeit Emma with a twist.

She stood up, blood pouring from her nose, one arm hanging limply at her side. She spat into the dirt.

"Come get me, fucker."

Chapter 42: Vain figures out the answer to life, the universe, and everything.

Before the dust Roman raised when Eventide threw him into the garden even had time to settle, Vain was already halfway to him. Her heart slammed against her chest in time with her footfalls. That part of the garden had been flattened by Hotel detritus, and she leaped over huge sections of wall that still smoldered from the explosion. In a distant part of her brain, she realized she'd burned her hand climbing over the rubble, but she couldn't make herself care. All that mattered was Roman.

She spotted him behind an azalea bush, getting to his feet and holding his chest. She threw herself at him.

"Are you okay?"

"Yeah. This thing really works." He held up his hand to show her the Thimble on his finger. "But being thrown through the air is terrifying."

"Why did you fight Eventide, you big ninny? Leave that to Emma and me."

"I didn't actually, he attacked me."

"We have to hurry back. Emma's going to need us. How's your energy level?"

"Insane. I'm soaking it up through the air. Pull as much as you need."

"Stay behind me, okay? Thimble or no, I don't want you to get hurt again."

He nodded, and they ran back towards Emma and the

battle for the Hotel. Vain's mind twisted and turned with ideas. What could she possibly do? Some people, jerks mostly, insinuated her plans were crazy, and maybe those jerks had a point. But her plans were never stupid. And attacking Eventide with the meager power she and Roman could summon would be suicide. But she couldn't stand there and do nothing.

A group of figures huddled behind some ruined shrubbery in the distance. Pairs. Maybe that was something she could do.

"We have to get the pairs to help." She pointed and tugged Roman by the shirt. "Come on."

Ferocious booming explosions sounded in the distance, and Vain picked up the pace, hoping she wasn't too late. No telling how long Emma could stand up against that onslaught.

The pairs hugged each other, looking terrified, and they flinched when Vain approached. She thought she recognized a few of them.

"Hey Termite." She waved at a Utility she knew, a young kid with pale hair.

"It's Terabyte," he said.

"What'd I say?"

"Termite."

"Are you sure?"

"Vain, there's no time for this." Roman appeared behind her. "Hi everyone. Long time, no see. We need your help if we're going to beat that thing that's attacking us."

"How are we supposed to fight against that thing?" Terabyte's Conduit, Stable, spoke up. She was normally a timid one.

"Terabyte can make shields." Roman said. He pointed as he went around the group. "Zizek can throw fire. Whisper heals people. It's enough. If we all work together, maybe we can do something."

Vain was losing patience. Time to bring out the big guns. She raised her hands to get everyone's attention.

"Listen to me. In less than an hour, aircraft from here will join others from around the world. And you will be launching the largest aerial battle in this history of mankind. Mankind. That word should have new meaning for all of us today. We can't be consumed by our petty differences anymore. We will be united in our common interests. Perhaps it's fate that today is the 4th of July."

"Come on, Vain, seriously?" Roman interrupted. "Are you doing the speech from Independence Day?"

"Should I have done Rocky Four?"

"You shouldn't do any of it," he snapped. Well, someone put sand in his cornflakes. "Look, everyone. I know you're scared. I am too. But we can do this if we work together, I promise. Terabyte, if you and Vain put a shield up in front of us, we can approach safely. Zizek, you throw fire when you get a clean shot. Whisper, you heal anyone who goes down. I promise, we can do this. Together. Okay?"

Strangely, Roman's quite bland speech got them moving, and she wondered if the rule of cool was as broken as time here in the Hotel. Because honestly, the Independence Day speech ruled.

As a group, they ran towards Emma and the battle. Coming up over the crest, she spotted Trick and the rest of her friends, also with a much larger group of pairs. She ran to Trick and gave him a fast hug. God, look at her, she may as well have been starring in pornos at that point, for all the performances she was putting on.

"Are you okay?"

"Yeah."

"Where's Mark?"

"I'm sorry. He didn't make it."

Vain's vision blurred and she couldn't catch her breath. What was the last thing she'd said to him? Why hadn't she told him how much she loved being his friend, how much she relied on him for strength and support?

Hush said, "Is that Emma? Jesus Christ, he's killing her."

Vain pushed thoughts of Mark aside. If she survived this, then she could unpack how she'd treated him. First, she needed to make sure her friends were safe.

Eventide threw Emma across the rubble towards the Hotel. Emma looked like a disaster, blood streaming from basically every part of her body. Somehow, she was still standing.

And smiling.

"Everyone!" Vain yelled. "Attack!"

Pairs pulled from their Conduits, and she pulled from Roman and threw everything she could at Eventide. Their collective volley took him by surprise and energy blasts and fire slammed into his back, hurling him over Emma's head, close to the Elevator. The group ran forward, at least twenty of them, all pushing with whatever power they had, trying to stop that horrible thing from doing any more damage.

Vain noticed right away that the energy blasts didn't seem to do anything. It was like they vanished when she threw them at Eventide. But it for sure did not like the fire. It snarled and flailed about as a few flame-wielding pairs doused it in thick gouts. They continued like that, one step at a time, getting closer to Emma, progressing further through the Hotel rubble, forcing Eventide back.

"Oh Jesus," Roman said.

Emma was a complete ruin, and Vain didn't understand how she was standing. Blood poured from... well, trying to identify the individual sources of blood would be pointless. Roman and Flute both rushed to her side while the pairs continued to hammer at Eventide.

"No energy," Emma croaked. "It eats energy."

That made sense and Vain kicked herself for not thinking of that. She raised her voice.

"Fire only, everyone. Energy users put up shields."

Flute ran to Emma's side and grabbed her by the head. She closed her eyes and Sunrise slumped to the ground, but Emma's back straightened and the blood dried and color returned to her face.

"Thank you." Emma said.

Roman gave her a fierce hug.

Vain approached with caution. "Are you going to force choke me again? Lucas and his lawyers might want to have a word with you if you try that. Ha, ha?"

"No." Emma gave her an Arctic smile, but Vain's neck remained un- choked, so she could live with the tradeoff. "We need to finish this. The fire seems to be working. Keep pouring it on. I can generate enough for it to absorb at once, but I won't be able to keep up that level for long."

They descended on Eventide, attacking from every direction. Eventide roared and pushed back with a stupendous wave of energy. Vain got a shield up in time, but not all the pairs were so lucky. Several were cut down while others were knocked unconscious. Eventide lashed out again, pushing them all back.

"It's still too strong." Arthur appeared from nowhere, with Charm trailing behind him. A single line of blood poured down his cheek. "This isn't working. We have to get out of here."

"Keep going," Emma growled. She shot a staggering pulse of energy at Eventide that would level cities. It stumbled back and glared at Emma with hatred. "We're beating it."

Vain wasn't sure if that was the case, but it was possible that Eventide also felt that way, because it cowered and scrambled away from them. It seemed like it was on the defensive. But there wasn't really any place to go. The Hotel was destroyed and Vain didn't think Eventide would want to get back in the Well. That only left one place.

"The Elevator," she gasped.

Eventide unleashed a furious wave of power at them, and while they ducked behind Emma's shield, it skittered towards the open Elevator. It got as far as putting one hand on the gold gating, gripping the door so hard with its black-taloned hand that the metal warped.

"Stop it," Vain yelled.

Vain wasn't sure what Emma did, but she made a gesture and Eventide stopped, for some reason unable to move any further. Emma leaned back like she was pulling on a rope. Eventide writhed, unable to take a single step forward. Emma had him tethered. The pairs continued to douse him with fire that he fended off with one hand.

"I can't hold him long!"

"Let him go," Arthur said. "Who cares if he escapes? It's not our problem."

"We can't." Emma's voice was strained and breaking.

"Then I will." Arthur raised his hand and Vain realized what was coming.

He attacked Emma, trying to break her concentration,

trying to snap the invisible energy thread that was so tenuously keeping Eventide from escaping permanently. Emma cried out and held up a hand to block the power. Vain pulled from Roman by instinct and threw everything she could at Arthur. It knocked him back, the unexpected attack not doing a lot of damage, but distracting him enough that he stopped going after Emma.

"You miserable bitch," he said, and wiped his mouth.

Before Vain could do anything, Charm came up behind him, brandishing a two by four like a bat. Arthur didn't see her, he was so busy explaining to Vain what a bitch she was. Beside her, Trick opened his mouth, but didn't say anything. Charm swung from the hip and slammed it into the side of his head. Hot, salty blood sprayed across Vain's face and Arthur tumbled to the ground, his skull a ruin of gore and bone.

"Holy shit," Vain said. Charm dropped the two by four with a startled cry and looked at Vain with pleading eyes.

"I didn't mean it." she managed to say.

"Holy shit." Trick stood over top of Arthur, staring down at the body. Blood from Arthur's skull soaked into the dirt. There was no possible way for him to have survived that.

"Please do something." Emma continued to pull back on her invisible rope tethering Eventide. "I can't keep this up."

The pairs were exhausted too. They'd stopped shooting fire at Eventide, their Conduits completely spent. And without that pressure, Eventide would regain the upper hand. Even now it seemed to be getting its strength back.

Vain pushed Arthur from her head and looked around for something she could use. A rock. Maybe a two by four as that seemed to work pretty well for Charm. Sunrise seemed to have the same idea. He brandished a broken guitar he must have found in the rubble and bellowed. Flute yelled at him to stop and reached out to grab him by the collar of his t-shirt but he slipped from her grasp.

He attacked Eventide with the broken guitar, slamming it against Eventide's back, and in that moment of confusion, Emma pulled back and hauled Eventide a step away from the Elevator. The monster still had one had on the grate, though. Sunrise slammed the guitar against Eventide, again and again and again, and Vain had a momentary thought that his insane attack might work. Fuck, maybe Eventide was allergic to musical instruments? Why even the hell not? She scanned the ground for a violin or harmonica or something.

"Sunrise, get away from him," Flute yelled. She tried to rush forward to help, but Trick grabbed her by the wrist.

"Let go of me." She tried to struggle out of his grip.

"He'll kill you," Trick said. "It's too late."

Eventide snarled at Sunrise and knocked the guitar from his hands. It grabbed him by the throat and picked him up off the ground.

"No!" Flute yelled.

Vain fired a salvo of energy shots at Eventide's wrist, hoping that she could maybe force him to drop Sunrise, but it didn't work. It held fast and shook Sunrise like a dog, as if he weighed no more than a pound. Sunrise's face turned bright red. Eventide held him up above his head and squeezed. Vain heard bones break like the crack of a starter's pistol. With a final twist, Eventide threw him to the ground. Flute fell to her knees with a broken wail.

"I can't feel him," Flute said. "I can't feel Sunrise."

Eventide took another step inside the Elevator. He was halfway in now. Emma was almost parallel with the ground, she was pulling so hard, but she was only one person. The pairs were spent. Arthur was dead. Christ, what could Vain do? There had to be something. She couldn't stand there and do nothing. If she was going to die, she wanted to participate, not simply watch it happen to her. She scanned the ground for anything she could use. Rocks. A broken table leg. A jagged piece of floor tile. A flexi-hose connector.

Wait. A flexi-hose connector?

She picked it up and turned it over. It was the Device that connected pairs. An idea began to form. A super perfect idea. A stupendously fantastic plan that would completely and totally work.

"Vain, what are you doing with that?" Trick said.

"I can use this on Eventide. Connect to him, make him my Conduit somehow. Then I'd have all his energy."

Trick shook his head. "It doesn't work. You're both Utilities. We've tried it before."

"What happens then?"

"It kills both the Utilities."

Vain slightly altered her stupendously fantastic plan that would completely and totally work. Maybe not exactly the way she wanted, but Trick had told her what she needed to hear.

"Vain, did you hear me? It kills both people."

She leaned over and gave him a quick peck on the cheek. "I'm really glad we kissed, Trick."

Trick stared at her for a beat. He wasn't stupid.

"I'm going with you, then."

"You can't."

He shrugged. "I told you I wouldn't leave you. If we're doing this, let's do this."

Her heart melted a bit. Boyfriends ruled, maybe.

"Take the Thimble." Roman held out the Device Emma had created. "It will protect you. You don't have to actually die."

Brilliant, brilliant Roman. For the third time, she modified her plan. Man, was she ever getting good at incorporating feedback.

She slipped it on her finger.

With the Device in her hand, she ran towards Eventide. Emma had dropped to a single knee, and it looked like she didn't have much time left. Eventide was almost fully in the Elevator.

So far, jumping on people's backs had not served her very well. The two times she'd tried it with Wyatts, she'd kind of gotten her ass kicked. Still, third time was the charm, so the saying went, and every kick-ass hero needed a signature move.

It didn't notice her approaching, so invested it was in trying to get away. With a cry that she hoped sounded brave, she jumped as high as she could and landed on his back. The smell of rot and maggots made her heave, and its cloak was somehow cold and hot at the same time. This was completely wild. She was riding a demon. She could feel the bones in its neck. So gross. It bucked and spun around, trying to shake her free. She wouldn't have much time. Trick's face was slack with surprise.

Eventide still held on to the Elevator with one hand while

it clawed at her with the other. Roman was yelling at her, and she was so glad she got to see him one last time. She kissed the Thimble on her finger and said the one thing that had been bothering her all this time.

"How did you even buy a cloak?"

Okay, maybe not the best exit line. It would have to do.

With a yell of triumph, she stabbed the flexi-hose into its eye.

The world crumbled into blackness, an absence of light so profound she thought it had struck her blind. Her body shook with tension, and she couldn't catch her breath. Thick, wet pressure surrounded her. Across the endless void, she perceived Eventide; not seeing it, but experiencing it as a physical presence in her mind, both repellent and intimate.

Power ripped through both of them, and she instantly understood what Trick had meant. It was like two positive forces hitting each other. She screamed as energy tore through her body, pain assaulting her from every direction. Eventide also screamed, and she felt the power growing within him, growing like pus in a pimple that was about to pop. But it was killing him. She felt it. The Thimble grew hot on her finger—lava-hot—but she was already in so much agony that she hardly noticed.

Smoke billowed out of Eventide's rapidly melting eyes. Then Trick was there beside her, grabbing her, trying to pull her from Eventide's back. And even though she was in agony and these were her last moments alive, she did what she always did. What she always would do. Make sure Roman was safe. Her eyes found him, standing beside Blunt, his arm around the big man's shoulders. He was alive. Good enough.

From somewhere that seemed miles away, she heard Trick yell, "It's still holding the Elevator!" His hands were on her back. Had Trick mentioned something about a backlash of energy? But if Eventide was holding the Elevator, that meant the backlash might be—

"Ah, shit."

There was a huge explosion, and then her world went black.

<u>Epilogue</u>

Vain felt hard pavement under her body. Her body didn't hurt. It was warm. Time existed. She was no longer clinging to Eventide's back. Rather than open her eyes, she put SARCAC into practice.

She opened a single eye. Feet. City sounds reached her ears; the car honks and steady buzz that meant thousands of people. She was on a sidewalk. An incredibly busy sidewalk. People stepped around her and Trick.

Mark dead. Sunrise dead. Arthur dead. Eventide, maybe dead. But she was alive. She opened her other eye. Wherever she was, it wasn't the Hotel. Trick lay beside her, still breathing. She rolled him over and slapped him lightly on the face.

He coughed and sat up, opening both eyes at the same time.

"That's a terrible SARCAC," she told him, in case he was open to feedback, and immediately felt guilty about Mark. She had a feeling she was going to spend many, many years feeling guilty about Mark. Maybe it was what she deserved, though.

Trick groaned and put his head in his hands. Pedestrians swore at them to move as they stepped over their bodies. Hundreds of pedestrians. Tall skyscrapers surrounded them. It was bedlam. He rubbed his eyes.

"Why are we alive? Is this New York? It looks like Times Square. God, my head. I remember you on Eventide and then there was a huge, blinding flash."

"Trick, why are we in New York?" She pulled him against

the side of a building, getting out of the way of traffic. It looked to be mid-day.

"The Elevator," Trick said. "I told you, creating Utility to Utility pairings creates a massive energy backlash. When you killed Eventide, he was holding the Elevator. So all that energy killed him and then, I guess, created an Elevator-like wave?"

"Are you saying he traveled us?"

"It seems like it, yeah. I guess because I was touching you, we went together."

"All of us?"

"Presumably."

Vain remembered her last image of Roman holding Blunt. At least he wouldn't be alone. Wherever he was, he'd have someone. She clung to that.

"What world are we in?"

"I have no idea."

Vain stood up and tried to get a better look. Wherever they were, at least it looked like normal New York, and not cannibal New York. People looked like normal people, wearing flannel shirts and listening to Discmans and carrying boom boxes.

Wait, none of that seemed right.

She took a closer look at the ads flashing on the buildings. One for the movie Reservoir Dogs, except, weirdly, it seemed to star Bill Murray. Another showed the R.E.M. album, Automatic for the Humans. Something wasn't right.

"Oh, you're kidding me," she said. She poked at a random guy in a suit. "Hey, buddy. Where am I?"

He stopped, maintaining his distance with a sour and guarded expression. "Rough night?"

She probably didn't look great, what with being exploded to a new location and waking up on the sidewalk. She ran her fingers through her short, choppy hair to smooth it, but stopped, experiencing profound Deja vu.

"Very rough. Help me out, okay? This is New York, right?"

"Yeah." He eyed her suspiciously.

"What year is it?"

"Am I on America's Funniest Home Videos?"

"Oh no," she groaned. "It's like nineteen ninety something, isn't it?"

"Ninety-two. Yeah."

Vain dropped to the ground, stunned, and leaned against Trick.

"Trick," she said.

"I heard."

"We're trapped in nineteen ninety-two."

"Yup."

"On a weird planet where it's sort of the same as ours but not entirely."

"Yup."

"Do we have any possible way to get back that you can think of?"

"No Elevator. No Padlock. So, nope."

She frowned at him. "You're taking this rather well."

He shrugged. "You did it. You killed Eventide. There's no way he survived the blast. Apparently, he's also scattered us, and probably all your friends, to the cosmic winds, but it's over. At least we're together."

"I can't feel Roman," she said. "Trick, what are we going to do?"

"Adjust to our new lives? At least we know not to open a video store, right? If we can buy some Apple stock, we should be fine."

"Are you kidding me? That's your plan? Trick, if Eventide's blast scattered them all, they could be anywhere. Anywhen. We have to get back. We have to find them."

"How?"

"Well." She leaned back against the side of the building and rested her head on his shoulder. "I have some ideas about that."

The End, Book two of the Hotel.

Acknowledgements

No one writes a book by themselves.

More accurately, everyone writes books by themselves, but they lean on the support and strength from those around them to get them over the finish line. The original idea for this book was about a group of people who had devoted their lives to protecting the Hotel and one of them carried a space hammer and spoke exclusively in Nicholas Cage quotes, and in retrospect, that's the book I should have written.

Anyway, there's a whole bunch of people who helped me get through this and put up with me as I hammered away at the story and figured out what writing a book is all about.

Of course, my wife and kid, mostly for dealing with me. I haven't been easy to be around through covid.

My writing group. All of you. You're the best thing to come out of this year. You guys kept me writing and that was enough to make sure this book got written.

And of course, a special thank you to my editor and friend, Alex Woodroe, without whom this book wouldn't exist. I said that about the last book, but it's even more true about this one. I mean it literally. Without Alex, this book does not exist. Thank you for all your help and patience. You are a wonderful editor and you make me sound like I know what I'm doing. What more can anyone ask for?

www.ingramcontent.com/pod-product-compliance
Lightning Source LLC
Chambersburg PA
CBHW051419170626
46809CB00006B/2237